Praise for Mr. Ambler and *Epitaph for a Spy:*

"This is a tale well worth acquaintance."
                    —*New York Herald Tribune*

"An uncommonly good story of international intrigue."
                    —*The Atlantic*

"Ambler successfully combines excitement, entertainment and social significance."
                    —*The New York Times Book Review*

EPITAPH FOR A SPY

ERIC AMBLER

Carroll & Graf Publishers, Inc.
New York

Copyright © 1938 by Eric Ambler. Copyright © renewed 1966
by Eric Ambler.

Published by arrangement with Alfred A. Knopf, Inc.

First Carroll & Graf edition 1991

Carroll & Graf Publishers, Inc.
260 Fifth Avenue
New York, NY 10001

ISBN: 0-88184-716-X

Manufactured in the United States of America

Preface

RECENTLY, literary critics on both sides of the Atlantic have made attempts to explain the sudden, extraordinary and (by implication) preposterous popularity of the spy novel. The consensus seems to be that it has something to do with the public's need to discharge accumulated Cold War tensions; and, since the Cold War has already been blamed successfully for so many far weightier social ills, the wretched thing can probably support this small additional burden of guilt.

However, one of the critics, Mr Jacques Barzun, who is Dean of Faculties and Provost of Columbia University, has gone more deeply and more bitterly into the matter. Writing in *The American Scholar*, he says that, 'The soul of the spy is somehow the model of our own; his actions and his trappings fulfil our unsatisfied desires.' He also discovers 'a pre-established harmony: the novel as a genre has been prurient and investigative from the start ... from Gil Blas to Henry James's "observer" somebody is always prying.' Mr Barzun probes yet further. 'The novel,' he declares, 'is dedicated to subversion: the novelist is a spy in enemy country. No reason, then, to be surprised that his ultimate parable should be the tale with a declared, certified spy in it, one who like the original *picaro* sees society from below, and resentfully.'

When *Epitaph for a Spy* was written spy stories were generally considered a very low form of literary life indeed, and few self-respecting critics were prepared to notice them. When they were noticed, the word 'novel' was scarcely ever used; they were 'yarns'. For a scholar of Mr Barzun's reputation to contribute to a learned journal an article about the spy novel, even for the purpose of denouncing it, would then have been unthinkable. The spy novel had to become a social phenomenon before it could draw academic fire.

Mr Barzun's references to my own work were not, in their context, wholly unfriendly and I suppose it ought to be gratifying to be at last legitimised, if only as one of the puny, conscienceless and morally-defective heirs of a great tradition, one of those responsible for the 'contamination that the sophisticated and the spies have brought into the story of detection'. I must admit, nevertheless, that I was more puzzled than gratified; and when this new edition of *Epitaph for a Spy* was projected, I read the book again in the light of Mr Barzun's strictures.

At least part of the charge is true. *Epitaph for a Spy* is basically a kind of detective story, and I have brought spies into it. However, whether or not this constitutes contamination and, if so, who (apart from Mr Barzun) cares, are questions that I gladly leave to the reader.

The reappraisal was useful in one respect. As I don't make a habit of reading my own books, and as it had been some years since I had corrected the proofs of this one, I found that much of it I had quite forgotten and that even the names of the characters seemed unfamiliar to me. I also found traces of padding and some unnecessary adjectives and adverbs. These I have removed. A few paragraphs have been revised for the sake of greater clarity.

A final note. 'St Gatien' and 'Hôtel de la Réserve' are

6

the names I used to conceal the identity of a real French village and hotel in which I had stayed during the nineteen thirties. Twenty years later I revisited the place. It was in one of the few areas of the Côte d'Azur to suffer extensive damage during the allied landings of August 1944. I found that the hotel, which had been used by the Germans as a headquarters, had been totally destroyed. The pine trees and the red rocks were still there, but they were no longer peaceful. Campers with motor scooters and portable radios were everywhere. Most of the old buildings had gone. Only one remained completely undamaged and just as it is described in the book. It was, inevitably, the ugliest; the police station.

ERIC AMBLER

I

I ARRIVED in St Gatien from Nice on Tuesday, the 14th
of August. I was arrested at 11.45 a.m. on Thursday, the
16th, by an *agent de police* and an inspector in plain
clothes and taken to the Commissariat.

For several kilometres on the way from Toulon to La
Ciotat the railway runs very near to the coast. As the train
rushes between the innumerable short tunnels through
which this section of the line has been built, you catch
quick glimpses of the sea below, dazzlingly blue, of red
rocks, of white houses among pine woods. It is as if you
were watching a magic-lantern show with highly coloured
slides and an impatient operator. The eye has no time to
absorb details. Even if you know of St Gatien and are
looking for it, you can see nothing of it but the bright
red roof and the pale yellow stucco walls of the Hôtel de
la Réserve.

The hotel stands on the highest point of the headland
and the terrace runs along the south side of the building.
Beyond the terrace there is a sheer drop of about fifteen
metres. The branches of pines growing below brush the
pillars of the balustrade. But farther out towards the point
the level rises again. There are gashes of red rock in the
dry green scrub. A few windswept tamarisks wave their
tortured branches in silhouette against the intense ultra-
marine blue of the sea. Occasionally a white cloud of spray
starts up from the rocks below.

The village of St Gatien sprawls in the lee of the small headland on which the hotel stands. The walls of the houses are, like those of most other Mediterranean fishing villages, coated with either white, egg-shell blue, or rose-pink washes. Rocky heights, whose pine-clad slopes meet the seashore on the opposite side of the bay, shelter the miniature harbour from the mistral that sometimes blows strongly from the northwest. The population is seven hundred and forty-three. The majority depend for their livelihoods on fishing. There are two cafés, three bistros, seven shops and, farther round the bay, a police station.

But from the end of the terrace where I was sitting that morning the village and the police station were out of sight. The day was already warm and the cicadas were droning in the terraced gardens at the side of the hotel. By moving my head slightly I could see, through the balustrade, the small Réserve bathing beach. Two large coloured sunshades were planted in the sand. From under one of them two pairs of legs protruded, a woman's and a man's. They looked young and very brown. A faint murmur of voices told me that there were other guests out of sight in the shady part of the beach. The gardener, his head and shoulders sheltered from the sun by a huge straw hat, was painting a blue band round the gunwale of an upturned dinghy resting on trestles. A motorboat was coming round the headland on the far side of the bay and making for the beach. As it came nearer, I could distinguish the thin, lanky figure of Köche, the manager of the Réserve, drooping over the tiller. The other man in the boat was one of the fishermen from the village. They would have been out since dawn. Maybe we would have red mullet for lunch. Out at sea a Nederland-Lloyd liner moved on its way from Marseilles to Villefranche. It was all very good and peaceful.

I was thinking that tomorrow night I would have to pack my suitcase and that early Saturday morning I would have to go by bus into Toulon and catch the train for Paris. The train would be near Arles in the heat of the day, my body would stick to the hard leather seats of the third-class compartment, and there would be a layer of dust and soot over everything. I would be tired and thirsty by the time we reached Dijon. I must remember to take a bottle of water with me, with, perhaps, a little wine in it. I would be glad to get to Paris. But not for long. There would be the walk from the platforms of the Gare de Lyon to the platforms of the Métro. My suitcase would be heavy by then. *Direction* Neuilly to Concorde. Change. *Direction* Mairie d'Issy to Gare Montparnasse. Change. *Direction* Porte d'Orléans to Alésia. Exit. Montrouge. Avenue de Châtillon. Hôtel de Bordeaux. And on Monday morning there would be breakfast standing at the counter of the Café de l'Orient and another Métro journey, Denfert-Rochereau to Étoile, and a walk down the Avenue Marceau. Monsieur Mathis would be already there. 'Good morning, Monsieur Vadassy! You are looking very well. This term you will take elementary English, advanced German, and elementary Italian. I myself will take the advanced English. We have twelve new students. There are three businessmen and nine waiters. All are for English. There is none who wishes Hungarian.' Another year.

But meanwhile there were the pines and the sea, the red rocks and the sand. I stretched luxuriously and a lizard darted across the tiled floor of the terrace. It stopped suddenly to bask in the sun beyond the shadow of my chair. I could see the pulse beating in its throat. Its tail lay curved in a neat semicircle, making a tangent of the diagonal division between the tiles. Lizards have an uncanny sense of design.

It was this lizard which reminded me of my photographs.

I possess only two objects of value in this world. One of them is a camera, the other a letter dated February 10, 1867, from Deák to von Beust. If someone were to offer me money for the letter I would accept it thankfully; but I am very fond of the camera, and nothing but starvation would induce me to part with it. I am not a particularly good photographer; but I get a lot of pleasure pretending that I am.

I had been taking photographs at the Réserve and had, the previous day, taken an exposed spool into the village chemist's shop to be developed. Now, in the ordinary way, I would not dream of letting anyone else develop my films. Half the pleasure of amateur photography lies in doing your own darkroom work. But I had been experimenting, and if I did not see the results of the experiments before I left St Gatien, I would have no opportunity of making use of them. So I had left the film with the chemist. The negative was to be developed and dry by eleven o'clock.

The time was eleven thirty. If I went to the chemist's now, I would have time to get back, bathe, and have an apéritif before lunch.

I walked along the terrace, round through the gardens, and up the steps to the road. By now the sun was beating down so fiercely that the air above the asphalt was quivering. I had no hat and when I touched my hair it was burning hot. I draped a handkerchief over my head and walked up the hill, and then down the main street leading to the harbour.

The chemist's shop was cool and smelt of perfumes and disinfectant. The sound of the doorbell had barely died away before the chemist was facing me over the counter. His eyes met mine, but he seemed not to recognise me.

'Monsieur?'

'I left a spool of film yesterday to be developed.'

'It is not ready yet.'

'It was promised for eleven o'clock.'

'It is not ready yet,' he repeated steadily.

I was silent for a moment. There was something curious about the chemist's manner. His eyes, magnified by the thick pebble-glasses he wore, remained fixed on mine. There was an odd look in them. Then I realised what the look was. The man was frightened.

I remember that the realisation gave me a shock. He was afraid of me—I who had spent my life being afraid of others had at last inspired fear! I wanted to laugh. I was also annoyed, for I thought I knew what had happened. He had spoiled the film.

'Is the negative all right?'

He nodded vehemently.

'Perfectly, Monsieur. It is a question only of the drying. If you will be good enough to give me your name and address, I will send my son with the negative as soon as it is ready.'

'That's all right, I'll call again.'

'It will be no trouble, Monsieur.'

There was a strange note of urgency in his voice now. Mentally I shrugged. If the man had spoiled the film and was so childishly anxious not to be the bearer of the bad news it was no affair of mine. I had already resigned myself to the loss of my experiments.

'Very well.' I gave him my name and address.

He repeated them very loudly as he wrote them down.

'Monsieur Vadassy, Hôtel de la Réserve.' His voice dropped a little, and he ran his tongue round his lips before going on. 'It shall be sent round to you as soon as it is ready.'

I thanked him and went to the door of the shop. A man in a panama hat and an ill-fitting suit of Sunday blacks was standing facing me. The pavement was narrow, and as he did not move to make way for me, I murmured an apology and made to squeeze past him. As I did so he laid a hand on my arm.

'Monsieur Vadassy?'

'Yes?'

'I must ask you to accompany me to the Commissariat.'

'What on earth for?'

'A passport formality only, Monsieur.' He was stolidly polite.

'Then hadn't I better get my passport from the hotel?'

He did not answer but looked past me and nodded almost imperceptibly. A hand gripped my other arm tightly. I looked over my shoulder and saw that there was a uniformed *agent* standing in the shop door behind me. The chemist had disappeared.

The hands propelled me forward, not too gently.

'I don't understand,' I said.

'You will,' said the plain-clothes man briefly. '*Allez, file!*'

He was no longer polite.

2

THE journey to the police station was accomplished in silence. After the initial demonstration of authority the *agent* dropped a few paces to the rear and allowed me to walk on ahead with the plain-clothes man. I was glad of this, for I had no wish to be marched through the village as though I were a pickpocket. As it was, we drew some curious glances, and I heard a jocular reference by two passers-by to the *violon*.

French slang is very obscure. Anything less like a violin than the Commissariat de Police would be difficult to imagine. The only really ugly building in St Gatien, it is a forbidding cube of dirty concrete with small windows like eyes. It lies some hundreds of metres away from the village round the bay, and its size is accounted for by the fact that it houses the police administration of an area of which St Gatien happens to be the centre. The facts that St Gatien is also one of the smaller, more law-abiding, and least accessible villages in the area had been ignored by the responsible authorities.

The room into which I was taken was bare except for a table and some wooden benches. The plain-clothes man retired importantly, leaving me with the *agent*, who sat down on the bench beside me.

'Will this business take long?'

'It is not permitted to speak.'

I looked out of the window. Across the bay I could see

the coloured sunshades on the Réserve beach. There would not, I reflected, be time for a swim. I could, perhaps, have an apéritif at one of the cafés on my way back. It was all very annoying.

'*Levez-vous!*' said my escort suddenly.

The door opened and an elderly man with a pen behind his ear, no cap, and an unbuttoned tunic beckoned us out. The *agent* with me did up his collar, smoothed out his tunic, straightened his cap and, gripping my arm with unnecessary force, marched me down the passage to a room at the end of it. He rapped smartly on the door and opened it. Then he pushed me inside.

I felt a threadbare carpet beneath my feet. Sitting facing me behind a table littered with papers was a spectacled, businesslike little man. This was the Commissaire. Beside the table, wedged in a small chair with curved arms, was a very fat man in a tussore suit. Except for a clipped mouse-coloured bristle on the rolls of fat round his neck, he was bald. The skin of his face was loose and hung down in thick folds that drew the corners of his mouth with them. They gave the face a faintly judicial air. The eyes were extraordinarily small and heavily lidded. Sweat poured off his face and he kept passing a screwed-up handkerchief round the inside of his collar. He did not look at me.

'Josef Vadassy?'

It was the Commissaire who spoke.

'Yes.'

The Commissaire nodded to the *agent* behind me, and the man went out, closing the door softly behind him.

'Your identity card?'

I produced the card from my wallet and handed it over. He drew a sheet of paper towards him and began making notes.

'Age?'

'Thirty-two.' It was on the identity card; he was being officious.

'You are, I see, a teacher of languages.'

'Yes.'

'Who employs you?'

'The Bertrand Mathis School of Languages, one hundred and fourteen *bis*, Avenue Marceau, Paris, six.'

While he was writing this down I glanced at the fat man. His eyes were closed and he was fanning his face gently with the handkerchief.

'*Écoutez!*' said the Commissaire sharply. 'What is your business here?'

'I am on holiday.'

'You are a Yugoslav subject?'

'No; Hungarian.'

The Commissaire looked startled. My heart sank. The long and involved explanation of my national status, or rather, lack of it, would have to be given yet again. It never failed to arouse officialdom's worst instincts. The Commissaire rummaged among the papers on his table. Suddenly he gave an exclamation of satisfaction and flourished something in front of my face.

'Then how, Monsieur, do you explain this?'

With a start I realised that 'this' was my own passport— the passport that I had believed to be in my suitcase at the Réserve. That meant that the police had been to my room. I began to feel uneasy.

'I am waiting, Monsieur, for your explanation. How is it that you, a Hungarian, are using a Yugoslav passport? A passport, moreover, that has not been valid for ten years?'

Out of the corner of my eye I saw that the fat man had

stopped fanning his face. I began to give the explanation I knew by heart.

'I was born in Szabadka in Hungary. By the treaty of Trianon in 1919 Szabadka was incorporated in Yugoslav territory. In 1921 I went as a student to the University of Buda-Pesth. I obtained a Yugoslav passport for the purpose. While I was still at the University my father and elder brother were shot by the Yugoslav police for a political offence. My mother had died during the war and I had no other relations or friends. I was advised not to attempt to return to Yugoslavia. Conditions in Hungary were terrible. In 1922 I went to England, and remained there, teaching German in a school near London until 1931, when my labour permit was withdrawn. I was one of many other foreigners who had their labour permits withdrawn at that time. When my passport had expired I had applied for its renewal to the Yugoslav legation in London, but had been refused on the grounds that I was no longer a Yugoslav citizen. I had afterwards applied for British naturalisation, but when I was deprived of my labour permit I was forced to find work elsewhere. I went to Paris. I was allowed by the police to remain and given papers with the proviso that if I left France I should not be permitted to return. I have since applied for French citizenship.'

I looked from one to the other of them. The fat man was lighting a cigarette. The Commissaire flicked my useless passport contemptuously and looked at his colleague. I was looking at the Commissaire when the fat man spoke. His voice made me jump, for from those thick lips, that massive jowl, that enormous body, came a very light, husky tenor.

'What,' he said, 'was the political offence for which your father and brother were shot?'

18

He spoke slowly and carefully, as though he were afraid that his voice was going to crack. When I turned to answer him he was lighting the cigarette like a cigar and blowing a jet of smoke at the burning end of it.

'They were social-democrats,' I said.

The Commissaire said 'Ah!' as though all was now ominously clear.

'Then that perhaps explains . . .' he began unpleasantly.

But the fat man held up a repressive hand. It was small and puffy, with a roll of fat at the wrist like a baby's.

'What languages do you teach, Monsieur Vadassy?' he said gently.

'German, English, and Italian, occasionally Hungarian also. But I am afraid that I cannot see what these questions have to do with my passport.'

He ignored the last remark.

'You have been to Italy?'

'Yes.'

'When?'

'As a child. We used to spend our holidays there.'

'You have not been there during the present regime?'

'For obvious reasons, no.'

'Do you know any Italians in France?'

'There is one where I work. He is a teacher like myself.'

'His name?'

'Phillipino Rossi.'

I saw the Commissaire write this down.

'No others?'

'No.'

'You are a photographer, Monsieur Vadassy?'

It was the Commissaire again.

'An amateur—yes.'

'How many cameras do you possess?'

'One.' This was fantastic.

'What make is it?'

'A Zeiss Contax.'

He opened a drawer in his desk.

'Is this it?'

I recognised my camera.

'It is,' I said angrily, 'and I should like to know what right you have to remove my belongings from my room. You will please give it back to me.' I stretched out my hand for it.

The Commissaire put the camera back in the drawer.

'You have no other camera but this?'

'I have already told you. No!'

A grin of triumph spread over the Commissaire's face. He opened the drawer again.

'Then how, my dear Monsieur Vadassy, do you explain the fact that the chemist in the village received from you this length of cinematograph film for development?'

I stared at him. Between his outstretched hands was the developed negative of the film I had left with the chemist. From where I sat I could see against the light of the window my experimental shots; two dozen of them with but one single subject—lizards. Then I saw the Commissaire grin again. I laughed as irritatingly as I could.

'I can see,' I said patronisingly, 'that you are no photographer, Monsieur. That is not cinematograph film.'

'No?'

'No. I admit that it looks a little like it. But you will find that cinematograph film is a millimetre narrower. That is a standard spool of thirty-six twenty-four by thirty-six millimetre exposures for the Contax camera.'

'Then those photographs were taken by this camera here, the camera that was in your room?'

'Certainly.'

There was a pregnant pause. I saw the two exchange looks. Then:

'When did you arrive in St Gatien?'

It was the fat man once more.

'On Tuesday.'

'From?'

'Nice.'

'At what time did you leave Nice?'

'I left by the nine twenty-nine train.'

'At what time did you get to the Réserve?'

'Just before dinner, at about seven o'clock.'

'But the Nice train arrives at Toulon at three thirty. There is a bus for St Gatien at four. You should have arrived at five. Why were you late?'

'This is ridiculous.'

He looked up quickly. The small eyes were coldly menacing.

'Answer my question. Why were you late?'

'Very well. I left my suitcase in Toulon station and went for a walk down to the waterfront. I had not seen Toulon before and there was another bus at six.'

He wiped the inside of his collar thoughtfully.

'What is your salary, Monsieur Vadassy?'

'Sixteen hundred francs a month.'

'That is not very much, is it?'

'Unfortunately, no.'

'The Contax is an expensive camera?'

'It is a good one.'

'No doubt; but I am asking you how much you paid for it.'

'Four thousand, five hundred francs.'

He whistled softly. 'Nearly three months' pay, eh?'

'Photography is my hobby.'

'A very expensive one! You seem to be very clever with your sixteen hundred francs. Holidays in Nice and at the Hôtel de la Réserve, too! More than we poor policemen can afford, eh, Commissaire?'

The Commissaire laughed sardonically. I could feel myself getting very red in the face.

'I saved my money to buy the camera,' I said. 'As for this holiday, it is the first I have had for five years. I saved my money for that also.'

'But naturally!' The Commissaire sneered as he said it.

The sneer aroused me.

'Now, Monsieur,' I protested angrily. 'I have had enough of this. It is my turn to demand explanations. What exactly do you want? I am prepared to answer questions about my passport. You are within your rights in asking them. But you have no right to steal my private property. Neither have you any right to question me in this way about my private affairs. As for those negatives to which you seem to attach some mysterious importance, I have yet to learn that it is forbidden to photograph lizards. Now, Messieurs, I have committed no crime, but I am hungry, and it is time for lunch at the hotel. You will please return to me my camera, my photographs, and my passport immediately.'

For a moment there was dead silence. I glared from one to the other. Neither moved.

'Very well,' I said at last, and turned to the door.

'One moment,' said the fat man.

I stopped.

'Well?'

'Please don't waste your time and ours. The man outside the door will not allow you to leave. There are a few more questions we have to ask you.'

22

'You may keep me here by force,' I said grimly, 'but you cannot force me to answer your questions.'

'Naturally,' said the fat man slowly; 'that is the law. But we can recommend you to do so—in your own interests.'

I said nothing.

The fat man picked up the negative from the Commissaire's desk and, holding it up to the light, ran it through his fingers.

'Over two dozen photographs,' he commented, 'and all practically the same. Now that, I think, is curious. Don't you think so, Vadassy?'

'Not in the least,' I replied curtly. 'If you knew anything at all about photography, or if you were just ordinarily observant, you would notice that each one is lighted differently, that in each one the shadows are massed in different ways. The fact that the object photographed in every case is a lizard is unimportant. The differences lie in the way each is lighted and composed. Anyway, if I like to take a hundred shots of lizards in the sun I don't see that it is any business of yours.'

'This is a very ingenious explanation, Vadassy. Very ingenious. Now I will tell you what I think. My idea is that you were not in the least interested in what you photographed with those twenty-six exposures and that you were merely exposing the film as quickly as you could to complete the spool and get the other ten exposures developed.'

'The other ten? What are you talking about?'

'Isn't it a waste of time to pretend any longer, Vadassy?'

'I really don't know what you mean.'

He heaved himself out of the chair and stood close to me.

'Don't you? What about the first ten exposures, Vadassy? Would you like to explain to the Commissaire and myself why you took *those* photographs? I feel sure we should be interested!' He tapped me on the chest with his finger. 'Was it the lighting, Vadassy, or was it the massing of the shadows that so interested you in the new fortifications outside the naval base of Toulon?'

I gaped at him.

'Is this a joke? The only other photographs on that spool are some I took in Nice of a carnival that was held the day before I left.'

'You admit taking the photographs on this film?' he said deliberately.

'I have already said so.'

'Good. Please look at them.'

I took the negative, held it up to the light and ran it slowly through my fingers. Lizards, lizards, lizards. Some of the shots looked promising. Lizards. More lizards. Suddenly I stopped. I looked up quickly. Both of them were watching me.

'Go on, Vadassy,' said the Commissaire ironically; 'don't trouble to look surprised.'

Unable to believe my eyes, I looked at the negative again. There was a long shot of a section of coastline partly obscured by what looked like a twig close to the lens of the camera. There was something on the coastline—a short grey strip. Another shot, closer this time and from a different angle, of that same grey strip. There were things that looked like trap-doors along one side of it. More shots. Two of them were from the same angle; another had been taken looking down and nearer still. Then came three almost wholly obscured by a dark mass in front of the camera. The edge of the mass was blurred

24

and very faintly patterned like a piece of cloth. Then there was one of what looked like a concrete surface out of focus and very near to the camera. The last of them was overexposed, but only one corner of it was obscured. It was taken from one end of what looked like a wide concrete gallery. There were some curious arrangements of highlights. They puzzled me for a moment. Then at last I understood. I was looking at the long, sleek barrels of siege guns.

3

THE formalities of my arrest were attended by the examining magistrate, a harassed little man who, prompted by the fat detective, subjected me to a perfunctory interrogation before instructing the Commissaire to charge me. I was, I learned, charged with espionage, trespassing in a military zone, taking photographs calculated to endanger the safety of the French Republic, and of being in possession of such photographs. After the charges had been read out to me and I had signified that I had understood them, I was deprived of my belt (lest, presumably, I should hang myself) and the contents of my pockets, and taken, clutching my trousers, to a cell at the rear of the building. There I was left alone.

After a bit, I began to think more calmly. It was ridiculous. It was outrageous. It was impossible. Yet it had happened. I was in a police cell under arrest on a charge of espionage. The penalty, should I be convicted, would be perhaps four years' imprisonment—four years in a French prison and then deportation. I could put up with prison—even a French one—but deportation! I began to feel sick and desperately frightened. If France expelled me there was nowhere left for me to go. Yugoslavia would arrest me. Hungary would not admit me. Neither would Germany or Italy. Even if a convicted spy could get into England without a passport he would not be permitted to work. To America I would be merely another undesirable alien. The South American republics would demand sums of money that I would not possess as surety for my good behaviour. Soviet Russia would have no more use for a convicted spy than would England. Even the Chinese wanted your passport. There would be nowhere I could go, nowhere. And after all, what did it matter? What happened to an insignificant teacher of languages without national status was of no interest to anyone. No consul would intervene on his behalf; no Parliament, no Congress, no Chamber of Deputies would inquire into his fate. Officially he did not exist; he was an abstraction, a ghost. All he could decently and logically do was destroy himself.

I pulled myself together sharply. I was being hysterical. I was not yet a convicted spy. I was still in France. I must use my brains, think, find the very simple explanation that must exist for the presence of those photographs in my camera. I must go very carefully over the ground. I must cast my thoughts back to Nice.

I had, I remembered, put the new spool in the camera and taken the photographs of the carnival on Monday. Then I had gone back to my hotel and put the camera in my suitcase. It had still been there when I packed later that night. It had remained in my suitcase until I had unpacked at the Réserve on Tuesday evening. While I had been in Toulon the suitcase had been in the *consigne* at the station. Could anyone have used it during the two hours I was walking about Toulon? Impossible. The suitcase was locked and no one could break it open in the *consigne*, steal the camera, take those dangerous-looking photographs, and restore the camera to the suitcase in two hours. Besides, why put the camera back again? No, that would not do.

27

Then another thought struck me. The photographs I was supposed to have taken were the first ten on the spool. They must have been, for my last lizard shot had been number thirty-six. There were no double exposures on the film. Therefore, as I had started a spool at the carnival in Nice, a new spool must have been put in before the Toulon photographs were taken.

I jumped up in my excitement from the bed on which I had been sitting, and my trousers sagged down. I rescued them and, with my hands in my pockets, marched up and down the cell. Of course! I remembered now. I had been slightly surprised to notice when I had started on the lizard experiments that the exposure counter on the camera had registered number eleven. I had thought that I had made only eight exposures at Nice. But it is very easy to forget odd shots, especially when there are thirty-six exposures on the spool. Yes, the spool had certainly been changed. But when? It couldn't have been done before I arrived at the Réserve, and I had started on the lizards the following morning after breakfast. It came to this, then: that between 7 p.m. Tuesday and 8.30 a.m. (breakfast-time) Wednesday, somebody had taken my camera from my room, put a new spool of film in it, gone to Toulon, penetrated a carefully guarded military zone, taken the photographs, returned to the Réserve and restored my camera to my room.

It didn't sound possible or probable. Quite apart from any other objections, there was the simple question of the light. It was practically dark by eight o'clock, and as I had not arrived until seven, that disposed of Tuesday. Even supposing that the photographer had gone by night and started work at sunrise, he would have had to be very quick and clever to get my camera back into my room while I was lying in bed looking out of the window. And, anyway, why return it to me with the spool still inside it? How had the police got into the business? Had the taker of the photographs told them anonymously? There was, of course, the chemist. The police had obviously been in ambush for the owner of the negative. Perhaps the chemist had been caught with the photographs and sworn that they had belonged to me. But then, that didn't account for their being with my experimental shots. There had been no sign of a join in the negative. It was hideously puzzling.

I was feverishly going over the ground for the third time when there was the sound of footsteps in the corridor outside and the door of my cell opened. The fat man in the tussore suit came in. The door closed behind him.

For a moment he stood wiping the inside of his collar with his handkerchief, then he nodded to me and sat down on the bed.

'Sit down, Vadassy.'

I sat down on the only other piece of furniture in the room, an enamelled iron *bidet* with a wooden lid on it. The small, dangerous eyes surveyed me thoughtfully.

'Would you like a bowl of soup and some bread?'

This I had not expected.

'No, thank you. I am not hungry.'

'A cigarette, then?'

He proffered a crumpled packet of Gauloises. This solicitude was, I felt, highly suspicious; but I took one.

He gave me a light from the end of his own cigarette. Then he carefully wiped the sweat from his upper lip and from behind his ears.

'Why,' he said at last, 'did you admit that you took those photographs?'

'Is this another official interrogation?'

He brushed cigarette ash off his stomach with the now sodden handkerchief.

'No. You will be interrogated officially by the *juge d'instruction* of the district. That is no business of mine. I am of the Sûreté Générale and attached to the Department of Naval Intelligence. You may speak quite freely to me.'

I did not see why he should expect a spy to speak quite freely to a member of the Department of Naval Intelligence, but I did not raise the point. I had, indeed, every intention of speaking as freely as I was allowed to.

'Very well. I admitted taking the photographs because I did take them. That is, all those on the spool with the exception of the first ten.'

"Quite so. Then how do you account for those first ten photographs?"

'I think the spool in my camera was changed.'

He raised his eyebrows. I plunged into a long account of my movements since leaving Nice and the deductions I had made concerning the origin of the incriminating photographs. He heard me out, but was obviously not impressed.

'This, of course, is not evidence,' he said when I had finished.

'I don't offer it as evidence. I am just trying to find a rational explanation of this fantastic affair.'

'The Commissaire thinks that he has found the explanation. I do not blame him. On the face of things the case against you is perfectly good. The photographs are on a negative which you have admitted to be yours. You are also a suspicious person. Simple!'

I looked him in the eye.

'But I take it that you are not satisfied, Monsieur?'

'I didn't say that.'

'No, but you would scarcely be here talking to me in this way if you were satisfied.'

His jowl distorted into the beginnings of a grin.

'You overrate your importance. I am not interested in spies, but in who employs them.'

'Then,' I said angrily, 'you are wasting your time. I am not the person who took the photographs, and my only employer is Monsieur Mathis, who pays me to teach languages.'

But he did not appear to be listening. There was a pause.

'The Commissaire and I agreed,' he said at last, 'that you were one of three things—a clever spy, a very stupid one, or an innocent man. I may say that the Commissaire thought that you must be the second. I was inclined from the first to think you innocent. You behaved far too stupidly. No guilty man would be such an imbecile.'

'Thank you.'

'I am not in the least desirous of your thanks, Vadassy. It was a conclusion that I disliked exceedingly. In any case, I can do nothing for you now. Understand that, please. You have been arrested by the Commissaire. You may be innocent, but it will not disturb my rest in the slightest if you are sent to prison.'

'I feel sure of that.'

'On the other hand,' he continued thoughtfully, 'it is essential that I should know who *did* take the photographs.'

There was another silence. I felt that I was expected to make some comment. But I waited for him to go on. After a few moments he did so.

'If the real criminal is discovered, we may, Vadassy, be able to do something for you.'

'Do something for me?'

He cleared his throat noisily.

'Well, of course, you have no consul to intervene on your behalf. It is our responsibility to see that you are treated properly. Providing, naturally, that you co-operate with us in a satisfactory manner, you need have no fears.'

'I have already told you all I know, Monsieur ...' I stopped. There was a lump in my throat and the words would not come. But the fat man evidently thought that I was waiting to be supplied with his name.

'Beghin,' he said, 'Michel Beghin.'

He paused and looked at his stomach once more. The cell was insufferably hot and I could see the sweat from his chest staining through his striped shirt. 'All the same,' he added, 'I think you may be able to help us.'

He got up from the bed, went to the cell door and banged on it once with his fist. The key clicked in the lock and I saw the uniform of an *agent* outside. The fat man muttered something I did not hear and the door closed again. He remained standing there and lit another cigarette. A minute later the door opened again and he took something from the *agent*. As the door closed once more he turned round. In his hand was the camera.

'You recognise this?'

'Of course.'

'Take it and examine it very closely. I want to know if you find anything curious about it.'

I took it and did as I was told. I tried the shutter, the viewfinder, and the focusing; I took out the lens and undid the back; I peered in every nook and cranny of the instrument. Finally I put it back in the case.

'I don't see anything curious about it. It is just as I left it.'

He put his hand in his pocket and drew out a piece of folded paper. He held it up.

'This, Vadassy, we found in your pocketbook. Have a look.'

I took the paper and opened it. Then I looked at him.

'Well, what about it?' I said defensively. 'This is merely the insurance policy on the camera. As you reminded me, it is an expensive instrument. I paid a few francs to insure myself against its loss or,' I added pointedly, 'theft.'

He took the paper from me with a patient sigh.

'It is lucky for you,' he said, 'that French justice takes care of imbeciles as well as criminals. This insurance policy indemnifies Josef Vadassy against the loss of the Zeiss Ikon Contax camera, serial number F/64523/2. Please look at the serial number on the camera you have there.'

I looked. The serial number was different.

'Then,' I exclaimed excitedly, 'this isn't my camera. Why were my photographs on that negative?'

'Because, my dear imbecile, it was not the films that were changed, but the cameras. This camera is a standard production and widely used. You used this camera with the Toulon exposures already made to photograph your stupid lizards. You even noticed that the number of the exposure was different from that in your own camera. Then you removed the film and took it to the chemist. He saw these ten photographs, saw, as any fool would see, what they were, and brought them to the police. Now, imbecile, do you see?'

I did.

33

'So,' I said, 'when you so generously proclaimed your faith in my innocence you were perfectly well aware of it. In view of that I should like to know what right you have to keep me under arrest like this.'

He wiped the top of his head with his handkerchief and surveyed me from beneath lowered lids.

'Your arrest is no affair of mine. I can do nothing. The Commissaire is annoyed with you, as this evidence has spoiled his charge sheet; but he has agreed, in the interests of justice, to strike out three of the charges. Only one remains.'

'What is that?'

'You were in possession of photographs calculated to endanger the safety of the Republic. That is a serious offence. It remains, unless,' he added significantly, 'unless means can be found to strike it out also. I shall naturally intercede with the Commissaire on your behalf, but I am afraid that unless I can offer some good reason for this irregular step the charge will go forward. It would mean deportation at the very least.'

My brain went as cold as ice.

'You mean,' I said steadily, 'that if I do not agree to co-operate, as you call it, this ridiculous charge will be pressed?'

He did not answer. He was lighting his fourth cigarette. When he had finished he let it hang lightly between his loose lips. He blew smoke past it and gazed contemplatively at the blank wall as though it were a painting and he were a collector wondering whether to bid.

'The cameras,' he said thoughtfully, 'could have been changed for one of three reasons. Someone might have wished to do you an injury. Someone might have wished to get rid of the photographs in a hurry. Or it could

34

have been done accidentally. The first hypothesis, I think, we can dismiss. It is too elaborate. There was no guarantee that (a) you would take the film to be developed and that (b) the chemist would go to the police. The second hypothesis is unreal. The photographs were valuable and the possibility of retrieving them remote. Besides, they were safe enough inside the camera. No, I think it was accidental. The cameras are of an identical pattern and in standard cases. But where and when were they changed? Not at Nice, for you told me that you took your camera back to the hotel and packed it. Not on your journey, because it was under lock and key in your suitcase during the entire time. It was at the Réserve that the change was made. If the change was accidental, then it could only have been made in one of the public rooms. At what time? You brought your camera down at breakfast-time yesterday, you tell me. Where did you have breakfast?'

'On the terrace.'

'Did you take the camera with you?'

'No. I left it in its case on one of the chairs in the hall to pick up as I went through into the garden afterwards.'

'At what time did you go to breakfast?'

'At about half past eight.'

'And to the gardens?'

'About an hour later.'

'And then you took photographs?'

'Yes.'

'At what time did you return?'

'It was nearly twelve.'

'What did you do?'

'I went straight to my room and removed the exposed spool.'

35

'Then you did not leave your camera before you started photographing your lizards except for an hour between eight thirty and nine thirty?'

'No.'

'And during that time it was on a chair by the door leading to the garden.'

'Yes.'

'Now think carefully. Was the camera in the same position when you picked it up as it was when you put it down?'

I thought carefully.

'No, it was not,' I said at last. 'I left it hanging by the strap of the case on the back of one of the chairs. When I picked it up it was lying on the seat of another chair.'

'You did not look to see if it was still hanging where you had left it?'

'Why, no. I saw it on the seat of the chair and took it. Why should I look?'

'You might have noticed if there was still a camera hanging on the back of the chair.'

'It would be easy not to. The strap is long so that the actual camera case would hang below the seat level of the chair.'

'Good. So it amounts to this: you hang a camera on the back of a chair. When you return you see an identical camera on the seat of another chair. Thinking that this is your property, you take it, leaving your camera where you put it on the back of the original chair. Presumably, then, the owner of the second camera later arrives, finds his camera missing from the seat of the chair, looks round and discovers yours.'

'It seems likely.'

'Were all the guests down to breakfast?'

36

'I don't know. There are only eighteen rooms at the Réserve and they are not all occupied, but I had only arrived the previous night. I would not know. But everyone going downstairs and through the hall would pass the chairs.'

'Then, my dear Vadassy, we can say with reasonable confidence that one of those now staying at the Réserve is the person who owns this camera and who took those photographs. But which? I think we may leave out the waiters and servants, for they are all from this village or near-by villages. We shall, of course, make inquiries, but they will, I think, give us nothing. There are, besides, ten guests, the manager Köche and his wife. Now, Vadassy, the guilty one had your camera, a Zeiss Ikon Contax identical to this one here. It is, you will realise, obviously quite impossible for us to arrest the entire *pension* and search everyone's luggage. Apart from the fact that several are foreigners whose consuls would be troublesome, we might fail to find the camera. In that case the guilty one would be on his guard and we should be helpless. Inquiries,' he went on pointedly, 'must be made by someone whose presence would arouse no suspicion, who could find out discreetly who has been seen with a Contax camera.'

'You mean me?'

'You might proceed very simply by finding out which of them have cameras. Those that have cameras but not Contax cameras may be less under suspicion than those who have no cameras. You see, Vadassy, the person who has your camera may know by now that the change has been made. In that case he would hide your camera lest he should be identified as the owner of the camera with the Toulon photographs in it. There is also the possibility,' he added dreamily, 'that he might try to get his own camera back again. You must be on the watch for that.'

'You don't put this suggestion forward seriously?'

He glanced at me coldly.

'Believe me, my friend, if I had any alternative I should be glad. You do not seem to me very intelligent.'

'But I am under arrest. Surely,' I said acidly, 'you will not be able to persuade the Commissaire to release me?'

'You will remain under arrest, but you will be released on parole. Only Köche knows of your arrest. We visited your room. He did not like it, but it was explained that it was an affair of passports and that you had given permission. You will state that there was a misunderstanding and that you were detained by mistake. You will report to me by telephone here every morning. Telephone from the post office in the village. If you wish to find me at any other time you will telephone to the Commissaire.'

'But I have to leave on Saturday morning for Paris. I am expected to start the new term on Monday.'

'You will stay until you have permission to go. Also you will make no attempt to get into touch with anyone outside the Réserve except the police.'

A sickening sense of helplessness crept over me.

'I shall lose my job.'

Beghin got up and stood over me.

'Listen, Vadassy,' he said; and in his absurd voice there was an ugly note far more menacing than the Commissaire's bluster. 'You will stay at the Réserve until you are told to go. If you try to leave before then, you will be re-arrested and I shall make it my personal business to see that you are deported by steamer to Dubrovnik and that your dossier is handed to the Yugoslav police. And

38

get this into your head. The quicker we find out who took those photographs the sooner you can go. But don't try any tricks and don't write any letters. Either you do what you are told or you will be deported. You will be very lucky if you avoid deportation, anyway. So be careful. You understand, eh?'

I did—clearly.

An hour later I walked back along the road from the Commissariat to the village. The Contax was slung over my shoulder. When I put my hand in my pocket I could feel a small piece of paper with a list of the guests at the Réserve typed on it.

Köche was in his office when I got there. As I passed by to go to my room he came out. He was in blue jeans, sandals, and a *maillot,* and, to judge from his wet hair, had just been swimming. With his tall, thin, stooping figure and his sleepy manner he looked very unmanagerial.

'Ah, Monsieur,' he said with a faint smile. 'You are back. Nothing serious, I hope. The police came here this morning. They said they had your permission to take your passport.'

I looked as disgruntled as I could.

'No, nothing serious. A question of identity and a mistake which they took a fantastic time to discover. They were apologetic, but what can one do? The French police are wholly ridiculous.'

He looked serious, professed amazement and indignation, complimented me on my forbearance. He was clearly unconvinced. I could scarcely blame him. I was feeling too weak to play the outraged citizen with any hope of success.

'By the way, Monsieur,' he said casually, as I made for the stairs, 'it is Saturday morning that you are leaving, I believe?'

So he wanted to get rid of me. I affected to consider the question.

'I had thought of doing so,' I said; 'but I may decide to stay a day or two longer. That is,' I added, with a wintry smile, 'if the police have no objection.'

He hesitated barely a second.

'A pleasure,' he said, but without enthusiasm.

As I turned again to go, it may have been my fancy, but I thought that his eyes were on the camera.

4

I FIND it difficult now to remember much of the next two hours. But I do know that when I reached my room there was for me only one question in the world—was there a train from Toulon to Paris on Sunday afternoon? I remember that I rushed to my suitcase and searched feverishly for the timetable.

You may find it odd that, faced with utter and complete disaster, I should be concerned about so trivial a matter as the train services to Paris. But human beings do behave oddly in times of great stress. Passengers in a sinking ship will go back to their cabins as the last boat is casting off from the side, to save trifling personal possessions. Men on the point of death worry about small unpaid bills as they go forward to eternity.

What worried me was the prospect of being late on the Monday morning. Monsieur Mathis was very strict on the score of punctuality. Latecomers, whether pupils or teachers, incurred his grave displeasure. This was expressed in biting terms and a very loud voice at a moment when the additional embarrassment of an audience had to be suffered. The denunciation, moreover, usually followed some hours after the commission of the crime. The suspense could be very wearing.

If, I reasoned, I could catch a train from Toulon on Sunday afternoon and travel overnight to Paris, I might be at the school on time. I remember the feeling of relief I experienced on finding that there was a train which reached Paris at six o'clock on the Monday morning. My mind was working in a fog. Beghin had said that I should not be able to leave on Saturday. Terrible! Monsieur Mathis would be angry. Could I get to Paris in time if I left on Sunday? Yes, thank God, I could! All was well.

I think that if anyone had suggested to me at that moment that I should not be able to leave on the Sunday, I should have laughed disbelievingly. But there would have been hysteria in that laugh for, as I sat on the floor beside my open suitcase, fear was clutching at the mechanism inside my chest, making my heart thud and my breathing short and sharp, as though I had been running. I kept swallowing saliva, feeling for some curious reason that by doing so I would stop my heart beating so. It made me terribly thirsty and after a while I got up, went to the washbasin, and drank some water out of the tooth glass. Then I went back and pushed the lid of my suitcase down with my foot. As I did so I felt the piece of paper Beghin had given me crackle in my pocket. I sat down on the bed.

I must have sat staring blankly at Beghin's list for well over an hour. I read it and re-read it. The names became ciphers, meaningless arrangements of shapes. I shut my eyes, opened them, and read again, I did not know these people. I had spent one day in the hotel. It was a hotel with large grounds. I had exchanged nods with them at mealtimes. No more. With my bad memory for faces I could probably have passed all of them in the street without recognising one. Yet one of the persons represented by those names had my camera. One of those who had nodded to me was a spy. One of them had been paid to make his or her way secretly into military zones, to take

42

photographs of reinforced concrete and guns so that some day warships out at sea might safely and accurately fire shells to smash to pieces the concrete and the guns and the men who served them. And I had two days in which to identify that person.

Their names, I thought stupidly, looked very harmless.

Monsieur Robert Duclos	French	*Nantes*
Monsieur André Roux	French	*Paris*
Mademoiselle Odette Martin	French	*Paris*
Miss Mary Skelton . .	American	*Washington, D.C.*
Mr Warren Skelton . .	American	*Washington, D.C.*
Herr Walter Vogel . .	Swiss	*Constance*
Frau Hulde Vogel . .	Swiss	*Constance*
Major Herbert Clandon-Hartley	English	*Buxton*
Mrs Maria Clandon-Hartley	English	*Buxton*
Herr Emil Schimler .	German	*Berlin*
Albert Köche (manager)	Swiss	*Schaffhausen*
Suzanne Köche (wife) .	Swiss	*Schaffhausen*

A similar list of guests might have been compiled from almost any other small *pension* in the south of France. There was the inevitable English army man and his wife. There were the Americans, not quite so inevitable, but by no means unusual. There were the Swiss, and there was the sprinkling of French. The solitary German was odd, but not unduly so. Swiss hotel managers and their wives were common enough.

What was I to do? Where should I start? Then I remembered Beghin's instructions about the cameras. I was to find out which of them had cameras and then report. This at least was a positive line of thought.

The obvious method seemed to be to engage them in conversation one by one, or couple by couple, and bring up the subject of photography. But that was no use. Supposing the spy had already discovered that his photographs were missing, that instead of his pictures of concrete and guns he had some lively low-angle shots of a carnival at Nice? Even if he did not immediately realise that he had somebody else's camera, he would know that something had gone wrong and be on his guard. Anyone attempting to get conversational on the subject of photography would excite his suspicions. I must proceed by less direct means.

I glanced at my watch. The time was a quarter to seven. From the window I could see that the beach was still occupied. There were a pair of shoes and a small sunshade lying on the strip of sand visible from my room. I combed my hair and went out.

Some people can strike up casual acquaintances with the greatest ease. They possess some mysterious flexible quality of mind that enables them to adjust their mental processes rapidly to conform with those of the strangers facing them. In an instant they have identified themselves with the stranger's interests. They smile. The strangers respond. There is a question and a reply. A minute later they are friends, chatting away amicably of trifles.

I do not possess this engaging faculty. I do not speak at all unless spoken to. Even then, nervousness allied to a desperate wish to be friendly renders me either stiff and formal or over-effusive. As a result of this, strangers either think me morose or suspect me of trying to work a confidence trick.

As I walked down the stone steps to the beach, however, I made up my mind that, for once at any rate, I would have to shed my inhibitions. I must be confident and friendly, I must think of amusing things to say, I must manage the conversation, be subtle. I had work to do.

The small beach was now in complete shadow and a faint breeze off the sea was beginning to stir the tops of the trees; but it was still very warm. I could see the heads of two men and two women over the backs of the deck-chairs in which their owners were sitting; and as I neared the foot of the steps I could hear that they were attempting to carry on a conversation in French.

I walked across the sand, sat a few metres from them on the end of one of the trestles on which the dinghy was being painted, and gazed out across the bay.

From the quick look I had got in as I sat down I knew that in the two chairs nearest me were a young man of about twenty-three and a girl of about twenty. They had been swimming, and it was evidently their brown legs that I had seen from the terrace that morning. I judged from their French that these were the two Americans, Warren and Mary Skelton.

The other two were very different. Both were middle-aged and very fat. I remembered having noticed them before. The man had a beaming moonlike face and a torso that from a distance looked almost spherical. This illusion was due in some measure to the trousers he wore. They were of some dark material and had very short, narrow legs. The tops of them, already very high, were drawn up over his round belly almost to his arm-pits by very powerful braces. He wore a tennis shirt open at the neck and no jacket. He might have walked out of a cartoon in *Simplicissimus*. His wife, for these were the Swiss, was slightly taller than him and very untidy. She laughed a great deal and even when she was not actually laughing she looked as if she was about to do so. Her husband beamed in concert with her. They both appeared as simple and unselfconscious as a pair of small children.

It seemed that Skelton was trying to explain the American political system to Herr Vogel.

'*Il y a,*' he was saying laboriously, '*deux parties seulement, les Républicaines et les Démocrates. Ces sont du droit—tous les deux. Mais les Républicaines sont plus au droit que les Démocrates. Ça c'est la différence.*'

'*Ah oui, je comprend,*' said Herr Vogel. He hurriedly translated the sense into German. Frau Vogel grinned broadly.

'One hears,' pursued her husband in his clipped French, 'that the gangsters (he pronounced it 'garngstairs') have a decisive influence during the elections. Like a party of the centre, perhaps?' He had the air of one putting aside frivolous small talk in favour of graver matters.

The girl giggled helplessly. Her brother drew a deep breath and began to explain with great care, and to Herr Vogel's evident amazement, that ninety-nine point nine per cent of the people of the United States had never seen a gangster. But his French soon gave out.

'*Il y a, sans doute,*' he was admitting, '*une quantité de ... quelque ...*' He could get no farther. 'Mary,' he said plaintively, 'what the hell's the word for graft?'

At that moment fortune favoured me. It may be that teaching becomes a habit, that the impulse to instruct will, like hunger or fear, overcome social inhibitions. Out of the corner of my eye I saw the girl shrug her shoulders helplessly; a fraction of a second later the words were out of my mouth.

'*Chantage* is the word you want.'

They all looked at me.

'Thanks,' said the girl.

An eager light came into her brother's eye.

'Do you speak French as well as English?'

'Yes.'

'Then,' he said grimly, 'do you mind telling fatso here on our left that gangster is spelt with a small "g" in America, and they're not represented in Congress. At least, not openly. You might add, too, while you're about it, that all our food doesn't come out of cans, and that we don't all live in the Empire State Building.'

'Certainly.'

The girl smiled.

'My brother's not serious.'

'Aren't I, by heaven! He's an international menace. Someone ought to tell him.'

The Vogels had been listening to this exchange with bewildered smiles on their faces. I translated, as tactfully as possible, into German. They rocked with laughter. Between paroxysms, Herr Vogel explained that it was impossible not to tease Americans. A party of garngstair! The Empire State Building! There were fresh peals of laughter. The Swiss were evidently not quite so naïve as they looked.

'What's the matter with him now?' demanded Skelton.

I explained. He grinned.

'You wouldn't think they had any guile in them, would you?' he said, and leaned forward to get a better view of the Vogels. 'What are they, Germans?'

47

'Swiss, I think.'

'Poppa,' remarked the girl, 'looks exactly like Tenniel's illustration of Tweedledum and Tweedledee.'

The object of these criticisms was regarding us anxiously. He addressed himself to me.

'*Die jungen Leute haben unseren kleinen Spass nicht übel genommen?*'

'He says,' I explained to the Skeltons, 'that he hopes he hasn't offended you.'

Young Skelton looked startled.

'Hell, no. Look—' He turned to the Vogels. '*Nous sommes très amusés. Sie sind sehr liebenswürdig,*' he said heartily. Then: 'Oh, tell him, will you?'

I did so. There was a great deal of nodding and smiling. Then the Vogels began to talk between themselves.

'How many languages do you speak?' said Skelton.

'Five.'

He laughed disgustedly.

'Then would you explain very carefully,' put in the girl, 'just how you learn a foreign language? I don't want five. But if you could think in terms of ones for a moment, my brother and I would be interested.'

I muttered something about living in countries and cultivating a 'language ear', and asked them if they had been at the Réserve long.

'Oh, we've been here a week or so now,' he replied. 'Our parents are coming over from home next week on the *Conte di Savoia*. We're meeting them at Marseilles. You arrived Tuesday, didn't you?'

'Yes.'

'Well, I'm glad we can talk to someone in English. Köche is not bad with his English, but he's got no staying power. We've only had that British major and his wife. He's high-hat and she doesn't speak at all.'

'Which could be lucky, too,' said his sister.

She was, I was realising, though far from pretty, extremely attractive. Her mouth was too wide, her nose was not quite symmetrical, and her face was flat, with over-prominent cheekbones. But there was humour and intelligence in the way the lips moved, and the nose and cheekbones were good. The skin of her body was firm and clear and brown, while the thick mass of tawny fair hair crushed forward by the back of the deck-chair gleamed in a most interesting way. She was almost beautiful.

'The trouble with the French,' her brother was saying, 'is that they get mad if you can't speak their language properly. I don't get mad if a Frenchman can't speak English.'

'No, but that's because most ordinary Frenchmen like the sound of their language. They don't like listening to a bad French accent any more than you like listening to a beginner practising on a violin.'

'It's no use appealing to his musical ear,' commented the girl. 'He's tone deaf.' She got up and smoothed out her bathing suit. 'Well,' she said, 'I guess we'd better be getting some more clothes on.'

Herr Vogel heaved himself out of his chair, consulted an enormous watch, and announced in French that it was seven fifteen. Then he hitched up his braces another notch and began to collect his and his wife's belongings. We all went in procession to the steps. I found myself behind the American.

'By the way, sir,' he said as we started up, 'I didn't catch your name.'

'Josef Vadassy.'

'Mine's Warren Skelton. This is my sister Mary.'

But I barely heard him. Slung across Herr Vogel's plump back was a camera, and I was trying to recollect where I had seen another one like it. Then I remembered. It was a box-type Voigtlander.

On very warm nights, dinner at the Réserve was served on the terrace. A striped awning was put up for the purpose and illumination was provided by candles on the tables. It looked very gay when they were all alight.

I had made up my mind to be the first on the terrace that evening. For one thing, I was hungry. For another, I wanted to inspect my fellow guests one at a time. Three of them, however, were already in their places when I arrived.

One of them, a man sitting alone, was placed behind me so that I could not see him except by turning right round in my chair. I took in as much as possible of his appearance as I walked to my table.

The candle on his table and the fact that he was bending forward over his plate prevented my seeing much of him except a head of short, greying fair hair brushed sideways without a parting. He was wearing a white shirt and a pair of coarse linen trousers of obviously French manufacture.

I sat down and turned my attention to the other two.

They sat very stiffly, facing one another across their table, he a narrow-headed man with grizzled brown hair and a clipped moustache, she an impassive middle-aged woman with large bones, a sallow complexion, and a head of neatly dressed white hair. Both had changed for dinner. She wore a white blouse and black skirt. He had put on grey flannel trousers, a striped shirt with a regimental tie, and a tweed jacket. As I watched him he put down his soup spoon, picked up a bottle of Beaujolais from the table, and held it to the light.

'I do believe, my dear,' I heard him say, 'that the waiters drink our wine. I marked this bottle most carefully at luncheon.'

He had a penetrating upper-middle-class English voice. The woman shrugged her shoulders ever so slightly. Obviously she did not approve.

'My dear,' he replied, 'it's the principle of the thing that I look at. They ought to be pulled up about it. I shall drop a hint to Köche.'

I saw her shrug her shoulders again and dab her mouth with her napkin. This was evidently Major and Mrs Clandon-Hartley.

The other guests had by this time begun to arrive.

The Vogels sat at a table beyond the two English and beside the balustrade. Another couple made for the table against the wall.

These were unmistakably French. The man, very dark and with goitrous eyes and an unshaven chin, looked about thirty-five. The woman, an emaciated blonde in satin beach pyjamas and imitation pearl ear-rings the size of grapes, might have been older. They were very interested in one another. As he held the chair for her to sit down he caressed her arm. She responded with a furtive squeeze of his fingers, then looked round quickly to see if the other guests had noticed. I saw that the Vogels were convulsed with silent laughter at the incident. Herr Vogel winked at me across the tables.

The blonde woman, I decided, was probably Odette Martin. Her companion would be either Duclos or Roux.

51

Mary Skelton and her brother came next. They nodded amicably and went to a table behind me on my right. There was only one more to come. He proved to be an elderly man with a white beard and wearing pince-nez attached to a broad, black ribbon.

When the waiter took my soup plate I stopped him. 'Who is the gentleman with the white beard?'

'That is Monsieur Duclos.'

'And the gentleman with the blonde?'

The waiter smiled discreetly.

'Monsieur Roux and Mademoiselle Martin.' He placed a faint emphasis on the 'mademoiselle'.

'I see. Which, then, is Herr Schimler?'

He raised his eyebrows.

'Herr Schimler, Monsieur? There is no one of that name at the Réserve.'

'You are sure?'

'Perfectly, Monsieur.'

I glanced over my shoulder.

'Who is the gentleman at the end table?'

'That is Monsieur Paul Heinberger, a Swiss writer and a friend of Monsieur Köche. Will you take fish, Monsieur?'

I nodded and he hurried away.

For a second or two I sat still. Then, calmly but with a hand that trembled, I felt in my pocket for Beghin's list, enveloped it in my napkin, looked down and read it through carefully.

But already I knew it off by heart. The name of Heinberger was not on it.

5

I AM afraid that I lost my head a little. As I ate my fish my imagination began to run riot. I gloated over the scene with Beghin that would follow my revelation.

I would be cool and patronising.

'Now, Monsieur Beghin,' I would say. 'When you gave me this list I naturally assumed that it contained the names of all the visitors to the Réserve apart from the staff. The first thing I find is this Paul Heinberger unaccounted for. What do you know of him? Why is he not registered? Those are questions that should be answered without delay. And, my friend, I advise you to look over his belongings. I shall be extremely surprised if you do not find among them a Zeiss Ikon Contax camera and a spool of film with some photographs of a carnival at Nice on it.'

The waiter took my plate away.

'Another thing, Beghin. Investigate Köche. The waiter says that Heinberger is a friend of Köche. That means that this manager is implicated. I am not surprised. I had already noticed that he took a suspicious interest in my camera. He is well worth examination. You thought you knew all about him, eh? Well, I should investigate a little more carefully if I were you. Dangerous to jump to conclusions, my friend.'

The waiter brought me a large portion of the *coq au vin à la Réserve*.

'Always investigate a man with a name like Heinberger, my dear Beghin.'

No, too clumsy. Perhaps a mocking smile would be best. I experimented with a mocking smile and was in the middle of the fourth attempt when the waiter caught my eye. He hurried over anxiously.

'There is something wrong with the *coq au vin*, Monsieur?'

'No, no. It is excellent.'

'Pardon, Monsieur.'

'Not at all.'

Blushing, I got on with my food.

But the interruption had brought me to earth. Had I, after all, made such an important discovery? This Paul Heinberger might have arrived that very afternoon. If that was the case, the hotel could not yet have furnished the police with particulars of his passport. But where, then, was Emil Schimler? The waiter had been very positive that nobody of that name was staying at the hotel. Perhaps he had made a mistake. Perhaps the police had made a mistake. In any case, I could do nothing but report to Beghin in the morning. I must wait. And meanwhile time was going, I could not telephone until nine o'clock at the earliest. Over twelve hours wasted. Twelve out of about sixty. I had been crazy to think that I could get away by Sunday. If only I could write to Monsieur Mathis and explain, or lie, say that I was ill. But it was hopeless. What could I do? This man who had my camera—he wouldn't be a fool. Spies were clever, cunning men. What could I hope to find out? Sixty hours! It might just as well be sixty seconds.

The waiter took my plate away. As he did so he glanced disapprovingly at my hands. I looked down and found that my fingers, fumbling with a dessert spoon, had bent it. I straightened it hurriedly, stood up, and left the terrace. I was no longer hungry.

I walked through the house into the gardens. In one of the lower terraces overlooking the beach there was a small alcove. It was usually deserted. I went to it.

The sun had gone and it was dark. Above the hills across the bay stars were already shining. The breeze had stiffened a little and carried a faint smell of seaweed with it. I rested my hot hands on the cold brickwork of the parapet and let the breeze blow on my face. Somewhere in the garden behind me a frog was croaking. The sea lapping gently at the sand made scarcely a sound.

Out at sea a light winked and disappeared. Ships exchanging signals, perhaps. One, maybe, a passenger liner, rustling swiftly through the oily sea on its way east, the other a cargo boat, travelling light with a half-submerged screw, thrashing its way towards Marseilles. On the liner they might be dancing now or leaning on the rails of the promenade deck watching the moon on the wake and listening to the water bubbling and hissing against the plates. Below their feet, deep down, would be half-naked lascars sweating amidst the roar of oil-fired boilers and the thudding of propellers. The headlights of a car swept the road round the bay, gleamed on the water for an instant, and were lost among the trees as the car headed for Toulon. If only I . . .

A shoe grated on the gravel slope behind, and someone began to descend the steps leading to the terrace. The footsteps reached the bottom. I prayed that their owner would turn to the right, away from me. There was silence, a hesitation. Then I heard a rustle as a piece of creeper overhanging the path to the alcove was pushed aside and I saw a man's head and shoulders faintly outlined against the blue-black of the sky. It was the Major.

I saw him peer at me uncertainly. Then he leaned on the parapet and looked out across the bay.

My first impulse was to leave. I did not feel in the least like talking to Major Herbert Clandon-Hartley of Buxton. Then I remembered young Skelton's comment on the Major. The man was 'high-hat'. It was unlikely that he would speak first. But I was wrong.

We must have stood there leaning on the parapet for ten minutes before he spoke. I had, indeed, almost forgotten his existence when suddenly he cleared his throat and remarked that it was a fine evening.

I agreed.

There was another long silence.

'Cool for August,' he said at last.

'I suppose so.' I wondered whether he had been thinking the point over and really did consider it cool or whether the comment was purely formal. If he really thought it cool I ought for politeness' sake to draw attention to the breeze.

'Staying long?'

'A day or so.'

'May see something of you, then.'

'That would be pleasant.'

You would scarcely call this 'high-hat'.

'Shouldn't have thought you were a Britisher. But I heard you talking to that young American just before dinner. If you don't mind my saying so, you don't look British.'

'There is no reason why I should mind your saying so. I am a Hungarian.'

'Are you now! I thought you were British. My good lady said no, but she hadn't heard you speak.'

'I spent some years in England.'

'Oh, I see. That accounts for it. In the war?'

'I was too young.'

'Ah, yes, you would be. Difficult for us old stagers to realise now that the war's all ancient history. Went right through from fourteen to eighteen myself. Just got my battalion in time for the March offensive in eighteen. Got put out of action a week later. Just my luck. Reverted to second-in-command and invalided out. Never had anything to do with your lot, though. Heard the Austrians are damned good soldiers.'

This did not seem to call for a reply on my part, and there was silence again. He broke it with an odd question.

'What do you think of our respected manager?'

'Who? Köche?'

'That's how you fellows pronounce it, is it? Yes, Köche.'

'Well, I don't know. He seems a very competent manager, but—'

'Exactly! *But!* Slovenly, untidy, lets those damn waiters do what they like. They pinch your wine, you know. I've caught 'em at it. Köche ought to put some ginger into them.'

'The food is very good.'

'I dare say it is, but you've got to have more than good food to be comfortable. If this place was mine I'd put some ginger into things. Have you talked to Köche much?'

'No.'

'I'll tell you something funny about him. My good

lady and I were in Toulon the other day doing some shopping. We'd finished what we had to do and went into a café for an *apperitivo*. Well, we'd just ordered when along comes Köche, walking faster than I'd ever seen him move before. He doesn't see us, and I was just going to call him over for a drink when he crosses the road and ducks down the side street facing us. Then he walks two or three doors down, gives a quick look round to see if anyone's looking and goes through a doorway. Well, we had our drink and I kept my eye on that doorway, but he never came out. But what do you think? When we get to the bus terminus there he is, as large as life, sitting in the St Gatien bus.'

'Extraordinary,' I murmured.

'That's what we thought. And I must say we were a bit bowled over.'

'Naturally.'

'You haven't heard the best of it, though. You know his wife?'

'No.'

'A regular tartar. She's French and older than he is, and I think she's got a bit of money. Anyway, she keeps our Albert right under her thumb. He likes going down to the beach with the guests and bathing. Well, she's looking after the ordering and the chambermaids and likes to have him where she can keep her eye on him. So by the time he's been down on the beach for ten minutes she's usually hanging over the terrace at the top yelling at him to come up. In front of all the guests, too! That's the sort of woman she is. You can't help noticing it, and you'd think Köche would be embarrassed. But not he. He just grins—you know, that sleepy grin of his; mutters something in French which must be pretty hot,

58

judging by the way the Frogs start laughing, and does what he's told.

'Anyway, we got on the bus and said how do you do. Well, naturally we couldn't resist telling him that we'd thought we'd seen him in the town. I don't mind telling you I was watching him pretty closely, but, would you believe it, the fellow didn't bat an eyelid!'

I murmured amazement.

'It's a fact. Didn't bat an eyelid. Of course, I thought he was just going to deny the whole thing and say we'd been mistaken. You see, my good lady and I had thought at once that the place he'd gone to was one of those sailors' houses with two entrances, and that he'd got a bit of goods there. It was damned embarrassing.'

'How do you mean?'

'Well, you see, the fellow didn't deny it at all. He was as cool as you please. He said that he didn't care for his wife very much and that he had a brunette there he liked better. Well, that was a bit of a facer. But when he went on to tell us all about her charms in that sleepy, grinning way of his, I thought it was time to stop. My good lady's a bit religious, and I had to hint pretty broadly that we'd rather not hear about it.' The Major looked up at the stars. 'Women are a bit touchy about some things,' he added.

'I suppose so,' was all I could think of to say.

'Funny creatures, women,' he mused, then uttered a short, self-conscious laugh. 'Still,' he went on facetiously, 'if you're a Hungarian, you probably know more about women than an old soldier like me. By the way, my name's Clandon-Hartley.'

'Mine is Vadassy.'

'Well, Mr Vadassy, I shall have to be getting inside

59

now. Night air's supposed to be bad for me. Usually play Russian billiards in the evening with that old Frenchman, Duclos. As far as I can make out he's got a fruit-canning factory in Nantes. But my French is not too good. He may be only the manager. Nice old boy, but he's always giving himself a few extra points when he thinks you aren't looking. Get's on your nerves after a bit.'

'It must do.'

'Well, me for bed. Those young Americans have got the table this evening. Pretty girl, and a nice lad. But he talks too much. Do some of these young fellows good to be under my old colonel. Speak when you're spoken to was the rule for junior officers. Well, good night to you.'

'Good night.'

He went. When he reached the top of the steps he began to cough. It was an ugly sound. As his footsteps died away up the path he was still gasping and choking. I had heard a cough like that once before. The owner of it had been gassed at Verdun.

For a long time there was silence. I smoked several cigarettes. Investigate Köche! Well, Beghin certainly had something to investigate.

The moon had risen and I could see the outlines of the clumps of bamboo canes below. A little to the right of them there was a patch of beach. As I watched, the shadows moved and I heard a woman's laugh. It was a soft, agreeable sound, half amused, half tender. A couple came up into the patch of light. I saw the man stop and pull the woman towards him. Then he took her head in his hands and kissed her eyes and mouth. It was the un-shaven Frenchman and his blonde.

For a while I watched them. They were talking. Then they sat down on the sand and he lit a cigarette for her.

I looked at my watch. It was half past ten. I crushed out my cigarette and walked along the terrace and up the steps.

The path was steep and winding. I went up slowly with my hand before my face to ward off the twigs that projected from the bushes on either side. Between the top of the path and the entrance to the house there was a small paved forecourt. My leather sandals were soft with use and my footsteps made no sound. I was halfway to the door when I stopped and stood perfectly still. The hall was in darkness except for a light streaming through the glass partition of Köche's office. The door of the office was open and from inside came the sound of voices—Köche's voice and that of another man. They were speaking in German.

'I will try again tomorrow,' Köche was saying, 'but I am afraid it is useless.'

There was a pause. Then the other man spoke. He had a deeper voice, but he spoke so quietly that I could scarcely hear him.

'You must keep trying for me,' he said slowly. 'I must know what has happened. I must know what I have to do.'

Again a pause. When Köche spoke there was a curious quality of softness in his voice that I had not noticed before.

'There is nothing you can do, Emil. You can only wait.'

Emil! I could barely contain my excitement. But the other man, Emil, was speaking again.

'I have already waited too long.'

Another pause. There was an odd, emotional quality in those pauses.

'Very well, Emil. I will try again. Good night. Sleep well.'

But the other did not answer. There was a step in the hall and, my heart thumping against my ribs, I moved quickly into the shadow of the wall. A man came out and stood for an instant in the doorway. I recognised his clothes but his face I had not seen before. It was the man whom the waiter had called Heinberger.

He walked quickly down the path to the terrace, yet as the light shone for that brief instant on his face I had seen a thin, firm mouth, a strong jaw, sunken cheeks, a fine, broad forehead. But these things were incidental. I scarcely noticed them. For I had seen something else, something that I had not seen since I had left Hungary: the eyes of a human being with nothing left to hope for but death to end his misery.

When I got to my room I opened the shutters, drew the curtains and sank into bed with a sigh of relief. I was very, very tired.

For a time I lay with my eyes shut, waiting for sleep. But my mind was too busy for oblivion. My head was hot, and the pillow became warm and sticky. I turned and twisted. I opened my eyes, closed them again. Paul Heinberger was Emil Schimler. Emil Schimler was Paul Heinberger. Köche must keep trying. Schimler must know what had happened. Schimler and Köche. Spies, both of them. I had discovered the truth. Beghin must know. To-morrow morning. A long time to wait. Early. Six o'clock. No, the post office would not be open and Beghin would be in bed. Beghin in pyjamas. He should know immediately. Absurd. Heavens, but I was tired. Must go to sleep. Heinberger was Schimler. Spies.

I got out of bed, put on a bathing-wrap, and sat by the window.

Heinberger was Schimler. He must be arrested without

delay. On what charge? Giving the police a false name? The police had his correct name. Emil Schimler—German —Berlin. A waiter had told me that his name was Heinberger. Was it an offence to tell people that one's name was Heinberger if one's name was really Schimler? Could I, Vadassy, say that my name was Karl Marx or George Higgins if I wished? What did it matter? Schimler and Köche were spies. They must be spies. They had my camera. And now they were wondering what had become of their photographs.

Yet I could not quite rid myself of the suspicion that the look on Schimler's face had nothing to do with cameras or photographs. There was, too, something about the man, something about his voice, the look of him, that ... But then you couldn't expect a spy to look like a spy— however a spy was supposed to look. He didn't advertise his trade. All over Europe, all over the world, men were spying, while in government offices other men were tabulating the results of the spies' labours: thicknesses of armour plating, elevation angles of guns, muzzle velocities, details of fire-control mechanisms and rangefinders, fuse efficiencies, details of fortifications, positions of ammunition stores, disposition of key factories, landmarks for bombers. The world was getting ready to go to war. For the spies, business was good. It might be profitable to start a bureau of espionage, a sort of central clearing-house for all this vital information. I had a vision of Köche walking quickly down a side street, turning into a doorway, and leaving by another exit. Would he have been quite so ready to admit to a mistress if she had really existed? Anyone but a fool like this English major would have seen that. I knew better. Headquarters in Toulon. Köche and Schimler. Schimler and Köche. Spies.

I shivered. The night was getting cold. I went back to bed.

Then, as my eyes closed once more, a new fear began to gather in my mind, turning over and over, growing bigger, a terrible possibility. Supposing one of the guests left the hotel?

It might easily happen. Tomorrow, Herr Vogel or Monsieur Duclos or Roux and his blonde, any of them, might say: 'I have decided to leave at once.' For all I knew one of them might already have his luggage packed to leave in the morning. What could I do to stop him? Supposing I were wrong about Köche and Schimler. Supposing that Roux and his blonde were foreign agents with false French passports. Supposing that the Americans or the Swiss or the English were spies. They would slip through my fingers. No use to tell myself that I would deal with the question when it arose. That might be too late. What exactly should I do? Quickly now! Imagine they're all going, leaving you here alone in the morning. What would you do? Get a pistol from Beghin. Yes, that was it, get a pistol from Beghin. Stand no nonsense. 'Stand where you are or I'll fill your guts with lead.' Ten rounds in the magazine. 'One for each of you.' No, eight rounds in the magazine. It depended on the type of pistol. I would need two.

I threw back the clothes and sat up. At this rate I should be a lunatic by the morning. I went to the washbasin and sluiced my face with cold water. I must, I told myself, have been dreaming. But I knew perfectly well that I had not been to sleep.

I drew back the curtains and looked out at the pine trees with the moonlight on them. I must examine the facts calmly—coolly and calmly. What exactly had Beghin said?

I must have stood there a very long time. When I finally went back to bed the sky across the bay was beginning to lighten. I was stiff with cold, but my mind was at rest. For I had a plan, and to my tired brain it seemed infallible.

As I closed my eyes once more a thought crossed my mind. There was something that English major had said that I had found curious, something quite small. But I no longer cared. I went to sleep.

6

I AWOKE with a headache.

I had forgotten to redraw the curtains and the early morning sun streaming through the open windows was already hot. It was going to be a warm day. And I had a lot to do. At the first possible moment I must telephone to Beghin. Then I must put my plan into operation. I was pleased to find it appeared as foolproof now as it had in the darkness of the small hours. I began to feel better.

I was early down on the terrace, and as I ate my *croissants* and drank my coffee I congratulated myself. Here was I, a teacher of languages with a nervous disposition and a dread of violence, evolving within a few hours a neat, clever plan for the capture of a dangerous spy. And I had been harrying myself with fears of being unable to reach Paris by Monday morning! After my second cup of coffee even my headache began to disappear.

The Vogels were sitting down at their table as I passed on my way out. I stopped, and said good morning.

Then I noticed that they were both looking uncommonly serious. Their smiles as they acknowledged my greeting were automatic and very watery. Herr Vogel must have noticed my curious glance.

'We are not happy this morning,' he said.

'Oh, I'm sorry.'

'We have had bad news from Switzerland.' He patted

a letter lying on the table. 'A dear friend has died. You must excuse us, please, if we seem a little distrait.'

'Naturally. I am very sorry.'

They were obviously itching to be rid of me. I passed on. Then other things drove them from my mind. I was being followed.

The post office was situated in the grocer's shop at the bottom of the village. As I walked down the hill, I became conscious of a man sauntering along a few paces behind me. I stopped outside the first café and looked back. He had also stopped. It was the detective who had arrested me the day before. He nodded genially to me.

I sat down at one of the tables and he came over and sat two tables away. I beckoned to him. He moved up. His manner was friendly.

'Good morning,' I said. 'I suppose you have been told to follow me?'

He nodded. 'Unfortunately, yes. I find it very fatiguing.' He glanced down at his Sunday blacks. 'This suit is very hot.'

'Then why do you wear it?'

His long, cunning, peasant's face became suddenly solemn.

'I am in mourning for my mother. It is only four months since she died. She had a stone.'

The waiter approached.

'What will you have to drink?'

He thought for a moment, then asked for a *limonade gazeuse*. I told the waiter to get it, and stood up.

'Now then,' I said, 'I am going to the post office down the street to telephone Monsieur Beghin. I shall be out of your sight for less than five minutes. You sit here and have your drink. I will join you on my return.'

67

He shook his head. 'It is my duty to follow you.'

'I know, but everyone in the village will know that you are following me. I do not like that.'

A mulish look came into his face.

'My orders are to follow you. I am not to be bribed.'

'I am not attempting to bribe you. I am asking you to consider your own comfort and mine.'

He shook his head again.

'I know my duty.'

'Very well.' I walked out of the café and on down the street. As I went I heard him arguing with the waiter over the responsibility for the *limonade gazeuse*.

The telephone in the post office was public in every sense of the word. It was flanked on one side by a cascade of garlic sausages hanging from the ceiling; on the other side by a pile of empty meal sacks. There was no cabinet. As I cupped my hand round the transmitter and murmured 'Police Station' into the mouthpiece, it seemed to me that the whole of St Gatien stooped to listen.

'*Poste Administratif*,' said a voice at last.

'*Monsieur Beghin?*'

'*Il est sorti.*'

'*Monsieur le Commissaire?*'

'*De la part de qui?*'

'*Monsieur Vadassy.*'

'*Ne quittez pas.*'

I waited. Then the Commissaire's voice came on.

'Hello! Vadassy?'

'Yes.'

'Have you anything to report?'

'Yes.'

'Telephone Toulon Ville eighty-three, fifty-five and ask for Monsieur Beghin.

'Very well.'

He hung up. Evidently the Commissaire's responsibility ended with seeing that I remained in St Gatien. I asked for Toulon Ville 83-55. My request produced a curious effect. Within less than a minute I was connected. Another few seconds and I was speaking to Beghin. His voice squeaked irritably over the wire.

'Who gave you this number?'

'The Commissaire.'

'Have you obtained the information about the cameras?'

'Not yet.'

'Then why are you bothering me?'

'I have discovered something.'

'Well?'

'The German, Emil Schimler, is calling himself Paul Heinberger. I overheard a conversation between him and Köche which sounded suspicious. There is no doubt that Schimler is the spy and that Köche is his accomplice. Köche also visits a house in Toulon. He states that he has a woman there; but this may be untrue.'

Even as I said it I felt my self-confidence draining away like water from a sieve. How very stupid it all sounded. Over the wire came a sound that I could have sworn was a hastily suppressed laugh. But what followed showed me that I had been mistaken.

'Listen,' squeaked Beghin's voice angrily, 'you were given certain instructions. You were told to find out which of the guests had cameras. You were not asked to think or to play detectives. You had your instructions. They were clear and straightforward. Why have you not carried them out? Do you want to go back to your cell? I want no more of this nonsense. Return to the Réserve immediately, question the guests, and give me the information I require the moment you have it. In all other matters mind your own business. You understand?' He hung up abruptly.

The man who owned the grocery shop which accommodated the post office was looking at me curiously. In my anxiety to impress Beghin with the importance of discoveries I must have raised my voice. I scowled at him and left the shop.

Outside, red in the face with heat and annoyance, was my detective. As I stalked off furiously up the street he lumbered along at my elbow hissing in my ear that I owed him eighty-five centimes plus *pourboire*, one franc, twenty-five in all. I had commanded the *limonade gazeuse*, he kept repeating, it was my duty to pay for it. He himself would not have ordered a *limonade gazeuse* unless I had invited him to do so. He was not allowed expenses by the government. I must pay the one franc, twenty-five. There was eighty-five centimes for the *limonade gazeuse* with a *pourboire* of eight sous only in addition. He was a poor man. He knew his duty. He would not be bribed.

I scarcely heard him. So I was to question the guests and find out which of them had cameras! It was madness. Obviously the spy would take fright and leave. Beghin was a fool and I was in his hands. My whole existence depended upon him. Mind my own business! But the capture of the spy *was* my business. I had everything to lose if he escaped. One had always heard that Intelligence Departments were noted for their stupidity. Here was evidence of that fact. If I had to trust myself to Beghin and the Department of Naval Intelligence in Toulon my chances of getting to Paris on Monday were remote. No, I would do my own thinking. It was safer. Schimler and Köche must be unmasked. And I must do the unmasking. I would carry out my plan as I had originally intended.

Beghin would look very foolish when I presented him with the evidence he needed. As for finding out about the cameras, well, I was not going to do any direct questioning. I would get the information; there was no harm in that. But I would get it discreetly.

'Eighty-five centimes plus a *pourboire* of eight sous. . . .' We had reached the gates of the Réserve. I gave the detective a two-franc piece and went in.

At the entrance I met the Skeltons coming out. They wore bathing suits and were carrying wraps, newspapers, and bottles of sun oil.

'Hallo there!' said he.

The girl smiled a greeting.

I said hallo.

'Are you coming down to the beach?'

'I'll go and change and follow you down.'

'Don't forget to bring your English with you,' he shouted after me, and I heard his sister telling him to 'lay off the nice gentleman.'

A few minutes later I came down again and started across the gardens to the steps leading to the beach. Then I had my first piece of luck.

I had nearly reached the first terrace when excited voices were raised ahead. The next moment Monsieur Duclos appeared hurrying anxiously towards the hotel. A moment or two later Warren Skelton dashed up the steps and flew after him. As he passed by he flung a sentence over his shoulder. I caught the word 'camera'.

I hurried down to the terrace. Then I understood the reason for the stampede.

Sweeping into the bay under full sail was a big white yacht. Men in white jeans and cotton sun-hats were running along her spotless deck. As I caught sight of her she came up into the wind. The sails fluttered and the mainsail crumpled as the gaff came down. The topsail, jib, and staysail followed and the bubbling water at her bow subsided into a long, deep ripple. An anchor chain clattered.

An admiring group clustered at the end of the terrace. There was Köche in swimming trunks, Mary Skelton, the Vogels, the two English, the French couple, Schimler, and a plump, squat woman in an overall whom I recognised as Madame Köche. Some of them had cameras in their hands. I hurried over to them.

Köche was squinting through the sights of a ciné camera. Herr Vogel was feverishly winding a new film into position. Mrs Clandon-Hartley was examining the yacht through a pair of field-glasses slung round her husband's neck. Mademoiselle Martin was operating a small box camera under her lover's excited direction. Schimler stood slightly apart, watching Köche work the ciné camera. He looked ill and tired.

'Lovely, isn't she?'

It was Mary Skelton.

'Yes. I thought your brother was chasing that old Frenchman up the path. I didn't know what all the fuss was about.'

'He's gone to fetch a camera.'

At this moment her brother appeared holding an expensive Kodak. 'All this boyish enthusiasm!' he complained. 'Why I should want to take pictures of somebody else's yacht, I do not know.' Nevertheless, he took two shots of the yacht.

In his wake, clutching an enormous filmpack reflex of an ancient pattern, trotted Monsieur Duclos. Breathing heavily, he unfolded the hood of the reflex and clambered on to the parapet.

'Do you think he works with his beard inside that viewfinder or out?' murmured Skelton.

There was a loud clicking as Monsieur Duclos wound up the shutter of the reflex, a moment's silence, then a soft crash as he released it. He scrambled off the parapet with a satisfied air.

'I bet he's forgotten to put a plate in.'

'You've lost,' said the girl. 'Let's go back down.'

Major and Mrs Clandon-Hartley were leaning over the parapet at the top of the steps. He nodded to me.

'Nice little craft, that. British built, by the look of her. Spent a leave yachting on the Norfolk Broads in '17. Grand sport. Got to have money to do it like this, though. Ever go to the Broads?'

'No.'

'Grand sport. By the way, meant to introduce you to my good lady. This is Mr Vadassy, my dear.'

She glanced at me impassively, indifferently; yet I had the impression that she was weighing me. I wished somehow that I had more clothes on. She smiled slightly with one side of her mouth and nodded. I bowed. I had an uncomfortable feeling that any form of verbal greeting would be regarded as an impertinence.

'We might have a game of Russian billiards later,' put in her husband breezily.

'Delighted.'

'Good. See you later.'

Mrs Clandon-Hartley nodded curtly.

It was a dismissal.

I found the Skeltons lying on the sand under a sunshade at one corner of the beach. They made room for me and I sat down.

The girl sighed happily. 'Say, Mr Vadassy, did you ever see anything like those Switzers?'

I followed her gaze. Herr Vogel had mounted his camera on a long steel tripod. Blushing and giggling in front of the lens stood Frau Vogel. As I watched, Vogel operated the delayed action shutter and skipped round the tripod to strike a pose with his arm round his wife. There was a faint whir from the camera, the shutter clicked and the Vogels burst into roars of laughter. The dear, dead friend was evidently forgotten.

Watching these antics with undisguised amusement were the French couple and Köche. The latter glanced across at us to see if we had been watching. He walked over.

Skelton said: 'Do you hire those two to entertain the guests?'

He grinned. 'I'm thinking of asking them to stay on as a permanent attraction.'

'I get it. Les Deux Switzers. Good, clean fun and a laugh in every line. Straight from their New York success. Swell dressers on and off.'

Köche looked slightly bewildered, and was about to reply when the air was rent by a shrill call from the terrace above.

'Al-baire!'

I looked up round the edge of the sunshade. Madame Köche was leaning over the parapet, her hands cupped round her mouth.

'Al-baire!'

Köche did not look up.

'The voice from the minaret,' he remarked lightly, 'calling the faithful to prayer.' With a nod to me he started towards the steps.

'You know,' commented Skelton dreamily, 'if I were our Albert, I'd murder that old battle-axe.'

'Tut-tut!' murmured his sister, and to me: 'How about a swim, Mr Vadassy?'

Both she and her brother were excellent swimmers. By the time I had churned out fifty metres or so on my ponderous side-stroke they were paddling round the anchored yacht halfway across the bay. I swam slowly back to the beach.

The Swiss were now in the water. At least, Herr Vogel was in the water. Frau Vogel was lying on a rubber raft quivering with laughter while her husband cavorted round her, splashing furiously and yodelling at the top of his voice.

I went back to the sunshade and dried my hair on my wrap. Then I lay down and lit a cigarette.

The camera situation was becoming clearer. Mentally I sketched out the results of my observations.

Herr Vogel	} Voigtlander box-type
Frau Vogel	
Monsieur Duclos . . .	Obsolete reflex
Mr Skelton	} Kodak Retina
Miss Skelton	
Monsieur Roux	} Box-type (French)
Mademoiselle Martin . .	
Monsieur Köche	} Ciné camera (Pathé)
Madame Köche	
Herr Schimler	None
Major Clandon-Hartley .	} None
Mrs Clandon-Hartley . .	

I considered the last three names.

The two English were probably not the sort of people who took photographs. Mrs Clandon-Hartley would probably disapprove. As for Herr Schimler, I was beginning to think that it was hardly worth while bothering to collect more evidence against him. Still, Beghin had asked for the information; he should have it. Köche? Well, we would see. I rolled over on my stomach out of the shadow of the sunshade. The sand was hot and the sun very strong. I draped a towel over my head. By the time the Skeltons, dripping and exhausted, rejoined me I was asleep.

Young Skelton poked me in the ribs.

'Time to eat,' he said.

The essence of all good plans, I reminded myself as I ate my lunch, was simplicity. My plan was simple, all right.

One of twelve persons had my camera. I had an identical camera belonging to that same one person. Beghin had pointed out that when and if that person discovered the loss of his or her photographs, he or she would be anxious to recover them. Now, for all that person knew, they were still in the camera. Therefore, if that person saw an opportunity of re-exchanging the cameras, he or she would certainly take it.

My idea was to plant the Contax I had in some conspicuous place at a time when all the guests would have an opportunity of seeing it, retreat somewhere whence I could see the camera without being seen and wait for results. If nothing happened it meant that the exchange of cameras had not yet been discovered. In that case no damage would be done. If something did happen, then I would know beyond doubt the identity of the spy.

I had given much thought to the question of where to

set the trap. I had finally decided upon the chair in the hall on which the original exchange had been made. It was the logical spot and had the additional advantage of being easy to watch. In the writing-room that opened off the opposite side of the hall there was a small gilt-framed mirror, hanging from a hook in the wall and tilted slightly forward. By manœuvring one of the big armchairs in the room I could sit with my back to the door and see the hall chair in the mirror. It would be impossible to see me from the hall except by stooping down to chair level and looking through the writing-room door into the mirror. Nobody, however cautious, was likely to do that.

I finished my lunch hurriedly, left the terrace for the writing-room, and put the armchair in position. Then I fetched the camera. A minute later I sat down breathlessly to wait.

The other guests started to leave the terrace.

First came the Vogels. A longish interval followed. Then Monsieur Duclos walked past, removing a crumb from his beard as he went. There followed Roux and Mademoiselle Martin, Major and Mrs Clandon-Hartley and the Americans. Schimler came through last. I waited. If there were going to be any exchanging done, my own camera would have to be fetched first to replace the one on the chair.

Ten minutes went by. The clock on the mantelpiece chimed two. I stared at the mirror, trying not to blink lest in the infinitesimal fraction of a second during which my eyes were closed something happened. The effort made my eyes water. Five past two. Once I thought a shadow moved across the room as though something or someone had passed by outside the window. But the sun was on the other side of the house, so that I could not say for certain. In any case, I was looking for something more substantial than shadows. Ten past two.

I was beginning to get bored. I had relied too much on theories. There had been too many 'ifs' in my reasoning. My eyes were smarting with the strain. They began to wander.

There was a slight creak from somewhere behind me. I looked sharply in the mirror. There was nothing to be seen.

Then suddenly I leapt from the chair and hurled myself at the door. But I was not quick enough. My hand just missed it as it swung to. It slammed. A key turned quickly in the lock.

I tried the handle once, then looked round wildly. There was the window. I dashed over, fumbled for a second or two with the catch and flung it open. I trampled frantically over a couple of flowerbeds to the door of the hotel.

The hall was deserted and silent. The chair on which I had left the camera was empty.

My trap had worked. But it had caught me. I had lost the one piece of evidence that proved my own innocence.

7

I SPENT quite a long time in my room that afternoon trying to persuade myself that the best thing I could do would be to leave the Réserve, make my way across country to Marseilles, and ship as a steward or deck-hand in an east-bound cargo liner.

I had the whole thing planned. I would take Köche's motorboat and land at some deserted spot west of St Gatien. Then I would lock the rudder of the boat, start the engine and leave it to chug out to sea while I made off inland to Aubague. There I would catch a train for Marseilles.

At this point doubts began to creep in. One was always reading of young men running away to sea, of people shipping as deck-hands and working their passages. There seemed to be no special qualifications needed. No ropes had to be spliced. No rigging had to be climbed. All you did was paint the anchor, chip rust off the deck plating and say 'aye, aye, sir,' when addressed by an officer. It was a tough life and you met tough men. There were weevils in the ship's biscuits and you had little to eat but skilly. Quarrels were settled with bare fists and you went about naked to the waist. But one of the crew always had a concertina and there were sing-songs when the day's work was done. In after life you wrote a book about it.

Yet would it work out quite like that for me? I was

inclined to think that it wouldn't. I may be unlucky, but I find that my enterprises never proceed along classical lines.

Rust-chipping would probably prove to be a highly skilled trade. They would laugh at the idea of a landsman imagining that he could do it. There would be no vacancy. Or if there were a vacancy it would be on a coastal steamer bound for Toulon. Or there would be some strange permit that had to be obtained from the police three months prior to sailing. Or they would find that my eyesight wasn't sufficiently good. Or they would insist on previous experience. Reality is always so obstructive.

I smoked a cigarette and reconsidered my position.

One thing was clear. I must not let Beghin know that I had lost the second camera. To do so would be to invite immediate re-arrest. The Commissaire was out for convictions. Without the evidence of the camera I would stand no chance of proving my innocence before an examining magistrate. What a fool I had been! Now it was more than ever necessary that I should clear up the mystery for myself. I must take risks. I *must* know for certain that Schimler had the cameras. I must be in a position to convince Beghin. There was only one thing to do. I would have to search the German's room.

The idea scared me. If I were caught, a charge of thieving would be added to my present troubles. But the search had to be made. Besides, it was certain to be successful. Should I make it now? My heart beating a little faster than usual, I looked at my watch. Nearly three o'clock. I would have to find out first exactly where Schimler was at the moment. I must be cool and careful about it. The phrase comforted me. Cool and careful. I must keep my head. Soft shoes? Most necessary. A

revolver? Absurd! I didn't have one, and even if I had ...
A torch? Idiot! it wasn't dark. And then I remembered
that I didn't even know the number of his room.

A wave of relief swept over me, and immediately I
despised myself for it. It was no good telling myself that,
whatever I felt, annoyance or relief, the fact remained
that I did not know Schimler's room number. The point
was that an efficient person would have already found
out what it was. If this was the way I was protecting my
own interests—feeling relieved when difficulties arose—
then heaven help me.

It was in this frame of mind that I went down to the
terrace, I had hoped to find it empty. But it was not.
Sitting in a deck-chair at one end, smoking a pipe and
reading a book, was Herr Schimler.

Now, if I had but known the number of it, was the
time to search his room. I almost turned on my heel to
go back. But I stood where I was. I would have to let the
opportunity go. Still, there was no harm in engaging the
man in conversation, in finding out what sort of a person
I had to deal with. After all, one of the fundamentals of
good strategy was the study of your opponent's mind.

But it was easier to think about studying Herr
Schimler's mind than actually to do so. I moved a wicker
armchair into the shade near him, sat down, and cleared
my throat.

He shifted the pipe between his teeth and turned over a
page of the book. He did not even glance in my direction.

I had heard that if one stares intently at the back of a
person's head and wills that person to turn round, he will
very soon do so. I stared and willed at Herr Schimler for
a good ten minutes. I could still now make an anthro-
pometric drawing of the back of his head. But I made no

impression at all on him. I managed to see the title of the book. It was Nietzsche's *Birth of Tragedy*, in German, and one of several German books I had seen on the shelves in the writing-room. I abandoned the attempt to compete with Nietzsche and gazed out to sea.

The sun was incredibly hot. A smoky haze lay on the horizon. The air above the stone balustrade quivered in the heat. In the garden the cicadas were in full chorus.

I watched a huge dragonfly circle once round a piece of flowering creeper and soar off over the fir trees. It was not an afternoon for thinking of spies. I ought, I knew, to telephone to Beghin and give him the list of cameras. But he could wait. Perhaps later, when the day had grown cooler, I would walk down to the post office. The detective in his heavy black suit would be sweating in the shadow of the dusty palm trees outside the gate and longing for a *limonade gazeuse*. I envied him. In exchange for peace of mind, I would gladly wear black on hot summer afternoons and sweat and wait and watch and long for *limonades gazeuses*. A fine life that! Whereas mine was furtive like that of a criminal. I was the watched.

I wondered what Mary Skelton thought of me. Nothing, probably. Or if she did think anything it was, no doubt, that I was a polite, reasonably personable young man with a gift for languages that was useful. I remembered the phrase she had used when she had thought that I was out of earshot. 'The nice gentleman.' The intention had been facetious in a kindly way. Quite appropriate to a hotel acquaintance. It would be exceedingly pleasant to have Mary Skelton interested in you. She understood her brother perfectly. That was obvious. No less obvious was the fact that he thought he understood her. You could tell that by his manner towards her. But she ...

Herr Schimler shut his book with a snap and tapped his pipe on the arm of his chair.

I plunged.

'Nietzsche,' I said, 'is hardly the companion for a hot afternoon.'

He turned his head slowly and examined me.

His thin cheeks had more colour in them now than on the night before; but in his blue eyes there was no longer misery. They expressed a more immediate emotion—suspicion. I saw the muscles at the corner of his mouth tighten.

He removed his pipe and started refilling it. His voice when he spoke was casually deliberate.

'You are probably right. But I was not seeking companionship.'

At any other time this rebuff would have reduced me to miserable silence. Now I persevered.

'Do people read Nietzsche nowadays?'

It was a fatuous question.

'Why shouldn't they?'

I blundered on.

'Oh, I don't know. I thought he was unfashionable.'

He took his pipe out of his mouth and looked at me over his shoulder.

'Do you know what you are talking about?'

I was tired of this.

'Frankly, no. I merely wanted to talk.'

For a moment he glared at me; then his thin lips relaxed into a smile. It was a very good smile and infectious. I smiled, too.

'Years ago,' I said, 'a fellow student of mine used to spend hours telling me why Nietzsche was a great man. Personally, I foundered on Zarathustra.'

He put his pipe between his teeth, stretched himself, and looked at the sky.

'Your friend was wrong. Nietzsche *might* have been a great man.' He flicked the book lying on his knees with his forefinger. 'This is his earliest work and there are seeds of greatness in it. Fancy diagnosing Socrates as a decadent. Morality as a symptom of decadence! What a conception. But what do you think he wrote about it about twenty years later?'

I was silent.

'He said that it smelt shockingly Hegelian. And he was quite right. Identity is the definition only of a simple, immediate, dead thing, but contradiction is the root of all movement and vitality. Only in so far as a thing has in itself contradiction does it move, does it possess an impulse and activity.' He shrugged. 'But what the young Nietzsche perceived with Hegel, the old Nietzsche despised. The old Nietzsche went mad.'

I was having difficulty in following this. I said, rather uneasily: 'I haven't seen you bathing.'

'I do not bathe, but I will play you a game of Russian billiards if you like. Or perhaps you call it bagatelle?'

It was said distastefully. He had the air of a man bowing ungraciously to the inevitable.

We went inside.

The billiard table was in one corner of the lounge. We played in silence. In ten minutes he had beaten me easily. As he made the winning stroke he straightened his back and grinned.

'That wasn't very amusing for you,' he said. 'You're not very good at it, are you? Would you like another game?'

I smiled. His manner was abrupt, almost brusque, but

there was something tremendously sympathetic about him. I felt myself wanting to be friendly. I had almost forgotten that this was Suspect Number One.

I said I would like another game. He turned the scoring dials back to zero, chalked his cue, and leaned forward to make the first shot. The light from the window falling on his face threw the rather wide cheekbones into relief, modelled the tapering cheeks, put a highlight on to the broad forehead. It was a beautiful head for a painter. The hands, too, were good; large, but finely proportioned, and firm and precise in their movements. His fingers lightly grasping the cue moved it easily across the thumb of his left hand. His eye was on the red ball when he spoke.

'You've had some trouble with the police, haven't you?'

It was said as casually as if he were asking the time. The next moment there was a crash as three balls dropped in quick succession.

I tried to be equally casual.

'Good shot! Yes, there was a mistake over my passport.'

He moved round the table slightly to alter the alignment of the balls.

'Yugoslav, aren't you?'

Only one ball dropped this time.

'Hungarian.'

'Oh, I see. Treaty of Trianon?'

'Yes.'

His next shot knocked the pin over. He sighed.

'I was afraid that would happen. Total score—zero. Your shot. Tell me about Yugoslavia.'

I bent over the table. Two could play at this game.

'I haven't been near it for over ten years. You're German, aren't you?'

I managed to hole the red in a low number.

'Good shot! You're improving.' But he didn't answer my question. I tried again.

'It's unusual to meet Germans holiday-making abroad these days.'

I potted the red again.

'Splendid! You're doing very well. What were you saying?'

'I said it was unusual to meet Germans on holiday abroad these days.'

'Yes? But that doesn't worry me. I am from Basel.'

This was a direct lie. In my excitement I holed my own ball without cannoning off another.

'Bad luck! Where's the chalk?'

I passed it to him in silence. He chalked his cue carefully and started to play again. His score mounted rapidly.

'What's that now?' he murmured at last. 'Sixty-four, isn't it?'

'Yes.'

He bent over the table once more.

'Do you know Germany well, Herr Vadassy?'

'I've never been there.'

'You should go. The people are so nice.' The red ball hovered on the brink of a high number. 'Ah, not quite enough energy behind that one. Sixty-four.' He straightened his back. 'Your German is very good, Herr Vadassy. You might have lived there many years.'

'At the University of Budapest we spoke mostly German. Besides, I teach languages.'

'So? It is your shot.'

I played, but I played badly, for I could not keep my thoughts on the game. Three times I knocked the pin over. Once I missed the ball completely. Questions were twisting and turning in my mind. What was this man trying to get out of me? Those questions of his had not been idle. What was the point of them? Did he suspect me of taking the photographs intentionally? And mingled with those unanswerable questions was the thought that this man could not be a spy. There was something about him that made the idea seem absurd. A certain dignity. Besides, did spies quote Hegel? Did they read Nietzsche? Well, his own answer would do there: 'Why shouldn't they?' What did it matter, anyway? One might just as well ask: 'Do spies make good husbands?' Why shouldn't they? Why not, indeed?

'Your shot, my friend.'

'I'm sorry. I was thinking of something else.'

'Oh!' He smiled slightly. 'This can't be very entertaining for you. Shall we stop?'

'No, no. I had just thought of something I had forgotten to do.'

'Nothing important, I hope.'

'No, nothing important.'

But it was important. I would telephone Beghin, throw myself on his mercy, explain the loss of the camera, ask for Schimler's room to be searched as mine had been. There was the excuse of the false name. But if only I could get one concrete piece of evidence against him, something that would establish his connection with the camera, something that would satisfy me that I was not making a stupid mistake. Supposing I were to take a risk! Supposing I were to ask point-blank if he had a camera? After all, it could do no harm now. The person who had slammed the writing-room door and taken the second camera would have no doubts about my connection with the business.

I holed two balls simultaneously.

'I did not,' I said, 'expect that.'

'No, I thought not.'

'I am,' I went on, as I moved round for the next shot, 'a man of one hobby.'

I failed to score and he took his place at the table.

'Indeed?'

'Yes. It is photography.'

He squinted along his cue.

'How nice.'

I watched him narrowly as I asked the fatal question.

'Have you a camera?'

He stood up slowly and looked at me.

'Herr Vadassy, do you mind not talking while I make this shot? It is difficult. You see, I am going to hit the cushion there, graze that white, hit the cushion again, and send the red into maximum. The white should roll into a five.'

'I beg your pardon.'

'It is I who should beg yours. This absurd game interests me. It is an utterly antisocial device. It is like a drug. It deprives you of the necessity for thinking. As soon as you start to think, you play badly. Have I a camera? I have no camera. I cannot, indeed, remember the last time I held a camera in my hands. It should require no thought on my part to produce that answer. Yet the distraction is sufficient to break the spell. The shot would have failed.'

He spoke solemnly. The fate of worlds might have depended on the success of the shot. Yet in his eyes, those very expressive eyes, there was a gleam of mockery. I thought I knew the reason for that gleam.

'I can see,' I remarked, 'that I shall never be able to play this game.'

But he had bent over the table again. There was a pause, a soft click-click, and the sound of two balls rumbling down to the tray.

'Magnificent!' said a voice.

I turned round. It was Köche.

'Magnificent,' murmured Schimler, 'but it is not war. Herr Vadassy has been very patient with me. The game has no attraction for him.'

I fancied that I saw the two exchange a significant glance. What did Schimler mean by that pompous threadbare allusion? I protested hastily that I had enjoyed the game. Perhaps we could play again tomorrow.

Schimler assented without enthusiasm.

'Herr Heinberger,' said Köche jovially, 'is an expert at Russian billiards.'

But the atmosphere had changed in some curious way. The two were obviously waiting impatiently for me to go. I took my leave as gracefully as possible.

'I had already noticed that. You will excuse me? I have to go into the village.'

'Of course.'

They stood and watched me go. They would not, it was clear, utter a word until I was well out of earshot.

As I passed through the hall the Clandon-Hartleys were going up the stairs. I murmured a greeting, but neither replied. Then, something about them, something in their stony silence, made me pause and glance after them. As they turned at the top of the stairs I saw that she had a handkerchief held to her face. Mrs Clandon-Hartley

89

crying? Impossible. That sort of Englishwoman didn't know how. She probably had something in her eye. I walked on.

The detective waiting for me at the gate had been changed. Now it was a short, stout man in a flat straw hat who wandered after me down to the post office.

I got straight through to Beghin.

'Well, Vadassy? You have the particulars of the cameras?'

'Yes. But the question of Schimler ...'

'I have no time to waste. The cameras, please.'

I started to give him the list slowly so that he could write it down. He snorted with impatience.

'Hurry, please. We have not all day, and the call is expensive.

Nettled, I rattled off the list as fast as I could. After all, it was I who was paying for the call, not he. The man was impossible. I concluded the list, fully expecting to be asked to repeat it. But, no.

'Good! And these three without cameras?'

'I have questioned Schimler, that is, Heinberger. He says he has no camera. I have had no opportunity to check the English. They have, however, a pair of field-glasses.'

'A pair of what?'

'Field-glasses.'

'That is unimportant. You will concern yourself only with cameras. Have you anything else to report?'

I hesitated. Now was the time. . . .

'Hello, Vadassy. Are you still there?'

'Yes.'

'Then don't waste time. Have you anything else to report?'

'No.'

'Very well. Telephone the Commissaire as usual to-morrow morning.' He hung up.

I walked back to the Réserve with a heart as heavy as lead. I was a fool; a weak, cowardly fool.

The heat had made my shirt cling uncomfortably to my body. I went to my room to change it.

The key was in the lock where I had left it, but the door was not properly closed. As I touched the handle the latch clicked and the door swung ajar. I went in and got my suit-case out from under the bed.

But for one thing I should probably have noticed nothing unusual. That one thing was that it was my habit to fasten only one latch of the case. Now both were fastened.

I opened them and looked inside the case.

In the ordinary way I should have found nothing strange in the sight of a slightly crumpled shirt. Now I stood up quickly and went to the chest of drawers. Everything there was in its place; but a small pile of handkerchiefs in one corner of the top drawer caught my eye. I had only one handkerchief with a coloured border. It had been at the bottom of the pile. Now it was on the top. I looked round the room. A corner of the counterpane on the bed was caught up below the mattress. The chambermaid had not left it like that.

There was no longer any doubt in my mind. The room and my belongings had been searched.

8

To realise that one's property has been searched is an unpleasant sensation.

My first reaction to the knowledge was anger. It was monstrous that a stranger's hands should open my suitcase, fumble among its contents, prying. But for the latched suitcase I might never have known. Ah, that was it! That was what was so infuriating. Not so much the prying and the fumbling but the attempt at secrecy, the fact that the fumbler thought that I would not know, that careful fastening of both latches on the suitcase. Inefficiency! He should have noticed that I had only fastened one latch. He should have noticed that I had left the plain white handkerchiefs uppermost in the drawer. Clumsy, fumbling oaf!

I went to the drawer and arranged the handkerchiefs as I had left them. I refastened the suitcase—one latch. I straightened the counterpane on the bed. Then, feeling a little calmer, I sat down. There was only one person who would search my room and take nothing from it—the spy. Having retrieved his camera and found the film missing he would naturally try my room. Naturally? Yes, because he had seen me watching through the writing-room mirror and would assume that since I was laying a trap for him I had developed the film and discovered the nature of his photographs. And then I remembered that at the bottom of my suitcase I had left two undeveloped rolls of film that I had used at Nice. I had not thought to see if they were still there. I got out the suitcase again and went through it very carefully. The rolls were gone. The spy was evidently leaving nothing to chance. I would do well to remember that in future.

If only I could have returned and caught him in the act. I spent a pleasurable half minute contemplating the scene. There would, I decided, have been very little left of the spy to hand over to Beghin. In my mind's eye I dragged the whimpering wretch to his feet and flung him into the arms of the waiting *agents*.

It was with some surprise that I realised that this imaginary spy of mine was not Schimler. It was not even Köche. It was nobody at the Réserve. It was a vindictive rat of a man with an evil face, a revolver in his hip pocket, and a knife up his sleeve; a vicious, disgusting creature without a single redeeming quality; a sly, furtive wretch despised even by those who employed him.

Nothing, I thought bitterly, could have demonstrated more clearly my utter futility. It was perfect! Instead of trying to find out which of the twelve possible persons had searched my room, I was busily evolving a fairy-tale thirteenth. I deserved to fail.

'Now,' I said aloud; 'get this into your head. This spy, this man *or* woman who took those photographs and your precious camera, this person who saw you through the writing-room window and locked you in like the helpless fool you are while he took the camera off the chair, this person who came into this room looking among your clothes for his photographs, this person is real, he is alive, he is one of those people outside. He doesn't look like a spy, you nitwit. He hasn't got a vicious look and a revolver in his hip pocket. He's real. He may have a

93

white beard like old Duclos or bulging eyes like Roux. He may quote Hegel like Schimler or he may seem as sleepy as Köche. She may look austere and dry like Mrs Clandon-Hartley or young and attractive like Mary Skelton. She may laugh like Frau Vogel or yearn like Mademoiselle Martin. He may be as fat as Herr Vogel, as thin as Major Clandon-Hartley, or as brown as Warren Skelton. He may be a patriot or a traitor, a crook or an honest man, or a bit of each. He may be old or young. She may be dark or fair, intelligent or stupid, rich or poor. And, whoever it is, you incompetent ass, you're not doing yourself the slightest good sitting here.'

I got up and looked out of the window.

The Skeltons had just come up from the beach and were sitting down at a table on the lower terrace. Faintly I could hear their voices. Warren laughed once and struck a Napoleonic attitude. His sister shook her head vehemently. I wondered vaguely what they were talking about. If they had been down on the beach all the afternoon they might be able to give alibis to some of the other guests. For the searching of my room could have taken place only while I had been with Schimler or in the village telephoning Berghin. It had probably been the latter. I had, no doubt, been seen leaving the hotel. The path to the gate was visible from half the windows or from the writing-room. Perhaps while I had been planning to search Schimler's room, Schimler had been planning to search mine. A pretty irony. Schimler, however, had known the number of my room. That is if it had been Schimler who had latched my suitcase twice instead of once. Perhaps his mind had been busy with the *Birth of Tragedy* at the time. Perhaps Köche had made the search, or Herr Vogel or Monsieur Duclos or ...

But this was Friday. Only one day more and it would be time for me to go; and still I should be hoping, wondering, saying names to myself—'Köche, Schimler, Herr Vogel, Monsieur Duclos'—and still I should be here watching the hands of the clock move and doing nothing but wish. I must act. I must do something. I must hurry.

When I left my room I was very careful to lock the door and put the key in my pocket. Worry can play very neat tricks with the sense of humour.

I walked slowly down to the lower terrace. The Skeltons were still talking, but as I approached they looked up. They hailed me with unexpected eagerness.

'We've been looking for you.' He came towards me, took me by the arm and looked at me searchingly. 'Have you heard yet?'

'Heard what?'

He led me firmly towards their table.

'He hasn't heard,' he announced with satisfaction.

'Not heard?' echoed the girl. She rose and took my other arm. 'Sit down, Mr Vadassy, and listen.'

'The sensation of the week!' put in her brother.

'It's too good to be true.'

'Will you tell him or shall I?'

'You. I'll take the big scenes.'

Skelton suddenly pushed me into a chair and thrust a packet of cigarettes under my nose.

'Smoking steadies the nerves.'

'But what . . .?'

'A match?'

I lit the cigarette.

'You see,' put in the girl earnestly, 'we don't want you to think us completely crazy, but we have this afternoon witnessed such a sight as . . .'

'Will kill you,' supplied her brother. 'Moreover, we've been dying to tell someone about it. Thanks to you, Mr Vadassy, we live.'

I grinned sheepishly. I was beginning to feel a little embarrassed.

'One of us,' remarked the girl darkly, 'won't live much longer if you don't get on with it.'

'To business, then!' he announced. 'Mr Vadassy, you know that yacht that came in this morning?'

'Yes.'

'It's an Italian.'

'Is it?'

'It is. Well, we were down on the beach this afternoon with some of the others. There were the Switzers and the French couple and that old guy with the white beard. A bit later down come the British major and his wife.'

'Oh, hurry up!' said the girl.

'Wait! I want to recreate the atmosphere for Mr Vadassy. That's how it happened. They came down a while after everyone else. You know how hot it was. All of us were lying around half asleep in our chairs after that *poulet à la crème* they gave us at lunch. We just knew the British had come down because we'd heard him saying his chair was unsafe or something.'

'You see,' she broke in, 'they were sitting just a little to the right, so we were quite close and saw everything. Well . . .'

'Be quiet,' said her brother, 'you're spoiling it. Your part comes in a minute. As I was saying, Mr Vadassy, we were all sitting there wondering whether it was possible for the sun to get much warmer and whether we hadn't had too much to eat when Mrs Switzer says something to Mr Switzer. Well, you know how it is. Even if you don't know a language, you can often understand the intonation. So I open my eyes and see that the Switzers are looking out across the bay. Then I see that the yacht has lowered a dinghy and that a sailor is rowing it around to the gangway. Down the gangway comes a man in a yachting cap and white drill. He's got plenty of flesh on him, but he hops into the dinghy neatly enough and the sailor starts to row him towards the beach. Well, everybody perks up at this, probably because it takes their minds off the digesting of the *poulet à la crème* and starts talking.' He wagged a dramatic finger. 'Little do they know what is in store for them.'

'But for us,' interjected his sister, 'the plot is already thickening, for suddenly the two British start talking. The queer thing is that they're talking Italian. Queerer still, it's Mrs Clandon-Hartley who is doing most of the talking. What's more, she keeps pointing to the dinghy. Then the Major has a look and starts talking back. He doesn't seem to agree with what she's saying, for he shakes his head and says something that sounded like a girl's name, Kay something or other. She didn't seem to like it and started pointing again. But this time the dinghy is about twelve yards out and the man in the cap is standing up with a boat-hook to catch that iron ring on the rocks when suddenly she lets out a sort of whoop and runs down to the water's edge calling out something and waving to him.'

'The man with the boat-hook saw her at the same moment and nearly fell overboard with excitement,' said Warren Skelton; 'then he shouted, "Maria!" I don't understand a word of Italian, so I couldn't tell what they were talking about, but they were talking away as hard as they could go across the water until finally he got the dinghy alongside the landing rock and jumped ashore.'

97

'Then,' said the girl, 'he flung his arms round her and kissed her two or three times. They evidently knew each other *very* well indeed. Not that I would care to be kissed even once by this particular man. He was fattish, and when he took his cap off he had his hair cropped so that his head looked like a dirty grey egg. Also he had dewlaps, and if there's one thing I wish no part of it's a man with dewlaps. But what surprised me was her. We'd never heard her say a single word before, and here she was behaving like a teenager and grinning till we thought her face was going to crack. Obviously she hadn't expected Signor Dewlaps and it was all a beautiful surprise. He was pointing to the yacht and thumping himself on the chest as though to say, "Look what I've done," and she was pointing up at the hotel and telling him she was staying there. Then they started hugging and kissing again. Everyone on the beach was highly diverted.'

'That is,' qualified Skelton, 'all except the Major. He wasn't looking a bit pleased. In fact, he was looking pretty tight-lipped. When this second bout of hugging started he got up very slowly from his chair and walked over to them. He just walked, but there was something about the way he walked that made you feel that something was going to happen. The Switzers had started talking to the old Frenchman, but now they shut up. If it hadn't been for the sound of the sea you could have heard a pin drop on the sand. But nothing happened—then. Signor Dewlaps looked up and saw the Major and grinned at him. You could see they'd met before, but you could also see that they thought nothing at all of each other. They shook hands and Dewlaps went on grinning, but Mrs Major dried up again as though someone had put an extinguisher on her. Then they all started to talk quietly.

Well, I think most of the others lost interest at that point, but I kept on watching them. You see, I'm something of a student of human nature.'

'For goodness' sake,' interrupted his sister, 'get on with it. What he's trying to say, Mr Vadassy, is that they all looked as if they were saying everything except the one thing they wanted to say.'

'That was,' Skelton cut in, 'until somebody did say it. But we had to wait for that. I must admit that I was beginning to lose interest myself when suddenly they, at least the two men, began to raise their voices. You know how Italian sounds from a distance—like a car with plug trouble. Well, suddenly, somebody stepped on the gas. Dewlaps was jabbering away furiously and waving his hand in the Major's face. The Major had gone very white. Then Dewlaps stopped and half turned away as though he had finished. But just then he evidently thought of a really dirty crack because he turned back, said something and then put back his head and roared with laughter.

'The next moment I saw the Major bunch his fist and draw back his arm. Somebody yelped—that French girl, I think—then the Major let fly and caught Signor Dewlaps—*thwack!*—smack in the solar plexus. You ought to have seen it. Dewlaps stopped laughing with his mouth still open, made a noise like bath water running away, staggered back a pace and sat down—*squoosh!*—on the sand just as a spent wave was running across it. Mrs Clandon-Hartley let out a scream, then turned on the Major and started yelling at him in Italian. And he began to cough, of all things. He couldn't seem to stop. Of course, by this time everybody, including us, had rushed over. The sailor who had been sitting in the boat hopped out and splashed over to help the young Frenchman with

Dewlaps, while the Switzer and I fastened on to the Major. Mrs Switzer and the French girl and Mary surrounded Mrs Clandon-Hartley. The old boy with the beard just hopped round saying what a pity it was. Not that there was much for us to do, because the Major couldn't do anything but cough and gasp "swine!" and Mrs Clandon-Hartley had started crying and saying in broken English that she was very sorry, and that her husband was a mad wolf. He didn't look much like it to me. Dewlaps shook his fist and shouted a lot of Italian when he had the breath and trailed off in his wet pants to the dinghy. The Major finally got over his coughing and they both became dignified and went upstairs. Now, aren't you sorry you missed it?'

'You could have told us what it was all about,' said the girl wistfully.

But I was not thinking very much about what they were saying. I leaned forward anxiously.

'What time did all this happen?'

They both looked rather crestfallen. It must have seemed to them that I was not doing justice to the story.

'Oh, I don't know,' said Skelton impatiently; 'about half past three, I guess. Why?'

'And did anyone stay down on the beach the whole afternoon?'

He shrugged a trifle irritably.

'I wouldn't know. There was a lot of coming and going. After all the excitement had blown over a bit, one or two went up to change into swim suits.'

'I think Philo Vance has got a clue,' said the girl. 'Come on, Mr Vadassy, tell us what's on your mind.'

'Oh, nothing,' I said feebly. 'I just saw Major and Mrs Clandon-Hartley going upstairs as I went down to the village. She had a handkerchief to her eyes. She must just have been crying.'

'Well, well, well! And I was afraid that you had the whole thing explained. Thank goodness you haven't, because I've worked out a beautiful explanation.'

'*We've* worked out a beautiful explanation,' supplemented her brother.

'All right—*we*. You see, Mr Vadassy, we think that many years ago Mrs Clandon-Hartley was just a simple southern Italian peasant girl living in a simple southern Italian village—you know, all baroque and whitewash and no main drainage—with her parents. She is promised to old Dewlaps, young and handsome then, the son of another brace of peasants. Then to the village comes the bold, bad Major twirling his moustachios. Stop me if you've heard this one. What happens? The Major, with his slick city ways and his custom-made suits, dazzles the simple peasant girl. To make a long story short, he carries her off to the big city and marries her.'

'Hey!' said Skelton, 'that bit about marrying her wasn't in the script.'

'Well, he *does* marry her. Maybe she's not so simple after all.'

'All right. Let it go.'

'The years roll by.' She smiled at us triumphantly. 'Meanwhile the young Dewlaps, embittered and disillusioned—that accounts for his face looking the way it does—has worked and prospered. Starting right from the bottom and working up and up and up, he is now one of the biggest shysters in Italy.'

'It seems to me,' put in her collaborator, 'that this story ends all wrong. It ought to be Dewlaps who does the socking and the Major who gets his pants wet.'

The girl looked thoughtful.

'Maybe.' She looked at me. 'I guess you must think we're being mean over this. But, you see, the whole thing was so unnerving really that we should be feeling depressed if we didn't laugh about it.'

I did not know quite what to say.

'I see,' I mumbled, 'that the yacht has gone.'

'Yes, it went about an hour ago,' said Skelton gloomily.

At this moment the Vogels appeared at the top of the steps. There was a subdued air about them. They paused at our table.

'The young people have been telling you of this afternoon's affair?' he said to me in German.

'Yes, I have heard something of it.'

'An unfortunate business,' he said gravely. 'My wife gave Frau Clandon-Hartley some smelling salts, but I do not think they will help much. Poor man. His wife says that he was wounded in the war and that it has affected his brain. He is not, it seems, responsible for his actions. The man from the yacht had, it appears, landed to purchase some wine from Köche's cellar and beg some ice. Frau Clandon-Hartley recognised in him an old friend. That was all. The poor Major misunderstood.'

They went on up to the hotel.

'What did he say?' said Skelton curiously.

'He said that, according to Mrs Clandon-Hartley, the Major was badly wounded in the war and that he's not quite right in the head.'

They were silent for a moment. Then I saw the girl's forehead pucker thoughtfully.

'You know,' she said to neither of us in particular. 'I don't think that that can be true.'

Her brother snorted impatiently.

'Well, let's forget it, anyhow. What are you drinking, Mr Vadassy? Dubonnet *sec*? Good. That makes three. I'll toss you who goes up to get them.'

I lost.

As I went up to order the drinks I saw Monsieur Duclos talking excitedly to Köche. He was demonstrating a fierce uppercut to the jaw.

9

THE Clandon-Hartleys did not come down to dinner.

I was interested in them in spite of myself. So Mrs Clandon-Hartley was an Italian! That explained a lot. It explained the Major's use of the word '*apperitivo*' when he had been talking to me the night previously. It explained his wife's forbidding silence. She was shy of speaking broken English. It explained why 'my good lady' was a 'bit religious.' It explained her un-English appearance. And Clandon-Hartley himself was a shell-shock case not responsible for his actions. I remembered Mary Skelton's doubt of that. Well, if their account of the incident on the beach were accurate. I was inclined to doubt it too. It sounded as if there had been more to the affair than a mere neurotic outburst. But it was no affair of mine. I had more important things to think about. This wretched business of the Clandon-Hartleys had rendered the Skeltons useless from my point of view. There had been 'a lot of coming and going.' That presumably had taken place while I was in the village. It was hopeless.

Dinner was nearly over when Köche came on to the terrace and announced that a ping-pong table had been erected under the trees in the garden and that guests were invited to make use of it: By the time I had finished my dinner I could hear that the invitation had been accepted. I wandered towards the sound.

An electric light fixed in the branches above the green-topped table shed a hard light on the faces of the players. They were Skelton and the Frenchman, Roux. Sitting on a stone rockery watching them were Mademoiselle Martin and Mary Skelton.

Roux played crouching in an attitude of fierce concentration, his protuberant eyes watching the ball as if it were a bomb on the point of exploding. He leaped about a great deal. In contrast, Skelton's easy, lazy play looked wooden and ineffective. But I noticed that he seemed to gain most of the points. Mademoiselle Martin made no effort to disguise her chagrin at this, uttering loud cries of despair every time Skelton won. A Roux victory was received with corresponding jubilation. I saw that Mary Skelton was watching her with interest and amusement.

The game ended. Mademoiselle Martin cast a malevolent glance at Skelton and wiped her perspiring lover's forehead with his handkerchief. I heard her assuring him that his failure made no difference to her affection for him.

'What about a game?' said Skelton to me.

Before I could reply, however, Roux had bounded to the other end of the table, flourishing his bat, and announced with a flashing smile that he wanted his revenge.

'What does he say?' muttered Skelton.

'He says he wants his revenge.'

'Oh, all right.' He winked. 'I'd better see that he has it.'

They started to play again. I sat down beside Mary Skelton.

'Why is it,' she said, 'that I can't understand a word of what that Frenchman says? He seems to have a very peculiar accent.'

'He's probably a provincial. Even Parisians can't understand some provincial French.'

'Well, that's comforting. You know, I think that if he goes on playing much longer his eyes will drop right out.'

I forget what I replied, for I was trying, for my own satisfaction, to identify Roux's accent. I had heard another like it, and quite recently. I knew it as well as I knew my own name. A loud cry of delight from Mademoiselle Martin brought my thoughts back to the game.

'Warren can be a very convincing loser when he likes,' said the girl. 'He lets me win a game sometimes, and I always feel that it's my good play.'

He was convincing enough to lose by a very narrow margin of points, though not without having to referee a spirited argument between Roux and Monsieur Duclos, who had arrived on the scene halfway through the game and insisted on keeping the score. Mademoiselle Martin was triumphant, and kissed Roux on the lobe of the ear.

'You know,' murmured Skelton, 'that old so-and-so with the white beard is a menace. I've seen him cheating at Russian billiards, but I didn't think he'd try and cook other people's ping-pong scores. I was keeping count myself. I was five points down, not two. If we'd gone on any longer he'd have won the game for me. Maybe he's got some sort of inverted kleptomania.'

'And where,' the subject of his comment was demanding sportively, 'are the English major and his wife this evening? Why are they not playing ping-tennis? The Major would be a formidable opponent.'

'Silly old slob!' said Mary Skelton.

Monsieur Duclos beamed at her blankly.

'For goodness' sake shut up,' said her brother; 'they might understand you.'

Mademoiselle Martin, dimly comprehending that English was being spoken, said 'Okay' and 'How do you do?'

to Roux, dissolved into laughter, and was rewarded with a kiss on the nape. It was evident that nobody had understood. Monsieur Duclos buttonholed me and began to discuss the affair on the beach.

'One would not have thought,' he said, 'that in this cold military officer there was so much passion, so much love for this Italian woman, his wife. But the English are like that. On the surface, cold and businesslike. With the English it is always business, one thinks. But below, who knows what fires may slumber!' He frowned. 'I have seen much of life, but one can never understand the English and the Americans. They are inscrutable.' He stroked his beard. 'It was a beautiful blow, and the curious noise made by the Italian was very satisfactory. Straight to the chin. The Italian fell like a stone.'

'I heard that the blow was in the stomach.'

He looked at me sharply. '*And* to the chin, Monsieur. *And* to the chin. Two magnificent blows!'

Roux, who had been listening, intervened.

'There was no blow struck,' he said decidedly. 'The English major used jiu-jitsu. I was watching closely. I am myself familiar with the hold.'

Monsieur Duclos put his pince-nez on his nose and glowered.

'There was a blow to the chin, Monsieur,' he said sternly.

Roux threw up his hands. His eyes bulged. He scowled.

'You could not have seen,' he said rudely. He turned to Mademoiselle Martin. 'You saw, *ma petite*, did you not? Your eyesight is perfect. You have no glasses to confuse you like this old gentleman here. It was undoubtedly jiu-jitsu, was it not?'

'*Oui, chéri.*'

'There, you see!' jeered Roux.

'A blow to the chin, without a doubt.' Monsieur Duclos's pince-nez were quivering with anger.

'Bah!' said Roux savagely. 'Look!'

He turned to me suddenly, grasped my left wrist, and pulled. Instinctively I drew back. The next moment I felt myself falling. Roux grasped my other arm and held me up. There was amazing strength in his grip. I felt his thin, wiry body stiffen. Then I was standing on my feet again.

'You see!' he crowed. 'It was jiu-jitsu. It is a simple hold. I could have treated this Monsieur here as the English major treated the man from the yacht.'

Monsieur Duclos drew himself up and bowed curtly.

'An interesting demonstration, Monsieur. But unnecessary. I can see perfectly well. It was a blow to the chin.'

He bowed again and strode off towards the hotel. Roux laughed derisively after him and snapped his fingers.

'An old cretin, that one,' he said contemptuously. 'Because we pretend not to notice when he cheats, he thinks we see nothing.'

I smiled noncommittally. Mademoiselle Martin began to compliment him on his handling of the situation. The two Skeltons had begun a game of ping-pong. I wandered down to the lower terrace.

Beyond the inky darkness of the trees I could see two silent figures leaning against the parapet. It was the Major and his wife. As my footsteps grated on the path he turned his head. I heard him say something softly to her, then the two of them moved away. For a moment or two I stood listening to their footsteps dying away up the path, and was about to move to where they had been standing when I saw the glow of a pipe in the blackness near the trees. I went towards it.

'Good evening, Herr Heinberger.'

'Good evening.'

'Would you care for a game of Russian billiards?'

There was a shower of sparks as he tapped the pipe on the side of the chair.

'No, thank you.'

For some unaccountable reason my heart began to beat faster. Words and phrases were rising to my lips. I had an overwhelming desire to blurt out my suspicions of him there and then, denounce him, this man here sitting in the darkness, this invisible spy. 'Thief! Spy!' I wanted to shout the words at him. I felt myself trembling. I opened my mouth and my lips moved. Then, suddenly, a match spluttered and flared, and I saw his face, thin and drawn in the yellow light, curiously dramatic.

He raised the match to the bowl of his pipe and drew the flame into it. The match flamed twice and went out. The glowing bowl moved in a gesture.

'Why not sit down, Herr Vadassy? There is a chair there.'

And, indeed, I was standing gaping at him like a fool. I sat down, feeling as if I had only just escaped being run over by a fast car, and that it was the driver's skill rather than my own agility that had saved me. For sheer want of something to say I asked him if he had heard about the English couple and the incident on the beach.

'Yes, I have heard of it.' He paused. 'It is said that the Englishman is unbalanced.'

'Do you think that is true?'

'Not necessarily. The real question is just how far he

was provoked. Even a lunatic does not become violent unless he is stimulated.' Again he paused. 'Violence,' he went on, 'is a very odd thing. A normal man's mind has an extraordinarily complex mechanism inhibiting him from using it. But the power of that mechanism varies with different cultures. With the Western peoples it is less powerful than with the Eastern. I do not, of course, speak of war. There, different factors are operating. The Indian is a good example of what I mean. The number of attempted assassinations of English officials in British India is, not unnaturally, very high. The interesting thing is the very large number of those attempts that fail. Most of them fail not because Indians are specially bad shots, but because at the crucial moment the would-be assassin becomes immobilised by his instinct against violence. I once talked with a Bengali Communist about it. He said that the Hindu might go with hate in his heart and a good revolver to kill the local representative of his oppressors. He might escape detection, he might stand out of the crowd unobserved when the time came and his enemy approached and raise the revolver. The official would be at his mercy. Then the Indian would hesitate. He would see not the hated oppressor, but a man. His aim would falter and the next moment he would himself be shot down by the guards. A German or a Frenchman or an Englishman under the same hate-stimulus would have shot and shot straight.'

'And what sort of hate-stimulus do you think caused Major Clandon-Hartley to punch this Italian in the stomach?'

'Perhaps,' said he, with a touch of impatience, 'he did not like the man.' He rose to his feet. 'I have some urgent letters to write. You will excuse me?'

He went. For a time I remained seated in my chair, thinking. It was not of Major Clandon-Hartley that I thought, but of Herr Schimler's Indian. 'He would see not the hated oppressor, but a man.' I felt a bond of sympathy with that Indian. But that was not all, for 'the next moment he would himself be shot down by the guards.' There was the whole thing in a nutshell. Fear and be slain. Or were you slain anyway, whether you were afraid or not? Yes, you were. Good did not triumph. Evil did not triumph. The two resolved, destroyed each other, and created new evils, new goods that slew each other in their turn. The essential contradiction. 'Contradiction is the root of all movement and vitality.' Ah, that was Schimler's sentence. I frowned in the darkness. If I paid a little more attention to Herr Schimler's actions and less to what he said I should perhaps get somewhere.

I walked up to the house. The writing-room was empty. So much for Schimler's 'urgent letters'! As I walked through the lounge I passed Madame Köche carrying a pile of linen. I said: 'Good evening!'

'Good evening, Monsieur. You have seen my husband? No? He will be down playing ping-tennis without a doubt. There are the clever ones who pass their days agreeably and the fools who slave behind the scenes. But someone must do the work. At the Réserve it is left to the women.' She swept on up the stairs calling shrilly for 'Marie.'

I passed through the deserted lounge to the upper terrace.

Monsieur Duclos was sitting with a Pernod and a cigar at a table by the balustrade. He saw me, stood up, and bowed.

'Ah, Monsieur! I must apologise for leaving you all

so abruptly. It was impossible, however, to remain there to be insulted.'

'I understand and sympathise, Monsieur.'

He bowed again. 'You will take something to drink, Monsieur? I have here a Pernod.'

'Thank you, a vermouth-citron for me.'

He rang for the waiter and offered me a cigar, which I accepted.

'In spite of my years,' he said, pouring some water into his glass, 'I am a proud man. Very proud.' He paused to take another piece of ice. I did not quite see why pride should diminish with age, but, fortunately, he went on before I could say so. 'In spite of my years,' he repeated, 'I would have struck this Roux, but for one thing. There were women present.'

'You took the most dignified course possible,' I assured him.

He stroked his beard. 'I am glad you think so, Monsieur. But it is difficult for a proud man to curb his anger under such circumstances. When I was a student I fought a duel. The man disputed my word. I struck him. He challenged. We fought. Our friends arranged it.'

He sighed reminiscently. 'It was a cold November morning; so cold that my hands were blue and numb. It is strange how such trifles worry a man. We took a carriage to the meeting-place. My friend wished to walk, for neither of us could afford a carriage. But I insisted. If I were to be killed it would not matter. If I were not killed the relief would be so great that I should not care about the expense. So we took a carriage. But all the same I was worrying about my cold hands. I put them in my pockets and still they were cold. I was afraid to put them under my arms for fear that my friend should think from my hunched attitude that I was frightened. I tried sitting on them, but the leather of the seats was smooth and shiny and even colder. All my thoughts were centred in my hands. And do you know why?'

I shook my head. His eyes twinkled behind the pince-nez.

'Because, in the first place, I was afraid that I should not be able to shoot straight enough to hit my opponent and, secondly, because if his hands were as cold as mine he might have the luck to hit me.'

I smiled. 'I take it, Monsieur, that all went well, after all.'

'Perfectly! We both missed. We not only missed. We nearly shot our seconds.' He chuckled. 'We have laughed over it many times since. He is now the owner of the factory next to mine. He has five hundred workmen. I have seven hundred and thirty. He makes machinery. I make packing-cases.' The waiter arrived. 'A vermouth-citron for Monsieur.'

I was puzzled. Someone, Skelton or the Major, had told me that Monsieur Duclos had a canning factory. I must have been mistaken.

'Times are difficult,' he was saying. 'Wages rise, prices rise. The next moment prices fall, yet wages still must rise. I am forced to reduce wages. What happens? My workmen strike. Some of them have been with me for many years. I know them by their names, and as I walk through the factory I greet them. Then the agitators, the Communists, went among them, turning them against me. My men struck. What did I do?'

The waiter arriving with my drink absolved me from the necessity of replying.

'What did I do? I sat down to think. Why had my men

turned against me? Why? The answer was—ignorance. Poor fellows, they did not understand, they did not know. I resolved to call them together, to explain to them the simple truth. I, Papa Duclos, would explain. It needed courage, for the young men did not know me as well as the old ones and the agitators had done their work well.'

Monsieur Duclos sipped at his Pernod.

'I faced them,' he said dramatically, 'standing on the steps of the factory. I held up my hand for silence. They were silent. "My children," I said, "you wish for increased wages." They cheered. I held up my hand again for silence. I spoke again. "Let me tell you, my children, what will happen if I do this. Then you may make your own choice." They murmured and were silent again. I felt inspired. "Prices are falling," I continued. "Prices are falling. If I increase your wages the prices of the Duclos works will be higher than those of our competitors. We shall lose orders. For many of you there will no longer be work. Do you wish that?" There were shouts of "no!" Some agitators cried in their ignorant way that the profits must be reduced. But how can one explain to such imbeciles that interest must be paid on investments, that if there were no profits business would come to a stop? I ignored these shouts. I went on to tell them of my love for them, of my sense of responsibility for their welfare, of how I wished to do the best for all, of how we must co-operate for the sake of ourselves and of France. "We must all," I said, "make sacrifices for the common good." I appealed to them to accept a reduction in wages with stout hearts and the determination to work even harder. When I had finished they cheered me, and the older men agreed among themselves that all should go back to work. It was a great moment. I wept for joy.' His eyes glistened through the pince-nez.

'A great moment, as you say,' I said tactfully. 'But is it, do you think, quite as simple as that? If wages fall, do not prices fall still further for the reason that people have less to spend?'

He shrugged.

'There are,' he said vaguely, 'certain economic laws with which it is unwise for man to tamper. If wages rise above their natural level the delicate balance of the system is upset. But I must not bore you with these affairs. In my factory I am a businessman, alert, decisive, strong. Now I am on holiday. For the moment my great responsibilities are put aside. I am content to soothe my tired brain with contemplation of the stars.'

He flung his head back and looked at the stars. 'Beautiful!' he murmured raptly. 'Magnificent! Such quantities! Formidable!'

He looked at me again. 'I am very sensitive to beauty,' he said. He turned his attention to his glass, diluted the contents with some more water and drank it off. Then he looked at his watch and stood up.

'Monsieur,' he said, 'it is half past ten. I am old. I have enjoyed our discussion. Now, with your permission, I will retire to bed. Good night.'

He bowed, shook hands, put his pince-nez in his pocket, and walked, rather unsteadily, indoors. Only then did it occur to me to suspect that perhaps Monsieur Duclos had had more then one Pernod that evening.

For a time I sat in the lounge and read a fortnight-old *Gringoire*. Then, tiring of this, I went out into the garden to look for the Americans.

The ping-pong table was deserted, but the light was

still glaring down on it. The bats lay crossed, with a dented ball lying between the handles. I picked up the ball and bounced it on the table. It made an odd, cracked sound. As I replaced it between the bats I heard a step somewhere near at hand. I turned round expecting to see someone. The darkness beyond the pool of light round the table was intense. If there was anyone there I could not see him or her. I listened, but there was no further sound. Whoever it was must have passed by. I decided to go down to the alcove on the lower terrace.

I threaded my way through the bushes to the path and began to descend. I had nearly reached the steps and could see a narrow strip of starry blue-black sky between the cypresses when it happened.

There was a slight rustle in the bushes on my left. I went to turn. The next moment something hit me on the back of the head.

I don't think that I actually lost consciousness, but the next thing I realised at all coherently was that I was lying on my face, half off the path, and that something was pinning my shoulders to the ground with considerable force. Lights were flashing behind my eyes and my ears were singing; but behind the singing I could hear the sound of somebody's quick breathing, and I could feel hands fumbling in my pockets.

Almost before my stunned brain had begun to absorb these faces the whole thing was over. The pressure on my shoulders suddenly relaxed, a shoe grated on the path, then there was silence.

For several minutes I lay where I was, my hands clasping my head as waves of sickening pain began to surge through it. Then, as the waves subsided into a steady throb, I got slowly to my feet and struck a match. My note-case was lying open on the ground. It contained only money and a few odd papers. Nothing had been taken.

I started to walk towards the house. Twice I became dizzy and had to stop and wait for the fit to pass, but I gained my room without assistance and without meeting anyone. I sank on the bed with a sigh. The relief of being able to rest my head on a soft pillow was almost painful.

It may have been delayed concussion or it may have been sheer weariness, but in less than a minute I seemed to go to sleep. The inconsequence of my last conscious thought makes me think that it must have been concussion.

'I must remember,' I kept saying to myself, 'to tell Beghin that Mrs Clandon-Hartley is an Italian.'

10

LOOKING back on those next twenty-four hours is, I find, like looking at a stage through the wrong end of a pair of opera-glasses. The people on it are moving, but their faces are too small to see. I must try to turn the glasses the right way round. And yet, when I try to do that the figures are blurred at the edges and distorted. It is only by, so to speak, looking at one portion of the stage at a time that I can see things clearly.

I realise now, of course, that I had completely lost my sense of proportion. It is always quite easy to realise that afterwards. The remarkable thing is that during the day which followed I did not lose touch with reality altogether. It was, to put it mildly, a fantastic day. The first touch of fantasy was provided by, of all people, Major Clandon-Hartley.

I was late down to breakfast and only the Vogels were left on the terrace.

I had a swelling that felt the size of a cannon-ball on the back of my head. Though not unduly painful now, it was very tender, and when I walked it throbbed every time my heels touched the ground.

I went rather gingerly to the terrace and sat down. The Vogels were just getting up to go. They beamed at me and came over. We exchanged good mornings. Then Herr Vogel fired the first shot of the day.

'Have you heard,' he said, 'that the English major and his wife are leaving?'

My head throbbed violently. 'When?'

'We do not know. Monsieur Duclos had the news. He is very well informed. It is best, I think. Best, that is, that the English go. There would be difficulty after yesterday's affair. We shall be seeing you on the beach this morning?' He winked. 'The American miss is already down there.'

I made some vague reply and they passed on. The very thing that I had feared had happened. Not that there was the remotest possibility that Major Clandon-Hartley was a spy. That was too absurd. And yet there was the fact of Mrs Clandon-Hartley being an Italian. My mind went back to the Commissaire's room and Beghin's persistent questions as to my Italian acquaintances. It was not possible, but . . .

There was only one thing to do; telephone Beghin immediately. I gulped down my coffee and made my way through the lounge and the hall to the drive. I got no farther than halfway along it. Coming towards me from the gap in the trees that led to the garden was the Major; and he was showing every sign of wishing to intercept me.

'Been looking for you everywhere, Vadassy,' he greeted me when he was within talking distance. I stopped and he came up to me. He dropped his voice a trifle furtively. 'If you're not specially busy at the moment I'd like a private word with you.'

I must confess that, in spite of the obvious stupidity of the idea, the first thing that entered my head was the thought that the Major was going to confess to being a spy. I hesitated for a moment, then bowed formally. 'Certainly, Major. I am at your disposal.'

Without a word he led the way back to the house and into the writing-room. He drew up a chair. 'Damned uncomfortable, these chairs,' he said apologetically; 'but they're better than those in the lounge.'

This was untrue. It was obvious that he had chosen the writing-room because it was usually deserted. We sat down.

'I'm afraid I can't offer you a cigarette,' he said. 'I don't smoke.'

His embarrassment was painful. I lit one of my own cigarettes. He leaned forward in his chair, clasping and unclasping his hands. He kept his eyes on the floor.

'Look here, Vadassy,' he said suddenly, 'I wanted to have a word with you for a special reason.' He stopped. I waited, looking at the end of my cigarette. In the silence I began to hear the clock ticking on the mantelpiece.

'You weren't down on the beach yesterday afternoon, were you?' he asked unexpectedly.

'No.'

'I thought not. I couldn't remember having seen you.' He hesitated, fumbling with his words. 'You probably heard about what happened there. Lost my temper, I'm afraid. Damned unpleasant.'

'I did hear something about it.'

'Thought you might have. You can't expect people not to talk about a thing like that.' He stopped again. I began to wonder when we were coming to the point. Suddenly he raised his head and looked me in the eyes.

'They're saying that I'm mad, aren't they, that I'm not responsible for my actions?'

The question took me completely by surprise. I did not know what to reply. I felt myself reddening.

'I beg your pardon.'

He smiled faintly. 'Sorry to spring that on you, but I had to know where I stood. I can see by your face that the answer is yes. Well, that's what I wanted to have a word with you about, that and something else.'

'Oh, I see.' I tried to make the answer casual, as though I were used to people explaining why they were regarded as mad. He did not appear to be listening.

'I know,' he said, 'that it's damned bad form unloading one's private affairs on strangers, that is, on people one's just met; but I have a good reason. You see, Vadassy, you're the only man I can talk to here.' He regarded me sombrely. 'I hope you don't mind.'

I said, wondering what on earth it was all about, that I did not mind.

'It's good of you to say so,' he went on; 'these damned foreigners . . .' He stopped, evidently realising that this was scarcely tactful. 'You see, Mr Vadassy, it's about my wife.' He stopped again.

I was getting tired of this. 'Supposing,' I suggested, 'that you take my good will for granted and say what you want to say. You must remember that I have no idea what you are talking about.'

He flushed. There was a suggestion of a return to the military manner. 'Quite right. No good beating about the bush. I wouldn't be sitting here wasting your time at all if there wasn't a reason. Put my cards on the table. Tell you the whole story. Then you can judge for yourself. Don't want you to get the wrong idea.' He drove his fist gently into the palm of his other hand. 'I'll put my cards on the table,' he repeated.

'I met my wife early in 1918 in Rome.' He paused, and I was afraid that there were going to be more hesitations; but this time he went on.

'It was just after the Italians had folded up at Caporetto and retreated across the Piave. I'd been transferred to the staff as attaché to a divisional general. Well, the British and French War Offices were pretty worried about the Italian situation. Most of the people thought, of course, that the Austrians were after the industrial areas around Milan; but there were whispers, and pretty loud ones, that the Austro-German General Staff wouldn't have detached so many troops from the Western front for that alone and that their real plan was to outflank the Swiss barrier via the North Italian plain with Lyons as the objective. A sort of *Drang nach Westen*.' He stumbled over the German.

'Anyway, ourselves and the French sent guns and troops into Italy to stop the rot, and a few of us were drafted there to sort things out. I went to Pisa first. They'd got their railway system into a shocking mess. Of course, I knew damn-all about railways, but there was a promoted ranker with me who'd had some civilian experience in England, and together we got along famously. Later in '18 they sent me down to Rome.

'Have you ever been in Rome in winter? It's not at all bad. There was a pretty big British colony there at the time, but it was mostly army, and it was part of our job to mix with the Italians and get friendly. For two pins they'd have made peace. Well, I'd been there about a couple of months when I had a bit of bad luck. You know, some of those Italian cavalry officers are amazing riders and a bit mad. So are the horses. Anyway, I was out for a canter with one of these chaps one day, and he put his horse at a jump that I shouldn't like to try on a Grand National winner. My animal tried to follow, and I took a toss that busted a leg and a couple of ribs.

'I was living in a hotel, and as they couldn't look after me there I had to go into hospital. The trouble was that just about that time there'd been a dust-up in the north. The wounded were being sent down by the trainload from the base hospitals to make room for the fresh casualties. Beds were scarce and the place they took me to was overcrowded and hopelessly understaffed. I sent out an S.O.S. to an Italian staff officer I knew, and the next day I was moved to a huge private villa just outside Rome. It belonged to a family who had volunteered to nurse convalescent officers. Their name was Staretti.'

He glanced at me. 'I dare say you're wondering what the hell all this has to to do with what happened on the beach yesterday afternoon.'

I was actually wondering more than that. I was wondering what, in any case, the happenings on the beach had to do with me. But I merely nodded.

'I'm coming to that,' he said. He began to knead his fingers as though they were cold.

'The Starettis were a curious family. At least I thought so. The mother was dead. There were only the old man and his children—two daughters, Maria and Serafina, and a son, Batista. Maria was about twenty-five and Serafina was two years younger. Batista was thirty-two. Staretti himself was a dried-up, wizened old chap with a shock of white hair. He was seventy, a big banker in Rome, and as rich as Crœsus. Well, you know you can't live in somebody's house for weeks on end without getting a pretty good idea of how each one feels about the others. I used to sit out in the garden most of the day with my leg and ribs strapped up, and they used to come and talk to me. That is, all except old Staretti, and he was nearly always at his office or seeing ministers. He was quite important in Rome at that time. But Maria used to come out a lot and sometimes Serafina, though she used to talk about nothing except the Italian who'd got me in there. They were going to be married. Then Batista started coming.

'Batista hated the old man and the old man hadn't got much time for him. I think quite a lot of the trouble was because Batista had something wrong with his heart and wasn't fit enough for the army. The old man was very hot on smashing the Austrians. Anyway, Batista used to moan to me about how his father overworked him and kept him short of money, and tell me what he'd do when old Staretti died and the money came to him. It used to get a bit boring at times. He was a nasty piece of work, and fat and flabby even then; but I'd got nothing much to do except look at the scenery, and that was even more boring—just a long, flat plain with a clump of cypresses here and there, dull. But one thing struck me about Batista. He had his father's business instincts, a sort of complicated cunning that saw about three moves ahead of everyone else. I found out a bit more about that later.

'Those weeks went pretty quickly, all things considered. Maria and I got on pretty well together. It wasn't exactly a nurse-and-patient business, because they had a proper nurse in to look after me. But Maria didn't like all these young pups of Italian officers who used to prance round taking a darn sight too much for granted. She couldn't handle them like her sister. Anyway, in the end Maria and I arranged that when the war was over I would come back and that we would get married. But we said nothing about that to anyone, though I think Serafina had a pretty shrewd notion of the way things were. You see, she being a Catholic made it difficult, and we didn't want the

124

thing discussed until we were ready. In the spring I was drafted back to France.

'Well, things went all right with me until August, when I was caught in a gas-shell bombardment. It was latish in 1919 before they finally shot me out, with about half a lung in working order, and told me to live in a warm, dry climate. Well, that suited me, and I made tracks for Rome. They were all very pleased to see me, especially Maria. A few weeks later we announced our engagement.

'It seemed at first as if everything was fine. Old Staretti was delighted. I think he was a bit sorry that I hadn't an arm or a leg shot off instead of being gassed, but he promised us the earth. Plans were going ahead for the wedding and the climate was working wonders with my chest; and then the trouble started.

'By this time Batista was pretty high up in his father's business, and one day he came to me and asked me if I'd like to make a packet of money. Well, naturally, I wanted to hear more about it. It appeared that a lot of people were making comfortable little fortunes by buying up surplus machine-guns from the Italian government, cheap, and shipping them to Syria, where they fetched about six times as much from the Arabs. The only thing you needed was capital to buy the guns. That was the way Batista put it.

'Well, as you can imagine, I jumped at the chance. Batista moaned that he'd only got about a thousand quid in dollars and that we should need at least five to make it worth while. I agreed to put up the four. It was just about all I had apart from my pension and a small reversionary interest in an estate belonging to my cousin, and I was keen to multiply the four by six.

'I knew nothing about business. Never been able to

make head or tale of it. Give me some men and guns and a job to do with them and I'll do it. But I've got no head for pettifogging business dealings. I left all that side of it to Batista. He said that it had to be cash, so I got cash. He said that he'd look after the details. I let him. I even signed a lot of papers that he gave me to sign. I may have been a fool, but anyway my Italian wasn't so very good that I was in a position to check up on him even if I'd wanted to.

'Nothing happened for a time, then one day old Staretti sent for me. He said that it had been brought to his notice that I had engaged in a business deal with two men, whose names I had never even heard of, in connection with a shipment of machine-guns to Syria and that I had given them a written guarantee to pay them twenty-five per cent of the selling price in Syria. I said that I knew nothing about any twenty-five per cent, but that I had invested four thousand pounds with Batista in a shipment of machine-guns. I knew nothing more than that about the business side. He had better ask Batista.

'Well, he got very angry at that. There was my written guarantee. Had I or had I not signed it? I admitted signing it, but said that I had not known what I was signing. He told me not to play the fool and demanded an explanation. To cut a long story short, it turned out that the paper I'd signed had been a guarantee of twenty-five per cent to the two men at the Italian War Office responsible for selling the machine-guns—in other words, a large-scale bribe. Well, the political situation was a bit touchy then and the War Minister had come down on old Staretti like a ton of bricks, wanting to know what the hell his future son-in-law was playing at. Pretty embarrassing for the old boy, it was.

'Of course, I denied it absolutely, and then he sent for Batista. The moment Batista came into the room I knew that I'd been done to a turn. There was a smug grin on his face that made me long to knock him down. He pleaded complete ignorance of the whole affair. He said that he was very shocked.'

I saw the Major clench his fists until the knuckles showed white.

'There's not much more to it,' he went on at last. 'Apparently old Staretti had altered his will, leaving half his money to Maria. Batista was out to scotch that. And he did. He also relieved me of my four thousand. I had a dreadful scene with the old boy. He accused me of trying to blacken his son's name and of marrying his daughter for his money. He said that the marriage was off and that if I didn't get out of Italy within twenty-four hours he'd have me arrested and risk the scandal. I went,' he added slowly, 'but I hadn't finished being a damned fool yet because I let Maria go with me against her father's wishes. We were married in Bâle.'

He stopped. I said nothing. There was nothing to say. But he hadn't finished yet. He cleared his throat.

'Women are funny creatures,' he said inanely. He paused. 'I don't think my good lady knew just how little money I had when she said she wanted to go with me. She'd been used to something different from cheap hotels. We tried England for a bit, but my chest wouldn't stand it. Then we went to Spain. When the trouble started there we had to clear out. We went to Juan les Pins for a time, but it got too expensive in the season, so we moved along here. She hates it all. She should never have left her own people. We're all foreigners to her. She even hates speaking English. And sometimes I think she hates me. She's never really forgiven me for letting Batista put it across me. She says that I must be mad. Sometimes she tells other people that, too.' There was infinite weariness in his voice now.

'You should have seen her when she recognised Batista yesterday. She knows what he did to me, yet she was overjoyed to see him. It fairly bowled me over. And then he started. He's got the old man's money now, and he laughed at me. He made a joke out of the way he'd treated me. A joke! Good God, if I'd had a gun in my hand I'd have shot him. As it was, I just hit him and not even in his smug, grinning face, but in his fat belly. The swine!' His voice had risen and he began to cough. But he managed to stop himself. He looked at me challengingly. 'You probably think I'm a damned fool, eh?'

I muttered a denial.

He laughed bitterly. 'You aren't far wrong. And you're going to think me a damned outsider as well because I'm going to ask you to do something for me.'

For some reason my head throbbed painfully. At last we were coming to the point. I said, 'Yes?' and waited.

He had become formal and embarrassed again. He stumbled over the words as though each one was an effort. 'I wouldn't have told you all this, Vadassy, but I wanted you to understand the circumstances. Damned difficult thing to ask anyone. My good lady and I, we can't stay in this place after that business yesterday. Everybody gossiping. Embarrassing for all concerned. Climate doesn't suit my chest, either. There's a boat that leaves Marseilles every Monday for Algiers. Thought we'd catch it. Trouble is—' he hesitated. 'Hate to bother you with my private affairs like this, but the fact is I'm in a bit of a corner. Wasn't expecting this Algiers trip. Quite a bill from Köche as well. These things happen. Must sound to you horribly like a hard-luck story. Can't stand cadgers myself. But the fact is, Vadassy, that if you could possibly lend me a couple of thousand francs until the end of the month it would be helpful. Hate to ask you, but you know how it is.'

I had not the slightest idea what to say, but I opened my mouth to speak. He forestalled me.

'Of course, I shouldn't expect you to lend me money without security. I'll naturally give you a post-dated cheque on Cox's bank—that is, if you don't mind it in pounds. Safer than francs, what!' He gave a forced laugh. There were small beads of perspiration on his temples. 'Shouldn't dream of troubling you at all, of course, but as we've got to leave this place it puts me in a damned awkward position. Know you'll understand. You're the only person here I'd care to ask, and—well, I don't have to tell you how much I'd appreciate it.'

I stared at him helplessly. At that moment I would have given almost anything to have had in my pocket five thousand francs, to have been able to smile cheerfully, to produce my notecase, to reassure him. 'Good heavens, yes, Major! Why didn't you say so before? No trouble at all. Better make it five thousand. After all, it's only a matter of cashing a cheque, and a Cox's cheque is as good as a Bank of England note any day. Delighted to be of assistance. Glad you asked me.' But I had no five thousand francs. I had not even two thousand. I had my return ticket to Paris and just enough money to pay my bill at the Réserve and live for a week. I could do nothing but stare at him, and listen to the clock ticking on the mantelpiece. He looked up at me.

'I'm sorry,' I stammered, and then again: 'I'm sorry.'

He stood up. 'Quite all right,' he said, with ghastly unconcern; 'not really important. Just wondered if you could manage it, that's all. Sorry to have taken up so much of your time. Damned inconsiderate of me. Forget about the money. Just wondered, that's all. Enjoyed having a jaw, though. Not often I have a chance of speaking English.' He drew himself up. 'Well, I'll be getting along to do a little packing. Expect we shall be leaving early tomorrow. And I shall have to get a wire off. See you before we go.'

Too late I found tongue.

'I can't tell you how sorry I am, Major, that I can't help you. It's not a question of not wanting to cash a cheque for you. I haven't got two thousand francs. I've only just got enough to pay my bill here. If I had any money I should be only too delighted to lend it to you. I'm terribly sorry. I—' Now that I had started I wanted to go on apologising, to embarrass myself to restore his self-esteem. But I had no chance to do so for, even as I was speaking, he turned on his heel and walked out of the room.

When, some ten minutes later, I telephoned to the Commissariat and asked to speak to the Commissaire, Beghin's irritable voice answered.

'Hello, Vadassy!'

'I have something to report.'

'Well?'

'Major and Mrs Clandon-Hartley may be leaving tomorrow. He has tried to borrow money from me to pay his and his wife's fare to Algiers.'

'Well? Did you lend him the money?'

'My employers have not yet paid me for the Toulon photographs,' I retorted recklessly.

To my surprise this impertinence was greeted with a squeaky chuckle from the other end.

'Anything else?'

Rashly, I gave way to the impulse to deliver a further jibe.

'I don't suppose you'll think it important, but last night I was knocked down by somebody in the garden and searched.' Even as I said it I knew that I had been very foolish. This time there was no answering chuckle but a sharp order to repeat myself. I did so.

There was a significant silence. Then:

'Why didn't you say so at first instead of wasting time? Did you identify the man? Explain yourself.'

I explained myself. Then came the question that I had been dreading.

'Has your room been searched?'

'I think so.'

'What do you mean by "think so"?'

'Two rolls of film were taken from my suitcase.'

'When?'

'Yesterday.'

'Was anything else taken?' The question was very deliberate.

'No.' The camera, after all, had been taken from the chair in the hall.

There was another silence. Now he was going to ask me if the camera was safe. But he did not do so. I thought we had been cut off, and said: 'Hello!' I was told to wait a minute.

My head throbbing painfully, I waited two minutes. I could hear a murmur of voices, Beghin's squeak and the Commissaire's growl, but I could not catch what they were saying. At last Beghin returned to the telephone.

'Vadassy!'

'Yes?'

'Listen carefully. You are to go straight back to the Réserve, see Köche, and inform him that your suitcase has been forced open and that several things have been stolen—a silver cigarette-case and a box containing a diamond pin, a gold watch-chain and two rolls of film. Make a fuss about it. Tell the other guests. Complain. I want everyone at the Réserve to know about it. But don't ask for the police.'

'But—'

'Don't argue. Do as you are told. Was your suitcase forced?'

'No, but—'

'Then force it yourself before you tell Köche. Now understand this. You are to bring in the question of the films as an afterthought. You are annoyed principally about the valuables. Is that clear?'

'Yes, but I have no cigarette-case or diamond pin or gold watch-chain.'

'Of course you haven't. They have been stolen. Now get on with it.'

'This is impossible, absurd. You cannot force me to do this—' But he had already hung up.

I walked back to the hotel with murder in my heart. If there was a bigger fool than myself in this business, it was Beghin. But he had nothing to lose except a spy.

I I

I WENT about the business of concocting the evidence with bitter thoroughness.

I got out my suitcase and locked it. Then I looked round for something with which to force the latches open. I made the first attempt with a pair of nail scissors. The locks were flimsy enough, but it was difficult to get any leverage on the scissors. After five minutes' unsuccessful labour, I snapped one of the blades. I wasted several more minutes searching idly for a stronger tool. In desperation I took the key from the bedroom door and used the flat steel loop on it as a lever. The locks eventually yielded to this treatment, but I bent the key and had to spend more time straightening it. Then I opened the lid, stirred up the contents and, contorting my features into an expression of outraged innocence, hurried downstairs to find Köche.

He was not in his office. By the time I had traced him to the beach where he was lounging about in swimming trunks, my outraged innocence had relaxed into a sort of cringing anxiety. The Skeltons, the French couple, and Monsieur Duclos were down there with him. I played with the idea of awaiting a more opportune moment, but rejected it. I must remember that a robbery had been committed. Objects of value had been stolen from my room. I must behave as any normal person would behave under such circumstances; I must report to the manager even if he was clad only in a pair of swimming trunks. A sleek, black-coated manager would have been more appropriate to the occasion, but I must do the best I could with Köche.

I ran down the steps to the beach and started across the sand towards him. At this point, however, there was a disconcerting interruption. Skelton, hearing my footsteps on the stairs, had looked round the edge of his sunshade and seen me.

'Hey!' he called over. 'Haven't seen you all morning. Are you coming in the water before lunch?'

I hesitated; then, realising that there was nothing else for it, I went over. Mary Skelton, who was lying face downwards on the sand, turned her head and cocked an eye at me.

'We thought you'd deserted us, Mr Vadassy. You've no right to trifle with the kiddies' affections like that. Get into your swim suit and come and give us the dirt on the affair Clandon-Hartley. We saw you talking to him through the writing-room window after breakfast.'

'No finesse!' complained her brother. 'I was going to introduce the subject gradually. What about it, Mr Vadassy?'

'If you'll excuse me,' I said hurriedly, 'I must have a word with Köche. See you later.'

'That's a deal!' he called after me.

Köche was talking to Roux and Duclos. Evidently the quarrel of the previous night had been forgotten. I interrupted him in the middle of a disquisition on the virtues of Grenoble. I was tight-lipped and grave.

'Excuse me, Monsieur, but I should like to speak with you privately. It is rather urgent.'

He raised his eyebrows and excused himself to the others. We moved a little away.

'What can I do for you, Monsieur?'

'I regret to disturb you, but I am afraid I must ask you to step up to my room. While I was in the village just now, my suitcase has been broken open and several valuable objects stolen from it.'

The eyebrows went up again. He whistled softly between his teeth and glanced at me quickly. Then with a muttered 'excuse me' he walked across the sand, picked up his bathing wrap and sandals, put them on, and rejoined me.

'I will come with you immediately.'

Under the curious eyes of the others we left the beach.

On the way up to my room he asked me what was missing. I gave him Beghin's grotesque selection and added the tidbit about the films. He nodded and was silent. I began to feel apprehensive. True, there was no possible way of his discovering the whole business was a put-up job; yet, now that I had started the thing moving, I was uneasy. For all his lazy, indolent manner, Köche was no fool and I could not quite forget the fact that it was not impossible for Köche himself to have taken the films and also stunned me in the garden the night before. In that case he would know that I was lying. The consequences might be distinctly unpleasant for me. I cursed Beghin with renewed fervour.

Köche inspected my work on the suitcase locks with gloomy interest. Then he straightened his back and his eyes met mine.

'You say that you left your room at about nine o'clock?'

'Yes.'

'Was the suitcase all right, then?'

'Yes. The last thing I did before I went down was to lock the case and push it under the bed.'

He looked at his watch. 'It is now eleven twenty. How long ago did you return?'

'About fifteen minutes ago. But I did not go to the suitcase straight away. As soon as I saw what had happened, I came straight to you. It is disgraceful,' I added lamely.

He nodded and eyed me speculatively. 'Do you mind coming down to my office, Monsieur? I should like a detailed description of the missing objects.'

'Certainly. But I must warn you, Monsieur,' I mumbled, 'that I shall hold you responsible and that I shall expect the immediate return of the valuables and the punishment of the thief.'

'Naturally,' he said politely. 'I have no doubt that I shall be able to return your property to you within a very short time. There is no cause for you to worry.'

Feeling rather like an amateur actor who has forgotten his lines, I followed Köche down to his office. He closed the door carefully, drew up a chair for me and picked up a pen.

'Now, Monsieur. The cigarette-case first, if you please. It is, I think you said, a gold one.'

I looked at him quickly. He was writing something on the paper. I panicked. Had I said that it was a gold one when we were coming up from the beach? For the life of me I could not remember. Or was he trying to trap me? But I had an inspiration.

'No, a silver case, gold lines. It has,' I said, warming to my work, 'my initials, "J.V.", engraved in one corner and is machined on the outside. It holds ten cigarettes and the elastic is missing.'

'Thank you, and the chain?'

I remembered a second-hand chain I had seen displayed in a jeweller's window near the Gare Mont-parnasse.

'Eighteen-carat gold, thick, old-fashioned links, heavy. It has a small gold medallion on it commemorating the Brussels Exhibition of 1901.'

He wrote it all down carefully.

'And now the pin, Monsieur.'

This was not so easy. 'Just a pin, Monsieur. A tie-pin about six centimetres long with a small diamond about three millimetres in diameter in the head.' I gave way to a weak impulse. 'The diamond,' I said, with a self-conscious laugh, 'is paste.'

'But the pin itself is gold?'

'Rolled gold.'

'And the box in which these objects were left?'

'A tin box. A cigarette box. A German cigarette box. I cannot remember the brand. There was also in it two rolls of film, Contax film. They had been exposed.'

'You have a Contax camera?'

'Yes.'

He looked at me again. 'I assume that you made sure that the camera was safe, Monsieur. A thief would get a good price for a camera.'

My heart missed about two beats. I had blundered badly.

'The camera?' I said stupidly. 'I did not look. I left it in the drawer.'

He stood up. 'Then I suggest, Monsieur, that we go and look immediately.'

'Yes, of course.' I was, I felt, very red in the face.

We went upstairs again and along to my room. I pre-pared myself carefully for the emission of the suitable cries of dismay and anger that would be necessary.

I rushed anxiously to the chest of drawers, pulled open the top drawer and rummaged feverishly inside it. Then I turned round slowly and dramatically.

'Gone!' I said grimly. 'This is too much. That camera is worth nearly five thousand francs. The thief must be found without delay. I demand, Monsieur, that something is done immediately.'

To my surprise and confusion a faint smile appeared on his lips.

'Something will certainly be done, Monsieur,' he said calmly, 'but in the case of the camera, nothing will be necessary. Look!'

I followed the direction of his nod. There, on the chair beside the bed, was a Contax camera complete with case.

'I must,' I said stupidly, as we went downstairs again, 'have forgotten that I had left it on the chair.'

He nodded. 'Or the thief removed it from the drawer and then forgot to take it after all.' I thought it was my guilty conscience that detected a faint note of irony in his voice.

'Anyway,' I said, with unaffected gaiety, 'I have the camera.'

'We must hope,' he said gravely, 'that the other things will reappear as quickly.'

I agreed as enthusiastically as I could. We returned to the office.

'What,' he asked, 'is the value of the cigarette-case and the watch-chain?'

I thought carefully. 'It is hard to say. About eight hundred francs for the case and about five hundred for the chain, I should think. Both were presents. The pin, though intrinsically worthless, possesses great sentimental value for me. As for the films: well, I should be sorry to lose them, naturally, but—' I shrugged.

'I understand. They were insured, the case and the chain?'

'No.'

He put down his pen. 'You will appreciate, Monsieur, that in these affairs suspicion is bound to fall on the servants. I shall question them first. I should prefer to do it alone. I hope you will not think it necessary to call in the police at this stage and will trust me to handle the matter discreetly.'

'Of course.'

'Also, Monsieur, I would personally appreciate it if you would say nothing of this unfortunate affair to the other guests.'

'Naturally not.'

'Thank you. You will realise that considerable damage is done to the reputation of a small hotel such as this by such unpleasant affairs. I will report to you the moment I have completed my inquiries.'

I went, feeling distinctly uncomfortable. Köche had asked that the other guests should not be told; and for my part I would have been only too pleased to comply with the request. The less said about the business the better I should have been pleased. But Beghin had insisted on the news being broadcast to the other guests; he had been quite clear on the point. I must make a fuss. And there were the wretched servants to be considered. It was altogether a most unhappy situation; and, as far as I could see, utterly pointless as well: unless there was something going on about which I knew nothing. What cigarette-cases and watch-chains had to do with spies was beyond my comprehension. Did Beghin propose to use the alleged robbery as a pretext on which to arrest the spy? Absurd! Where was the evidence to come from? My two rolls of film were, no doubt, developed and thrown away by now; and the cigarette-case and watch-chain did not exist. There was only one sensible way of tackling the problems. Identify the spy first, then catch him with my camera in his possession.

My camera?

I took the last few stairs at a run and dashed for my room. It did not take me more than a few seconds to confirm my fears. This *was* my camera. The incriminating evidence had been politely returned.

I changed into my swimming trunks miserably. I could, of course, lie to Beghin. I could say that the cameras had been re-exchanged without my knowledge. I could plead ignorance. I could suggest that it had been done when my room had been searched. After all, I couldn't be expected to examine the number on the camera at hourly intervals throughout the day. If I was careful there was no reason why Beghin should know that for about eighteen hours I had had neither of the cameras. That was unless he caught the spy. Then the fat would be in the fire. Beghin might even have to release the man again. Not that there was the remotest chance of catching him with stories of forced suitcases and stolen watch-chains. Still, that was Beghin's affair. I was only a pawn in the game, a fly caught in the cog-wheels. A sickly, sticky steam of self-pity welled up into my mind. I stood in my shirt and looked at myself in the mirror. Poor fool! What skinny legs! I finished changing. As I went down the stairs I saw Schimler follow Köche into the office and shut the door. Schimler! I experienced an empty feeling inside my chest. That was another thing. Today I was to search Schimler's room.

The Vogels had now joined the French couple on the beach. The Americans were in the water. I went over to Monsieur Duclos, drew a deck-chair alongside his and sat down. For a minute or two we exchanged commonplaces. Then I began work.

'You, Monsieur, are a man of the world. I should be grateful for your advice in a delicate matter.'

A look of pure pleasure suffused his face. He stroked his beard gravely. 'My experience, such as it is, is at your disposal, Monsieur.' He rolled his eyes archly. 'It is, perhaps, concerning the American miss that you wish my advice?'

'I beg your pardon.'

He chuckled roguishly. 'You need not be embarrassed, my friend. If I may say so, your glances in her direction have been remarked by all. But the brother and sister are inseparable, eh? Believe me, Monsieur, I have some judgment in these affairs.' He lowered his voice and brought his head nearer mine. 'I have noticed that the miss also looks at you.' He dropped his voice still further and sprayed the next sentence right into my ear. 'She is especially interested when you are dressed as you are now.' He giggled into his beard.

I stared at him coldly. 'What I had to say was nothing to do with Miss Skelton.'

'No?' He looked disappointed.

'I am more concerned at the moment with the fact that several objects of value have been stolen from my room.'

His pince-nez quivered so much that they fell off. He caught them neatly and replaced them on his nose.

'A robbery?'

'Precisely. While I was in the village this morning my locked suitcase was forced open and a cigarette-case, a gold watch-chain, a diamond pin, and two rolls of film were stolen. The value of the property is over two thousand francs.'

'*Formidable!*'

'I am desolated by the loss. The pin was of great sentimental value.'

'*C'est affreux!*'

'Indeed it is! I have complained to Köche, and he is questioning the servants. But—and this, Monsieur, is the matter in which I should welcome your guidance—I am not satisfied with the way in which Monsieur Köche is conducting the affair. He does not seem to realise the gravity of the loss. Should I be justified in putting the matter before the police?'

'The police?' Monsieur Duclos wriggled with excitement. 'Why, yes! It is without a doubt an affair for the police. I will, if you wish, come with you now myself to the *Poste.*'

'And yet,' I said hurriedly, 'Köche was of the opinion that the police would be well left out of the affair. He is to question the servants. Perhaps it would be better to wait and hear the result of this questioning.'

'Ah, yes. Perhaps that would be better.' He was clearly reluctant to abandon the police so soon. 'But ...'

'Thank you, Monsieur,' I put in smoothly; 'I am grateful for your advice. It has confirmed my own inclinations in the matter.' I saw his eyes straying towards the Vogels and the French people. 'Naturally, you will appreciate that I speak in confidence. We must be discreet at this stage.'

He nodded portentously. 'Naturally, Monsieur. Please

consider my experience as a businessman at your disposal. You may trust me.' He paused, then tweaked the sleeve of my wrap. 'Have you any suspicions?'

'None. Suspicions are dangerous things.'

'That is so, but—' He dropped his voice and began to spray into my ear again: 'Have you considered this English major? A violent man, that! And what does he do for a living? Nothing. He has been there three months. I will tell you something more. This morning after breakfast he came to me on the lower terrace and requested a loan of two thousand francs. He needs money badly, that one. He offered five per cent interest per month.'

'You refused?'

'Naturally. I was very angry. He said that he required the money to go to Algiers. Why should I pay for him to go to Algiers? Let him work like other men. There was also something about his wife, but I could not understand. His French is incomprehensible. He is certainly a little mad.'

'And you think he stole from my room?'

Monsieur Duclos smiled knowingly and held up a protesting hand. 'Ah, no, Monsieur, I do not *say* that. I merely *suggest*.' He had the air of negotiating a very tricky legal subtlety. 'I point out merely that this man has no occupation, that he needs money, that he is desperate. No man who was not desperate would offer five per cent per month. He said something to me of expecting money that had failed to arrive. I do not accuse this Major. I merely suggest to you.'

I saw that the Americans had come out of the water. I stood up.

'Thank you, Monsieur. I will bear the suggestion in mind. Meanwhile, of course, we must be discreet. Perhaps we could discuss the matter further later in the day.'

'When,' he agreed, 'we have heard the results of the preliminary interrogations.'

'Precisely.' I bowed.

By the time I had got across the beach to the Skeltons he was deep in conversation with the French couple and the Vogels. I did not have to guess at the subject of the conversation. Monsieur Duclos could be relied upon to carry out Beghin's instructions to the letter.

In defiance of the printed notice in the bedrooms, Skelton was drying himself on one of the hotel towels.

'Ah!' was his greeting. 'The man with the news!'

His sister made room for me under the sunshade. 'Come and sit down, Mr Vadassy. No more sneaking off with Monsieur Köche. We want the truth—all of it.'

I sat down. 'I'm sorry I had to run off like that, but something rather nasty has happened.'

'What, again?'

'I'm afraid so. This morning, while I was down in the village, my suitcase was broken open and several things taken from it.'

Skelton sat down beside me as though his legs had given way. 'Phew! That *is* nasty. Anything valuable?'

I repeated the list.

'When did you say it happened?' It was the girl who spoke.

'While I was down in the village. Between about nine and ten thirty.'

'But it was about nine thirty when we saw you talking to the Major.'

'Yes, but I left my room at nine.'

Skelton leaned forward confidentially. 'Say, you don't

suppose the Major was engaging you in conversation while his wife did the job, do you?'

'Shut up, Warren. This is serious. It was probably one of the servants.'

Skelton snorted impatiently. 'Why should it be? It makes me tired. Whenever anything's stolen everybody always looks around for a servant or messenger-boy or somebody else who can't hit back to blame it on. If we're going to be serious, what was Papa Switzer doing gumshoeing about the corridor this morning?'

'That wasn't on Mr Vadassy's side of the house. What's the number of your room, Mr Vadassy?'

'Six.'

She began to rub oil into her arms. 'There you are! It was the other side of the house, the room next but one to mine. That friend of Monsieur Köche's has it.'

I grasped a handful of sand and let it trickle through my fingers. 'What number is that?' I said idly.

'Fourteen, I think. But the Switzer wasn't gumshoeing. He'd dropped a five-franc piece in the corridor.'

'What does Köche say about it, Mr Vadassy?'

'I'm afraid he suspects the servants.'

'Naturally,' said the girl vigorously. 'Warren's too darn fond of taking up the appropriate attitude. We all know that it *ought* to be a rich old meany with a touch of kleptomania. The fact of the matter probably is that it's some poor little underpaid chambermaid with a boy-friend in the village she wants to give a cigarette-case to.'

'*And* a gold watch-chain, *and* a diamond pin, *and* a couple of spools of film?' queried her brother sarcastically.

'Maybe it's a waiter.'

'Or maybe it's old Duclos or the Major. Incidentally, what about the Major, Mr Vadassy?'

I decided not to regale them with the Major's life story. 'He merely wanted to offer a general apology for the disturbance down here yesterday. The man from the yacht was his brother-in-law. He had had a quarrel with him over some money matter. The brother-in-law brought the question up again and the Major lost his temper. He explained that his wife was distraught and that she did not really mean that he was mad.'

'Is that all? Why did he tell you about it?'

'I think he was very embarrassed by the whole affair. As I was not here, he picked on me.' I was not going to tell them that Monsieur Duclos had received an abridged apology but the same request for money. 'The Major and his wife are, in any case, leaving, and . . .'

'In other words, Warren,' put in the girl, 'we're to mind our own business and not behave like a couple of nosey kids. Is that right, Mr Vadassy?'

It was, but I blushed and began to protest. Warren Skelton interrupted me. 'I smell drink! Come on. You can't go swimming now; it's nearly lunchtime.'

While he had gone to fetch the drinks the girl and I walked up to the tables on the lower terrace.

'You mustn't take any notice of anything Warren says,' she said, smiling. 'This is his first trip abroad.'

'You've been before?'

For a moment she did not reply, and I thought she had not heard me. She seemed to hesitate as though she were about to say something important. Then I saw her shrug her shoulders slightly. 'Yes, I've been before.' As we sat down she smiled at me. 'Warren says there's something mysterious about you.'

'Does he?'

'He says that you look like a man with something

to hide. He says, too, that it's not natural that a man should speak more than one language perfectly. I think he rather hopes you'll turn out to be a spy or something exciting like that.'

I felt myself reddening again. 'A spy?'

'I told you you mustn't take any notice of what he says.' She smiled again at me. Her eyes, intelligent and amused, met mine across the table. Suddenly I wanted to confide in her, to tell her that I was indeed a man with something to hide, to gain her sympathy, her help. I leaned forward across the table.

'I should like . . .' I began. But I never told her what I should like, and I have forgotten now what I was going to say, for at that moment her brother reappeared carrying a tray of drinks. It was, no doubt, as well that he did so.

'The waiters were busy on the terrace,' he said, 'so I brought them myself.' He raised his glass. 'Well, Mr Vadassy, here's hoping that the chambermaid's boy friend doesn't like your cigarette-case!'

'Or,' the girl added gravely, 'the two spools of film. We mustn't forget *them*.'

12

I DID not eat much lunch.

For one thing, my head had begun to ache again; for another, I received with my soup a message from Köche. The manager would be grateful if Monsieur Vadassy could spare the time to call in at the office after luncheon. Yes, Monsieur Vadassy could and would spare the time. But the prospect disturbed me. Supposing Köche had decided that some 'poor little underpaid chambermaid' was the culprit. What was I supposed to do? The idiotic Beghin had made no allowances for that contingency. The wretched girl would naturally deny the charge. What could I say? Was I to stand by and see some perfectly innocent person browbeaten by a zealous Köche and accused of a theft that had not taken place? It was an abominable state of affairs.

But I need not, as it happened, have worried about that. The chambermaid was perfectly safe.

Monsieur Duclos pounced on me as I left the terrace.

'Have you decided to call in the police, Monsieur?'

'Not yet. I am going to see Köche.'

He stroked his beard gloomily. 'I have been thinking, Monsieur. Every hour we delay is in the thief's favour.'

'Quite so. But ...'

'Speaking as a businessman, I counsel immediate action. You must be firm with Köche, Monsieur.' He thrust his beard forward ferociously.

'I shall be very firm, Monsieur, I . . .'

But before I could get away the Vogels came up, shook hands with me and expressed their sorrow at my loss. Monsieur Duclos was not in the least put out by this evidence of his treachery.

'We have agreed, Monsieur Vogel and I,' he stated, 'that the Commissaire of Police should be called in.'

'Five thousand francs,' nodded Herr Vogel weightily, 'is a serious loss. A matter for the police, without a doubt. Monsieur Roux is of the same opinion. There is the safety of the other guests' property to be considered. Mademoiselle Martin, a young lady of nervous disposition, is already frightened for her jewels. Monsieur Roux calmed her, but he informed me that unless the thief is discovered he will be forced to leave. Köche will be well advised to treat the matter more seriously. Five thousand francs!'—he requoted Monsieur Duclos's version of my loss—'It is a serious thing.'

'Yes, indeed!' said Frau Vogel.

'You see!' put in Monsieur Duclos triumphantly, 'the police must be called in.'

'With regard,' pursued Herr Vogel in a whisper, 'to the question of your suspicions, Herr Vadassy, we feel that at the moment the police should not be told of them.'

'My suspicions?' I glanced at Monsieur Duclos. He had the grace to avoid my eye and fumble a little ostentatiously with his pince-nez.

Herr Vogel smiled indulgently. 'I understand perfectly. It would be better to say nothing that might be construed as referring to'—he looked round swiftly and lowered his voice—'a certain person of English nationality, eh?' He winked. 'These affairs must be handled with discretion, eh?'

'Yes, yes!' echoed Frau Vogel cheerfully.

I mumbled something about having no suspicions at all and made my escape. Monsieur Duclos was proving a rather compromising publicity agent.

Köche was waiting for me in the office.

'Ah, yes, Monsieur Vadassy, please come in.' He shut the door behind me. 'A chair? Good. Now to business.'

I played my part. 'I hope, Monsieur, that you have satisfactory news for me. This suspense is most distressing.'

He looked very grave.

'I am very much afraid, Monsieur, that my inquiries have yielded no result whatever.'

I frowned. 'That is bad.'

'Very bad. Very bad, indeed!' He glanced at a paper before him, tapped it once or twice with his forefinger and looked up at me. 'I have examined every member of the staff, including the waiters and the gardener, hoping that one of them might, at any rate, be able to throw some light on the affair.' He paused. 'Frankly, Monsieur,' he went on quietly, 'I feel that they are all telling me the truth when they say that they have no knowledge of the theft.'

'You mean that it must have been one of the guests?'

He did not reply for a moment. I began, for no reason that I could identify, to feel even more uneasy. Then he shook his head slowly. 'No, Monsieur, I do not mean that it was one of the guests.'

'Then someone from outside?'

'Not that either.'

'Then . . .?'

He leaned forward. 'I have decided, Monsieur, that this is a case for the police.'

This was difficult. Beghin had made it clear that the police were not to be called in.

'But surely,' I protested, 'that is the last thing you would wish to do. Think of the scandal.'

His lips tightened. This was a new Köche, no longer easy-going and good natured, a very businesslike Köche. There was, quite suddenly, an ugly tension in the atmosphere.

'Unfortunately,' he said bitingly, 'the damage is already done. Not only are my guests aware of and discussing the affair, but one of them is actually being regarded by the others as a possible culprit.'

'I am sorry to hear that, I—'

But he ignored my interruption. 'I asked you, Monsieur, to remain silent until I could investigate this matter. I find that, far from remaining silent, you have discussed the affair with your fellow guests in the most unfortunate manner.'

'I asked the advice in confidence of Monsieur Duclos relating to the question of informing the police. If Monsieur Duclos has been indiscreet, I am sorry.'

There was something very much like a sneer in his voice as he answered. 'And what, pray, was Monsieur Duclos's advice?'

'He advised me to call in the police, but out of deference to your—'

'Then, Monsieur, we are in perfect agreement. You have your opportunity.' He reached for the telephone. 'I will communicate with the police at once.'

'One moment, Monsieur Köche!' His hand paused on the instrument. 'I merely repeated Duclos's advice. For my part I see no necessity for calling in the police.'

To my intense relief he took his hand from the telephone. Then he turned slowly and looked me in the eyes.

'I thought you wouldn't,' he said deliberately.

'I feel sure,' I said, with all the amiability I could muster, 'that you will handle this affair far more efficiently than the police. I do not wish to make a nuisance of myself. If the stolen articles are returned, well and good. If not—well—it cannot be helped. In any case, the police will be more of a hindrance than a help.'

'I believe you, Monsieur.' This time there was no doubt about the sneer. 'I can quite believe that you would find the police a very grave hindrance.'

'I don't think I understand you.'

'No?' He smiled grimly. 'I have been in the hotel profession for a number of years, Monsieur. You will not, I feel sure, think me impolite if I tell you that I have encountered gentlemen of your persuasion before. I have learned to be careful. When you reported this alleged theft you told me that you had lost a cigarette-case. Later, when I suggested to you that you had described it as a gold case, you hesitated and got out of your difficulties by saying that it was both gold and silver. A little too ingenious, my friend. When I went into your room I noticed a blade of a pair of scissors lying on the floor by the suitcase. On the bed was the rest of the scissors. You looked at them twice, but did not comment on them. Why? They had obviously been used to force the case. They were important evidence. But you ignored them. You saw nothing significant in them because you knew how the case had been forced. You had forced it yourself.'

'Preposterous! I—'

'Again, you showed real concern when the camera was

mentioned. When I pointed it out to you on the chair your emotion was quite genuine. No doubt you were afraid for the moment that something really had been stolen.'

'I—'

'You made another mistake over the valuation of the case. A case such as you described would be worth at least fifteen hundred francs. True, you said it was a gift, but even so you would scarcely undervalue it by fifty per cent. People who have lost things invariably go to the other extreme.'

'I have never—'

'The only thing that has puzzled me is your motive. The usual idea is for the injured guest to threaten the hotel with the police and the discomfiture of the other guests unless he or, more often, she receives compensation. It is well known that hotels are insured against such contingencies. But you are either new to the game or you have some other motive, for you told the guests immediately. Perhaps you would like to tell me what your motive really is.'

I had risen to my feet. I was genuinely angry now.

'This is a monstrous accusation, Monsieur. I have never been so insulted,' I stammered with rage. 'I . . . I shall . . .'

'Call in the police?' he put in solicitously. 'Here is the telephone.'

I put on as dignified a front as possible. 'I have no intention of prolonging this farce.'

'You are wise.' He tilted his chair. 'I have had suspicions of you, Vadassy, since your rather lengthy interview with the police on Thursday. The French police do not usually search a person's room unless they have very grave suspicions of him. The passport explanation was a little thin. I can appreciate your anxiety to avoid further encounters with the Commissaire. I am also in complete agreement with you concerning the undesirability of prolonging the present situation. I have, accordingly, made out your bill. Please do not interpret this as an act of mercy on my part. My own personal inclination is to hand you straight over to the police; or at any rate to tell you to clear out within an hour. My wife, however, is of the opinion that either of those courses would arouse still further comment among our guests. She is a more practical person than I am. I bow to her decision. You will leave the Réserve early tomorrow morning. Whether or not I then inform the police depends on your behaviour during the brief time you remain here. I shall expect you to inform the other guests that your complaint was unfounded, that you had merely mislaid the articles and that the damage to your suitcase was caused by your own carelessness in using the wrong key and jamming the locks. I have no doubt that you will be able to make your story convincing enough for inexperienced ears. It is understood?'

I did the best I could with the few shreds of self-possession that were left to me. 'I understand perfectly, Monsieur. I had, in any case, no intention of staying here after your fantastic impertinence.'

'Good! Here is your bill.'

I studied the bill ostentatiously for mistakes. It was a childish thing to do, but by this time I felt childish. He waited in silence. There were no mistakes. I had only just enough money. He took it with an air that told me that he had not expected to be paid in full.

While he was making out the receipt I stared blankly at an Istalia Cosulich Line sailing list pinned to the wall beside me. I had read it through twice before he handed me the receipted bill.

'Thank you, Monsieur. I regret that I cannot hope that we shall see you again at the Réserve.'

I went.

By the time I had got up to my room I was trembling from head to foot. The discovery that the towels, the fruit bowl, and every other portable object belonging to the Réserve, with the sole exception of the bedclothes, had been removed did not improve matters. I put my head under the tap, drank some water, lit a cigarette, and sat on the chair by the window.

I began to think of things I ought to have said to Köche, cool, bitter things. Then, after a bit, I ceased to tremble. This was Beghin's fault, not mine. He might have known that such a childish plot would fail. True it was my carelessness, my inefficiency, that had brought about its failure; but I was not used to behaving like a common crook. A wave of righteous anger swept over me. What right had Beghin to place me in such a despicable position? If I had been an ordinary person with a consul to defend my rights he would not have dared. Where was the sense in it, anyway? Or had it been his idea that I *should* be found out? Was I a sort of guinea pig, being used for the purpose of some crazy experiment? Maybe I was. What did it matter, anyway? The point was that unless Beghin liked to step in and exert his authority I should be out of the Réserve in the morning. What then? Presumably a cell at the Commissariat. Perhaps I should telephone to Beghin now and explain the situation. . . .

But even as the thought crossed my mind I knew that I could not do it. The truth was that I was afraid of him, afraid that he might blame me for my discovery by Köche. Above all, I was terrified of being taken back to the Commissariat and locked up again in that small, ugly cell.

I looked out of the window. The sea lay like a great sheet of rippled blue glass in the sun. It was infinitely peaceful. In its cool depths a man would have no more fears, no doubts, no uncertainties. I could go down to the beach and into the water and swim out beyond the bay into the sea. I could go on swimming until my arms were too tired to bring me back to the land. My strokes would get slower, more laboured. Then I would stop and sink. The water would rush into my lungs. I would struggle, the desire for life would surge up—life at any price!—but I would have made my preparations so that there would be no returning. There would be a moment or two of torment, then I would slide gently into oblivion. And what then? *A Yugoslav citizen named Joseph Vadassi* (they would misspell the name) *got into difficulties while bathing yesterday at St Gatien. Attempts to rescue him failed. His body has not yet been recovered.* Nothing else? No, nothing else. That was all. The body rotted.

My cigarette had gone out. I pitched it out of the window, went over to the mirror in the wardrobe and looked at myself. 'You're going to pieces,' I murmured. 'Better pull yourself together. Suicide one minute and now you're talking to yourself. Come on now. And don't be so damned hearty about it. It's no good squaring your shoulders like that. You're not going in for a weight-lifting contest. Muscle's no use to you. What you need is a little intelligence. This business probably isn't nearly as serious as you think. And for goodness' sake get this. It's about three o'clock. Between now and tonight you've got to find a person here with a Contax camera. That's all. It isn't difficult, is it? You've only got to look in their rooms. Now start with this man Schimler. He's the most likely. He's going under a false name. He says he's a Swiss when he's really a German. He's worried and he's got some understanding with Köche. You've got to bear in mind, too, that Köche may be in on the secret. Maybe that's the real reason why he's anxious to get rid of you without calling in the police. Yes that's an idea, isn't it? You're not beaten yet. But be careful. Use a little sense. You've been caught out once. Don't let it happen again. If he's the man, you've got to be clever to catch him. He's dangerous. He's the man who slugged you on the head last night and gave you this damnable headache. You know his room number. The girl gave you that. Number fourteen, and it's on the other side of the house. But first find out where he is. *You've got to be careful!* Now, get busy.'

I turned away from the mirror. Yes I must get busy. I must know where Schimler was. He usually sat by himself on the terrace. I would try there first.

I got to the lounge without meeting anyone and tiptoed over to the window. Yes there he was reading as usual, his pipe in his mouth, his head bent forward over the book in an attitude of concentration. For a moment I watched him. It was a fine head. It didn't seem possible that this man could be a spy.

But this time I hardened my heart. Get busy! It probably wouldn't seem possible that anyone was a spy—until you knew for certain that he was. Anyway it was my liberty or someone else's. Schimler was undoubtedly a suspicious character. Very well, then!

I went upstairs again. Outside my own room I paused.

Was there anything I wanted? A weapon? Nonsense! this wasn't going to be that sort of affair; just a quiet examination of the room, that was all. My heart beating furiously, I went on past my own room, along the passage. Then a new fear took hold of me. Supposing I met someone! The Skeltons or the Vogels! How should I explain my presence here? What was I supposed to be doing? Then I passed a door labelled *Salle de Bain*. If necessary I could go in there and pretend to be having a bath. But I met nobody. A few moments later I was outside room number fourteen.

Bridging the gulf between thought and action is often a very arduous process. It is easy to contemplate searching someone's room—standing before the mirror I had had no qualms—but when it comes to the mechanics of the business, the actual entry into the room, it is far from easy. It is not merely the fear of discovery that deters. It is the sense of privacy that is violated. There is a strange door, a strange door-handle and, beyond it, part of another person's life. To open the door seems as inexcusable an intrusion as spying on a pair of lovers.

I stood there for a second or two fighting down this sense of guilt, rationalising it into all sorts of minor objections. Perhaps Mary Skelton had been mistaken; perhaps this was the wrong room. It was too soon after lunch; I should have given Schimler longer to settle down. It was a waste of time; he would have hidden the camera. The door might be locked and someone might come along just as I was trying it. Someone might . . .

There was only one way to deal with this. I would make no attempt to go in stealthily. If the room were occupied or anyone saw me, then I had made a mistake. Monsieur Skelton had asked me to call in when I was ready to bathe. The wrong room? I was sorry. I would retire. That was unless it was one of the Skeltons who saw me. But if I stood outside here much longer I should be seen, anyhow. Drawing a deep breath, I rapped on the door, grasped the handle and turned it. The door was unlocked. Still standing on the threshold, I pushed it and let it swing open. The room was empty. I waited a second, then walked in and shut the door behind me. The deed was done.

I glanced round. The room was smaller than mine and looked out over the outhouse containing the kitchens. A clump of young cypresses near the window shut out a good deal of light. Keeping as far away from the window as possible, I looked for Schimler's suitcase. It did not take me long to establish the fact that there wasn't one. Perhaps he had transferred the contents to the chest of drawers and had the case taken to the storeroom. I tried the drawers. All with the exception of the top one were empty. The top drawer contained a white and very much laundered shirt, a grey tie, a small pocket-comb, a pair of socks with large holes in the heels, a set of clean but crumpled underclothes, a packet of soap flakes and a tin of French tobacco. There was no camera. I looked at the label on the tie. It bore the name and address of a Berlin manufacturer. The underclothes were of Czechoslovakian origin. The shirt was French. I went over to the wash-basin. The razor, shaving soap, toothbrush and paste were also French. I turned to the cupboard.

It was wide and deep, with a row of coat-hangers on a brass rail and a rack for shoes. There was one suit and a black raincoat in it. Nothing else. The suit was dark grey and threadbare at the elbows. The raincoat had a triangular tear near the bottom.

This, then, with the contents of the drawer, was 'Herr Heinberger's' wardrobe. Very odd! If the man had sufficient money to stop at the Réserve surely he would have more clothes than this?

That, however, was beside the point. I was looking for a camera. I felt under the mattress but this yielded nothing but a scratch on the hand from a projecting spring end. The room had begun to get on my nerves. I had failed to find what I had come for. It was time I went. There was, however just one more thing that I wanted to do.

I went back to the cupboard took the suit down and looked in the pockets. The first two I felt were empty; but in the breast pocket my fingers encountered what felt like a thin paper-covered book. I pulled it out. It was not one book, but two, and both were passports—one German and one Czech.

I examined the German one first. It had been issued in 1931 to Emil Schimler journalist, born in Essen in 1899. This was in itself surprising. I had assessed Schimler at well over forty. I turned to the visa pages. Most of them were blank. There were, however, two visas for France dated 1931 and a set of Soviet visas dated 1932. He had spent two months in Soviet Russia. There was also a Swiss visa for the previous December and a French one for May of that year. I turned to the Czech passport.

It contained an unmistakable photograph of Schimler, but was issued in the name of Paul Czissar, commercial representative, born in Brno in 1895. The date of issue was August 10, 1934. It contained a large number of German and Czech visa stamps. Herr Czissar seemed to have travelled extensively on the Berlin-Prague line.

After a little trouble I managed to decipher the most recent date stamp. It was for January 20 of the current year—just about eight months ago.

I was so engrossed with these significant discoveries that I did not hear the footsteps until they were practically outside the door. Even if I had have heard them I doubt whether I should have been able to do anything more. As it was, I just had time to cram the passport back into the pocket and bundle the suit into the cupboard behind me before the handle of the door turned.

In the few split seconds that followed, my brain and body seemed to go numb. I stood and gaped stupidly at the handle. I wanted to shout, hide in the cupboard, jump out of the window, scramble under the bed. But I did none of those things. I just gaped.

Then the door swung open and Schimler came into the room.

13

HE did not see me for a moment.

As he came through the doorway he tossed a book on the bed and made as if to cross to the chest of drawers.

Then our eyes met.

I saw him start. Then very slowly, he went on to the chest of drawers and took out the tin of tobacco. He started filling his pipe.

The silence was almost unbearable. A weight seemed to be pressing on my chest, stifling me. The blood was thumping in my head. Fascinated, I watched his fingers steadily pressing the tobacco into the bowl.

When at last he spoke, his voice was perfectly level, even casual.

'I'm afraid you will find nothing of value here.'

'I didn't—' I began huskily; but, pipe in hand he motioned me into silence.

'Spare me your protestations. Believe me you have my sympathy. Persons in your profession must of necessity take risks. It must be very galling to find that you have taken them for nothing. Especially', he added commencing to light the pipe 'when the risk lands you in prison'. He blew out a cloud of smoke. 'Now, would you prefer to see the manager here or in his office?'

'I do not wish to see the manager at all. I have taken nothing.'

'I am aware of that. There is nothing to take. But I must remind you that you are in my room, uninvited.'

My scattered wits were returning.

'As a matter of fact—' I began again but before I could get any further he had interrupted me.

'Ah! I was waiting for that. I find that when a person prefaces a statement with "as a matter of fact," the statement is nearly always a lie. But do go on. What is your fact?'

I flushed angrily.

'The fact is that earlier today some valuables were stolen from my suitcase. I suspected you of taking them. As Monsieur Köche did not take the matter seriously I decided to see for myself.'

He smiled acidly. 'Oh, I see. The best defence is attack. I threaten you, you threaten me. Unfortunately for you, I happen to have discussed with Herr Köche the subject of your complaint.' He paused significantly. 'Your bill is paid, I believe.'

'I am leaving under protest.'

'And is this part of your protest?'

'Put it that way if you wish. However, I see that I was mistaken. You are not the culprit. I can only apologise to you profoundly for taking the law into my own hands, and withdraw.' I made a move towards the door.

He moved over slightly to intercept me.

'I am afraid,' he said gravely, 'that that will not do. Under the circumstances I think it would be as well if we were to stay here and ask Herr Köche to come to us.' He went to the bell and rang it. My heart sank.

'I have taken nothing. I have done no damage. You cannot charge me with anything.' My voice rose.

'My dear Herr Vadassy,' he said wearily, 'you are already known to the police. That is sufficient. If it amuses you to quibble, do so. But, please save it for the Commissaire. You came here with the intention of stealing. You can make such explanations as you can think of to the detectives.'

I was desperate. I cast round wildly for a way out. If Köche came now I should be in the Commissariat within half an hour. I had only one thing left to say. I said it.

'And who' I snapped, 'is going to lodge the complaint? Herr Heinberger, Herr Emil Schimler of Berlin or Herr Paul Czissar of Brno?'

I had expected some reaction from this, but the extent of it took me by surprise. He turned round slowly and faced me. His hollow cheeks had gone deathly pale and the ironic expression in his eyes had changed to one of cold hatred. He walked towards me. Involuntarily, I took a step backwards. He stopped.

'So you are not the hotel sneak-thief after all.'

It was said softly, almost wonderingly, yet with a corrosive quality about it that scared me badly.

'I told you I wasn't a thief,' I said jauntily.

He stepped forward suddenly, gripped the front of my shirt, and pulled me towards him until my face was a few centimetres from his. I was so startled that I forgot to resist him. He shook me slowly backwards and forwards as he spoke.

'No, not a thief, not an honest rat, but a filthy little spy. A cunning spy, too.' His lip curled contemptuously. 'To the outside world a shy, ingenuous teacher of languages with a romantic appearance and sad Magyar eyes that would deceive a painter. How long have you been at the game, Vadassy, or whatever your name is? Did they pick you for the job or did you graduate from the flogging cells?' He gave me a violent push that sent me staggering back to the wall.

His fist was clenched and he was coming towards me again when there was a knock at the door.

For a moment we stared at each other in silence; then he straightened his back, walked to the door and opened it. It was one of the waiters.

'You rang, Monsieur?' I heard him say.

Schimler seemed to hesitate. Then:

'I am sorry,' he said; 'I did not mean to ring. You can go.'

He shut the door and, leaning against it, looked at me. 'That was a fortunate interruption for you, my friend. It is many years since I lost my temper so completely. I was going to kill you.'

I strove to keep the tremor out of my voice. 'And now that you have regained your temper, perhaps we can talk sense. A little while ago you remarked that the best defence is attack. I am afraid that your calling *me* a spy is a somewhat naïve way of putting that notion into practice. Don't you agree?'

He was silent. I began to regain my self-possession. This was going to be easier than I had thought. The main thing now was to find out what he had done with the camera. Then I would get the waiter back to telephone Beghin.

'If,' I went on, 'you knew the trouble you had caused me you would be far more sympathetic. I can still feel that crack on the head you gave me last night. And if you haven't already spoiled those two rolls of film I should like them back before the police come. You know, they talked of not letting me go back to Paris until the matter was cleared up. However, now that it *is* cleared up, I hope you are going to be sensible. By the way, what did you do with the camera?'

He was frowning at me uncertainly. 'If this is some sort of trick ...' he began, and paused. 'I haven't the least idea what you are talking about,' he concluded.

I shrugged. 'You're being very foolish. Have you ever heard of a man named Beghin?'

He shook his head.

'I am afraid you soon will. He is a member of the Sûreté Générale attached to the Naval Intelligence Department at Toulon. Does that suggest nothing to you?'

He came slowly to the middle of the room. I prepared to defend myself. Out of the corner of my eye I could see the bell-push. A couple of strides and I should be able to reach it. The next time he moved I would make a dash. But he stood still.

'I have a suspicion, Vadassy, that we are talking at cross purposes.'

I smiled. 'I don't think so.'

'Then I am afraid I do not understand you.'

I sighed impatiently. 'Is it really worth denying? Be sensible, please. What have you done with the camera?'

'Is this some sort of joke?'

'It is not, as you will soon find out.' Feeling that I was not handling the situation particularly well, I began to get annoyed. 'I propose to call the police. Have you any objections?'

'To the police? None at all. Call them by all means.'

He might be bluffing, but I felt a little uneasy. Without the evidence of the camera I was helpless. I decided to change my tactics. For a second or two I stared hard at him, then I broke into a crestfallen grin. 'Do you know,' I said sheepishly, 'I have an unhappy suspicion that I have made a mistake.'

His eyes searched mine warily. 'I feel quite sure that is the case.'

I sighed. 'Well, I am very sorry to have caused you all this inconvenience. I feel extremely foolish. Monsieur Duclos will be most amused.'

'Who?' The question was like a pistol shot.

'Monsieur Duclos. He is a pleasant old man, a little talkative, it is true, but sympathetic.'

I saw him control himself with an effort. He came nearer to me. His voice was dangerously calm. 'Who are you and what do you want? Are you from the police?'

'I am connected with the police.' This, I thought, was rather neat. 'You know my name. All I want is a piece of information. What have you done with that camera?'

'And if I still tell you that I don't know what you're talking about?'

'I shall hand you over for interrogation. What is more'—I watched him narrowly—'I shall make known what you seem so anxious to keep quiet—the fact that your name is not Heinberger.'

'The police already know it.'

'I know that. I regret to say that I have no confidence whatever in the intelligence of the local police. Now do you know what I am talking about?'

'No.'

I smiled and went to pass him to go to the door. He gripped my arm and swung me round.

'Listen, you fool,' he said savagely, 'I don't know what's the matter with you, but you seem to have got some idea into your head about me. Whatever it is, you seem to regard the fact that I am anxious to conceal my identity as some sort of proof that your idea is correct. Is that right?'

'Approximately.'

'Very well, then. My reasons for using the name Heinberger have nothing whatever to do with you. Köche is aware of them. The police have my correct name. You, who have no idea what those reasons are, propose to be wilfully indiscreet unless I give you some information which I do not possess. Is that correct, too?'

'More or less. Assuming, of course, that you haven't got the information.'

He ignored this last remark and sat down on the edge of his bed. 'I don't know how you found out. The police here told you, I suppose, and those passports in the wardrobe. In any case, I've got to stop the news getting any further. I am being perfectly frank with you, you see! I must stop you. The only way I can hope to do that is to give you my reasons. There is nothing very strange about them. My case is by no means unique.'

He paused to relight his pipe. His eyes met mine across the bowl. The ironic expression had returned to them. 'You look, Vadassy, as though you weren't going to believe a word of anything.'

'I don't know that I am.'

He blew the match out. 'Well, we'll see. But you must remember one thing; I am trusting you. I have, of course, no alternative but to do so. I cannot persuade you to trust me.'

There was a hint of a question in the pause that followed the remark. For one fleeting instant I weakened; but only for an instant.

'I am trusting nobody.'

He sighed. 'Very well. The explanation begins in 1933.

I was editor of a social-democrat newspaper in Berlin, the *Telegrafblatt*.' He shrugged. 'It is no longer in existence. It was not a bad paper. I had some clever men working for me. It was the property of a sawmill owner in East Prussia. He was a good man, a reformer, with a profound admiration for the nineteenth-century English liberals, Godwin and John Stuart Mill, people like that. He went into mourning when Stresemann died. He used sometimes to send me down leading articles about the brotherhood of man and the necessity of replacing the struggle between capital and labour with co-operation based on Christ's teaching. I must say he was on the best of terms with his own employees; but I have an idea that his mills were losing money. Then came the deluge.

'The trouble with postwar German social-democracy was that it supported with one hand what it was trying to fight with the other. It believed in the freedom of the individual capitalist to exploit the worker and the freedom of the worker to organise his trade union and fight the capitalist. Its great illusion was its belief in the limitless possibilities of compromise. It thought that it could build Utopia within the Constitution of Weimar, that the only sublime political conception was reform, that the rotten economic structure of the world could be shored up at the bottom with material from the top. Worst of all, it thought that you could meet force with good will, that the way to deal with a mad dog was to stroke it. In 1933 German social-democracy was bitten and died in agony.

'The *Telegrafblatt* was one of the first papers to be closed down. Twice we were raided. The second time the machine-room was wrecked with hand grenades. Even that we survived. We were lucky enough to find a printer who could and would print a newspaper of sorts for us. But three weeks later he refused to print any more papers for us. He had been visited by the police. The same day we had a telegram from the owner saying that owing to losses in his business he had been compelled to sell the paper. The purchaser was a Nazi official, and I happen to know that the price was paid with a draft on a Detroit bank. The following night I was arrested at my home and put in the police cells.

'They kept me there for three months. I was not charged. They did not even question me. All I could get out of them was that my case was being considered. The first month, while I was getting used to it, was the worst part. Those police weren't bad fellows. One of them even told me that he had sometimes read my stuff. But at the end of the three months I was moved to a concentration camp near Hanover.'

He paused for a moment.

'I dare say you've heard a lot about concentration camps,' he went on. 'Most people have; and their ideas are mostly wrong. To hear some talk you would imagine that the entire day was spent in knocking the prisoners' teeth out with rubber truncheons, kicking them in their stomachs and breaking their fingers with rifle butts. It isn't; at least it wasn't in the camp I was in. Nazi brutality is much less human. It's the mind they get at. If you'd ever seen a man come out of a fortnight's solitary confinement in a pitch-dark cell you'd know what I mean. Theoretically, it is possible to pass the time in a concentration camp no more uncomfortably than in any other prison—theoretically. No one, I should think, has ever done so. The discipline is fantastic. They give you work to do—shovelling piles of stones from one spot to another and then back again—and if you stop working, even to straighten your back for an instant—you get a flogging for disobeying orders and a week's solitary confinement. They never relax for a moment. They change the guards constantly so that they don't get tired of watching. They march you about the camp under cover of a machine-gun. They feed you on offal and cabbage stumps stewed in water and there's a machine-gun covering you while you eat the filth. One man there used to be so worried by the gun that as soon as he'd eaten he used to vomit. Some became so debilitated that they couldn't stand. When you were new to it you fought against it. They were ready for that. They used to get to work systematically to break your spirit. Regular floggings and long spells of solitary confinement soon did the trick. As long as you held out you were conscious that very gradually your mind was going. I pretended to knuckle under. It wasn't easy. You see, they can tell by your eyes. If you let them see you looking at them, let them see that your mind is still working like a human being's instead of a beast's, you're done for. You keep your eyes on the ground, never look at the guard who addresses you. I became quite expert; so expert that I began to think that I might be deceiving myself and that I was really no better off than the rest. I spent two years in that camp.'

His pipe had gone out. He tapped the bowl reflectively against the palm of his hand.

'One day I was taken to the commandant's office. They told me that if I would sign a paper renouncing my German citizenship, saying that I would leave Germany and would not return, I would be allowed to go. At first I thought it was merely another of their tricks for making you give yourself away. But it was no trick. Not even their People's Court could find anything to convict me of. I signed the paper. I would have signed anything to get out. Then I had to wait for three days for my permit to arrive. During that time they kept me away from the other prisoners. Instead of working with them I was put on to cleaning latrines. But at night we went to the same dormitory. And then something curious happened.

'Talking between the prisoners was forbidden, and the rule was enforced so savagely that the eyes-on-the-ground idea applied as much between prisoner and prisoner as between prisoner and guard. If you looked at another prisoner they might say you had been thinking of talking. The result was that you recognised the man next to you not so much by his face as by his shoulders and the shape of his feet. I had a shock when, as we were being marched into the dormitory on my last night there, I saw that the man next to me was trying to catch my eye. He was a grey-faced, heavy sort of man of about forty. He'd only been there six months, and by the way they'd singled him out for floggings I had guessed that he was a Communist. There was a guard near us and I was frankly terrified of giving them an excuse to cancel my permit. I got into my bunk as quickly as I could and lay still.

'It used to be quite common for the prisoners to have nightmares. Sometimes they would just mumble, sometimes they would shout and scream in their sleep. As soon as a man started one of the guards would get a bucket of water and empty it over him. I never slept much there, but that night I didn't sleep at all. I kept thinking of getting away the next day. I had been lying in the darkness for about two hours when this man next to me started to mumble in his sleep. One of the guards came over and looked at him, but the mumbling had ceased. When the guard moved away it started again, but now it was a little louder and I could hear what he was saying. He was asking if I were awake.

'I coughed a little, turned restlessly, and sighed so that he should know that I was. Then he began to mumble again, and I heard him telling me to go to an address in Prague. He only had time to say it once, for the guard had come over again and he was suspicious. The man turned over suddenly and began flinging his arms about wildly and shouting for help. The guard kicked him and, as the man pretended to wake up, threatened him with a bucket of water if he wasn't quiet. I heard no more from him. The following day I was given my permit and put on a train for Belgium.

'I won't attempt to tell you what it felt like to be free again. It worried me at first. I couldn't get the smell of camp out of my nostrils and I used to go off to sleep at all sorts of odd times during the day and dream that I was back there. But I got over that after a bit and began to think like a human being again. I spent a month or two in Paris doing a little work for the newspapers there, but the language difficulty made it almost impossible. I had to pay to have my stuff properly translated. I decided finally to try Prague. At the time I had no intention of going to the address that had been given me. I had, indeed, almost forgotten about it. Then something I heard from another German I met in Prague made me decide to investigate. That address turned out to be the propaganda organisation.'

He paused for a moment to relight his pipe. Then he went on.

'After a while, when they were sure of me, I started working for the underground. The principal activity was getting news into Germany, real news. We produced a newspaper—the name of it doesn't matter—and it used to be smuggled in small quantities over the frontier. It was printed on a very thin India paper and each one folded into a thin wad that a man could carry in the palm of his hand. Many different methods were employed for the smuggling, some of them very ingenious. The copies were even packed in small greaseproof bags and stuffed inside the axle boxes of the Prague-Berlin trains. They were collected by a wheel-tester at the Berlin end, but the Gestapo caught him after a while, and we had to think of something else. Then it was suggested that one of us should make an effort to get a Czech passport, pose as a commercial traveller and take the papers in with samples. I volunteered for the job, and after some trouble we were successful.

'I crossed into Germany over thirty times that year. It wasn't particularly risky. There were only two dangers. One was the chance of being recognised and denounced. The other was that the man who took the papers off me to pass them on to the distributing organisation might become suspect. He did become suspect. They didn't arrest him immediately, but watched. We used to meet in the waiting-room of a suburban station and then get into a train together. I would leave the parcel of paper on the luggage rack when I got out. He would pick it up. Then one day, just after the train had left the station, it stopped and a squad of S.S. men got in from the track. We didn't know for certain whether it was us they were after or not, so we went into separate compartments and sat still. I heard them arrest him and waited for my turn. But they just examined my passport and went on through the train. It was not until I was nearly back in

174

Prague the next day that I realised that I was being followed. Luckily I had the sense not to go back to headquarters. Luckily, that is, for my friends. It was less lucky for me. When they found that I wasn't going to lead them to the persons they wanted they decided that the best way would be to get me back to Germany and use their persuasive resources to extract information. You see, our newspaper had begun to worry them, and I was the only real clue they had to the people behind it. The German end of the organisation was concerned purely with distribution. It was the directing brains that they were after. I had to get away. And it had to be out of Czechoslovakia, too, for they had notified the Czech police that I was really a German criminal wanted for theft and that the Paul Czissar passport had been obtained under false pretences.

'In Switzerland they tried to kidnap me. I was staying on the shore of Lake Constance and got friendly with two men who said they were on a fishing holiday. One day they asked me to go out with them. I was bored. I said that I would go. Just in time and quite by accident I found out that they were Germans, not Swiss, and that their boat had been hired on the German side of the lake. I went to Zürich after that; I knew they would keep track of me, but they couldn't do any kidnapping so far away from the frontier. But I didn't stay there long. One morning I got a letter from Prague warning me that the Gestapo had somehow found out that my name was Schimler. They had known before, of course, that Paul Czissar was no Czech, but a German; but now that they knew my real name they would not have to kidnap me to get me back to Germany. I've been on the run ever since. Twice they've nearly caught up with me. Switzerland was swarming with Gestapo agents. I decided to try France. The people in Prague sent me to Köche. He's one of them.

'He's been an amazing friend. I arrived here without a penny, and he's given me clothes and kept me for nothing every since. But I can't run any more. I have no money and Köche can't give me any, for he has none himself. That wife of his owns the place, and it's all he can do to persuade her to let me stay. I offered to work, but she wouldn't have that. She's jealous of him and likes to have a hold over him. I should get away. It's dangerous here now. A few weeks back we heard that a Gestapo agent had been sent into France. It's amazing the way they ferret things out. When you are being hunted you develop an extra sense. You begin to *feel* when there's danger. I've managed to change my appearance a good deal, but I think I have been identified. I think, too, that I have spotted the agent they sent. But he won't act until he's sure. My only chance is to bluff him. You took me off my guard. For a moment I thought I had made a mistake. Köche had put you down as a petty crook.' He shrugged. 'I don't know what you are, Vadassy, but what I've told you is the truth. What are you going to do?'

I looked at him. 'Frankly, I don't know,' I said. 'I might have believed this story except for one thing. You didn't explain why the fact of their finding out that your name was Schimler should make your position very much worse. If they couldn't force you to return when they knew you as Czissar, why should they be able to do so when they had found your real name?'

His eyes were on mine; I saw the corners of his mouth twitch. It was the only hint of emotion he had betrayed. His voice when he replied was flat and toneless.

'It is very simple,' he said slowly, 'my wife and child are still in Germany.'

'You see,' he went on after a bit, 'when they expelled me from Germany they would not let me see my family. I had not seen them for over two years. Before I was sent to the camp I had heard that my wife had taken the boy to her father's house outside Berlin. I wrote to her from Belgium and Paris, and we arranged that as soon as I could establish myself in France or England they would join me. But I soon saw that it was all I could do to support myself in Paris. London would have been the same. I was just another German refugee. In Prague I met a man who told me that the Communists had ways and means of getting in and out of Germany undetected. I craved desperately to see my wife, to talk to her, to see the boy. It was that craving that sent me to the address I had been given in the camp. The story about getting in and out of Germany was nonsense, of course. I soon saw that; but when an opportunity did come I took it. On three of my trips with the Czech passport I met my wife in secret.

'She tried to persuade me to take her and the child to Prague with me, but I wouldn't. I was living on practically nothing, and while they could live in comfort with her father and the boy could go to school I thought it was best that they should do so.

'When the first blow fell I was glad that I had been so sensible. Let the Gestapo get me back if they could! Not, mind you, that it would have done them any good, because the Party knew that no matter how loyal a man was he might eventually be tortured into speaking. When I was followed to Prague the headquarters was moved. I don't know where they are now. Their address is Poste

Restante, Prague. But the Gestapo are very thorough. They wanted me back. And I underestimated them. My Czech passport was too dangerous to use, so I fell back on the old German passport that my wife had kept hidden safely and brought to me when we met. It must have been through my using it that they traced me.

'When I heard, I was terrified. In my wife and son they had hostages. I would have to return or know that my wife was imprisoned in my stead. I thought things over. Until they delivered their ultimatum she would probably be safe—under surveillance, no doubt, but safe. There was only one thing for me to do—go into hiding until I could get news of her. If she were all right and still with her father, I would stay in hiding until perhaps they had grown tired of looking for me, and I could get another passport with which to get her away.'

He stared at the old pile in his hand. 'I've waited over four months now, and I've heard nothing. I can't write myself for fear of the German censors. Köche has an accommodation address in Toulon, and he has tried to get letters through. But there has been no reply. I can do nothing but wait. If they find me here I cannot help it. Unless I hear from her very soon I must in any case go back. That is all there is for me to do.'

For a moment there was silence. Then he looked up at me and grinned very faintly. 'Can I trust you, Vadassy?'

'Of course.' I wanted to say more, but I could not.

He nodded his thanks. I got up and walked to the door.

'And what about your spy, my friend?' he murmured over his shoulder.

I hesitated. Then: 'I shall look for him elsewhere, Herr Heinberger.'

As I pulled the door to behind me I saw him slowly raise his hands to his face. I went quickly.

As I did so I heard another door close near at hand. I paid no attention to it, I had no reason to fear being seen leaving Herr Heinberger's room. Back in my own room, I took out Beghin's list and looked at it for a moment. Then I crossed off three names—Albert Köche, Suzanne Köche and Emil Schimler.

14

AT half past four on the afternoon of August the 18th I sat down with a sheet of hotel paper in front of me to solve a problem.

For a long time I stared at the blank paper. Then I held it up to read the watermark. At last I wrote on it, very slowly and clearly, this sentence:

'If it takes one man three days to eliminate three suspects, how long, other factors remaining constant, will it take the same man to eliminate eight more suspects?'

I considered this for a bit. Then I wrote below it: '*Answer: eight days*,' and underlined it.

After that I drew a gallows with a corpse suspended from it. The corpse I labelled 'SPY.' Then I added a fat stomach to it, pencilled in large globules of sweat, and altered the label to 'BEGHIN.' Last of all I deleted the stomach, added a lot of hair and semicircles under the eyes and rechristened it 'VADASSY.' I made a halfhearted attempt to sketch in the hangman.

Eight days! And I had less than eight hours! Unless, of course, Köche allowed me to stay after all. Schimler was his friend, and if Schimler told him that I was not a crook ... But did Schimler really know that I was not a crook? Perhaps I ought to go back to his room and explain. Though what was the use? I had practically no money left. I could not afford to stay any longer in the Réserve even if I were allowed to. That was another contingency that Beghin had omitted to provide for. Beghin! The man's incompetence and stupidity were monumental.

By the time I had destroyed the sheet of paper on which I had been scribbling and taken another, it was five o'clock. I looked out of the window. The sun had moved round so that now the sea looked like a shimmering pool of liquid metal. The sides of the hills across the bay glowed redly above their fringe of trees. A shadow had begun to move across the beach.

It would be good now, I thought, to be in Paris. The afternoon city heat would have gone. It would be good to sit under the trees in the Luxembourg, the trees near the marionette theatre. It would be quiet there now. There would be no one there but a student or two reading. There you could listen to the rustle of leaves unconscious of the pains of humanity in labour, of a civilisation hastening to destruction. There, away from this brassy sea and blood-red earth, you could contemplate the twentieth-century tragedy unmoved; unmoved except by pity for mankind fighting to save itself from the primeval ooze that welled from its own unconscious being.

But this was St Gatien, not Paris; the Réserve, not the Luxembourg Gardens; and I was an actor, not an onlooker. What was more, I should shortly become, unless I were very clever or very lucky, no more than a 'noise off.' I came back to business.

The Skeltons, the Vogels, Roux and Martin, the Clandon-Hartleys, and Duclos—I stared at the list miserably. The Skeltons, now! What did I know about them? Nothing, except that their parents were due to arrive the following week on the *Conte di Savoia*. That and the fact that this was their first trip abroad together. They could be eliminated straight away, of course. Then I paused. Why 'of course'? Was this the calm, dispassionate examination of all the available facts? No, it wasn't. I knew nothing of the Skeltons except what they had told me. Perhaps, for that matter, I had eliminated Schimler and Köche a little too readily. But then there were his passports and the conversation I had overheard between him and Köche to confirm what he had said. The Skeltons, however, had nothing to confirm their story. They must be investigated.

The Vogels? The temptation was to eliminate them also. No spy could be so grotesquely unlike a spy as Vogel. But they, too, must be questioned discreetly.

Roux and Martin? Except that Roux talked rather ugly French and that the woman was excessively affectionate there was nothing to single them out for special attention. To be investigated, nevertheless.

The Clandon-Hartleys looked more interesting. I knew a good deal about them. All of it was unconfirmed, of course, but it was interesting. And there was one very suggestive point. The Major was short of money. He had twice tried to borrow. Moreover, according to Duclos, he had been expecting money that had not arrived. Payment for the photographs? It was a distinct possibility. The Major, Duclos had insisted, was desperate. Well, that was possible, too. And Mrs Clandon-Hartley was an Italian. It all fitted together very nicely.

Old Duclôs, however, was by no means a reliable witness. His imagination was, as I knew only too well, extremely fertile. He himself could scarcely be classed as a suspect. He was too unlikely. But then they were all unlikely. What did I know about Duclos? Simply that he was, or appeared to be, a petty industrialist with a penchant for gossiping and cheating at friendly games. Where did that get me? Nowhere.

And then I made what I conceived to be a great discovery. Anyone but a hopeless nincompoop would have made it before. I decided that it was no use studying these persons' normal behaviour—nothing was easier than to play a part while everyone accepted you at your face value—the thing to do was to proceed on the assumption that every one of them was a liar and force them all into the open. I should not be friendly with them. I should quarrel. I should not calmly accept their own estimates of themselves, but question and analyse. I had been begging the whole question. It was time I adopted an aggressive policy.

But how did one carry out an aggressive policy in such circumstances? Was I to roam the grounds of the Réserve like a hungry mastiff snapping viciously at all who crossed my path? No, the thing to do was to question, to be inquisitive; and then, when the bounds of common politeness were reached, I must overstep them. I must blunder amiably but inexorably over people's feelings until they betrayed themselves. Then, I promised myself, I would swoop like a hawk on the guilty wretch.

At twenty-five past five I wrote the nine names down on my piece of paper, shut my eyes, moved my pencil in a circle and—stabbed. Then I opened my eyes and saw that the Vogels were to be my first victims. I combed my hair and descended in search of them.

They were, as usual, on the beach together with Duclos, the Skeltons, and the French pair. As I appeared Monsieur Duclos sprang from his deck-chair and hurried to meet me. Too late, I remembered that I had neglected to provide myself with a reasonable explanation for the recovery of the 'stolen' property.

I almost turned and ran. Then, as I was hesitating, I saw that it was too late for flight. Duclos was bearing down on me. I attempted to pass him with a genial nod, but he executed a swift outflanking movement and I found myself walking side by side with him towards the others.

'We expected to hear before,' he said breathlessly. 'The police have been called in?'

I shook my head. 'No. Fortunately they were not necessary.'

'The valuables have been found?'

'Yes.'

He ran on ahead to announce the fact. 'The thief,' I heard him saying, 'has been found. The missing valuables have been returned.'

As I came up they clustered round me excitedly, asking questions.

'Was it one of the servants?'

'The English major, without a doubt ...'

'The gardener?'

'The headwaiter?'

'Please!' I held up a repressive hand. 'There is no question of a guilty person. The valuables were not stolen.'

There was a gasp.

'The whole thing,' I said with uneasy gaiety, 'was a mistake ... a rather stupid mistake. It appears'—I racked my brain desperately for a way out of the difficulty—'it appears that the box was pushed out of sight under the bed when the room was cleaned.' It sounded inexpressibly feeble.

Roux pushed his way between the Vogels. 'Then how,' he demanded triumphantly, 'does it come about that the locks on the suitcase were broken open?'

'Ah, yes,' said Herr Vogel.

'Yes, indeed!' echoed his wife.

'What does he say?' said Skelton.

To gain time I translated. 'I don't,' I added, 'know what he's talking about.'

He looked puzzled. '*Weren't* the locks of your case burst open? I thought you said they were.'

I shook my head slowly. I had an idea.

Roux had been listening to this exchange with puzzled impatience. I turned to him.

'I was explaining, Monsieur, that you were under a misapprehension. I don't know where you gained your information, but there was certainly no question of the locks of my case being forced. I did discuss the matter, in confidence, with Monsieur Duclos here, but nothing was said of locks. 'If,' I went on severely, 'false rumours have been circulated by some person unaware of the true facts, a most unfortunate situation will have been created. Was it your impression, Herr Vogel, that the locks had been forced?'

Vogel shook his head hastily.

'No, indeed!' added Frau Vogel.

'Monsieur Roux,' I pursued heavily, 'I take it that you . . .' But he interrupted me.

'What is this nonsense?' he demanded irritably. 'It was the old one there'—he pointed to Duclos—'who told us all.'

Eyes turned on Monsieur Duclos. He drew himself up. 'I, Messieurs,' he said, sternly, 'am a businessman of long experience. I am not in the habit of betraying confidences.'

Roux laughed loudly and unpleasantly. 'Do you deny that you told Vogel and myself of the theft and that you stated that the locks were forced?'

'In confidence, Monsieur, in confidence!'

'Bah!' Roux turned to Mademoiselle Martin. 'In confidence! You heard him, *ma petite?*'

'*Oui, chéri.*'

'He admits it. In confidence, of course!' He jeered. 'But he admitted to having invented the affair of the locks.'

Monsieur Duclos bristled. 'That, Monsieur, is unjust!'

Roux laughed and put his tongue out very rudely. I began to feel sorry for Monsieur Duclos. After all, I *had* told him that the locks had been forced. But he was already rallying to his own defence. He stuck his head forward ferociously.

'If I were a young man, Monsieur, I should strike you!'

'Perhaps,' put in Vogel anxiously, 'we should discuss the matter calmly.' He hitched up his braces a further centimetre and laid a hand on Roux's shoulder.

It was shaken off impatiently. 'There is no point,' declared Roux loudly, 'in discussing anything with this old imbecile.'

Monsieur Duclos drew a deep breath. 'You are, Monsieur,' he said deliberately, 'a liar! It was you who stole the valuables from Monsieur Vadassy. Otherwise, how do you know that the locks of the suitcase were forced? I, Duclos, denounce you. Thief and liar!'

For a moment there was dead silence, then Skelton and Vogel together leaped on the enraged Roux as he sprang at his accuser, and grabbed his arms.

'Let me go!' Roux shouted furiously, 'and I will strangle him!'

As this was precisely what Vogel and Skelton feared, they hung on. Monsieur Duclos stroked his beard calmly and regarded the struggling Roux with interest.

'Thief and liar!' he repeated, as though we had not heard him the first time.

Roux yelped with rage and tried to spit at him.

'I think, Monsieur Duclos,' I said, 'that it will be better if you go upstairs.'

He struck an attitude. 'I will leave the beach, Monsieur, only when Roux has apologised.'

I was about to argue that the apology, if any, was due to Roux, when Mademoiselle Martin, who had been having hysterics in the background, created a diversion by flinging her arms round her lover's neck and exhorting him to kill. She was removed in floods of tears by Frau Vogel and Mary Skelton. By this time, however, Roux had found tongue and was hurling insults at all and sundry.

'Species of monkeys!'

Monsieur Duclos's calm deserted him. He leaped into the breach. 'Species of impotent goat!' he retorted hotly.

Mademoiselle Martin screamed. Roux, incensed, focused his attention once more on his enemy.

'Species of diseased camel!' he bawled.

'Misbegotten cretin!' roared Monsieur Duclos.

Roux licked his lips and swallowed hard. For a moment I thought he was beaten. Then I saw that he was gathering his forces for the *coup de grâce*. His lips worked. He drew a deep breath. There was a fraction of a second's silence. Then, with the full force of his lungs, he hurled the word in Monsieur Duclos's face.

'Bolshevik!'

Given the appropriate circumstances almost any word denoting a political or religious creed can become a deadly insult. At a conference of Moslem dignitaries the word 'Christian' could no doubt be used with devastating effect.

At a gathering of middle-aged White Russians the word 'Bolshevik' would probably be reckoned a virulent term of abuse. But this was not a gathering of White Russians.

For a moment there was not a sound. Then someone giggled. It was, I think, Mary Skelton. It was enough. We started to laugh. Monsieur Duclos, after one bewildered look round, managed to join in convincingly. Only Roux and Odette Martin did not laugh. For a moment he glared at us savagely. Then he wrenched himself free of Vogel and Skelton and stalked off across the beach towards the steps. She followed. As she caught up with him he turned and shook a fist at us.

'Well,' said Skelton, 'I don't know what it was all about, but we certainly do see life at the Réserve.'

Monsieur Duclos was preening himself—a Ulysses after the fall of Troy. He shook hands all round.

'A dangerous type, that!' he commented at large.

'A type of garngstair!' said Herr Vogel.

'Yes, indeed!'

To my relief they seemed to have forgotten the original point at issue. Not so, however, the Skeltons.

'I followed most of that,' said the girl. 'The old Frenchman was right, wasn't he? You *did* say that the locks were forced, didn't you?' She looked at me curiously.

I felt myself reddening.

'No. You must have been mistaken.'

'In other words,' said Skelton slowly, 'it *was* one of the guests.'

'I don't understand you.'

'O.K. We get it.' He grinned. 'The stuff returned and no questions asked. Say no more.'

'Speak for yourself, Warren. As between friends, Mr Vadassy, *wa*s it one of the servants or wasn't it?'

I shook my head miserably. This was very difficult.

'You don't mean to say it *was* one of the guests?'

'It wasn't anybody.'

'You're most unconvincing, Mr Vadassy.'

This I could well believe. Fortunately, Monsieur Duclos chose this moment to announce in penetrating tones that he was going to make a formal complaint to the manager.

I excused myself to the Skeltons and took him aside.

'I should be most grateful, Monsieur, if you would say nothing further about the matter. The whole affair has been most unpleasant and in a sense I am responsible. I am anxious for it to be forgotten. I should esteem it a personal favour to myself if you would overlook this unfortunate occurrence.'

He stroked his beard and shot a quick glance at me over the top of his pince-nez.

'The man insulted me, Monsieur. And in public.'

'Quite so. But we all saw how you dealt with the fellow. He came out of the affair very badly. I cannot help feeling that you would lose face by prolonging the issue. It is best to ignore such types.'

He considered the point. 'You may be right. But he had no right to say that the locks were forced when I had told him quite clearly that there was no question of violence.' His eyes met mine without a flicker.

One could only bow to such devastating mental agility. 'His behaviour demonstrates,' I agreed, 'that he was well aware of being in the wrong.'

'That is true. Very well, Monsieur, at your request I take the matter no further. I accept your assurance that my honour has been upheld.'

We bowed. He turned to the others.

'At this Monsieur's request,' he announced impressively, 'I have agreed to take the matter no further. It is concluded.'

'A wise decision,' said Vogel gravely and winked at me.

'Yes, indeed!'

'This Roux, however, must take care,' added Monsieur Duclos ominously. 'I will suffer no further insults from him. A dirty type, beneath contempt. You observe that he is not married to Mademoiselle. Poor child! That such a type should lure her from the path of virtue!'

'Yes, yes.' Herr Vogel hitched up his trousers, winked at me, and wandered off, followed by Duclos.

'A dirty type,' I could hear the old man saying; 'a very dirty type.'

The Skeltons were anointing each other with sun oil. I lay back on the sand and thought of Roux.

A bad-tempered, unpleasant man; and yet you could see why the woman found him attractive. There was a lithe precision in his movements; probably he was a good lover. He gave the impression of possessing both rat-like cunning and rat-like simplicity. A small, quick mind and a dangerous one. You would know what he thought when he acted. Yes, he would be dangerous all right. Physically strong, too; his body was amazingly wiry. He reminded you of a ferret.

Ferret! That was a word that Schimler had used. 'It's amazing the way they ferret things out.' I could hear him saying it. 'We heard that a Gestapo agent had been sent into France.' Fool! I ought to have thought of that before. The Gestapo agent, the man who had been sent into France to 'persuade' a German to return to Germany, the man who Schimler thought had identified him, the

man who would not act until he was sure of his prey—
Roux. It was as clear as daylight.

I shut my eyes, smiling to myself.

'What's the joke, Mr Vadassy?' said Mary Skelton.

I opened my eyes. 'There's no joke. I was just
thinking.'

It felt good, too. I had had another idea.

15

THE beach was deserted earlier than usual. A cool wind had sprung up and, for the first time since I had left Paris, I saw the sky heavy with cloud. The sea had changed in colour to a dingy grey. The red rocks no longer glowed. It was as if, with the going of the sun, the life of the place had also gone.

As I went up to put on some warmer clothes I saw that the waiters were laying the tables in the dining-room on the first floor. In my room I heard the first drops of rain patter through the leaves of the creeper outside my window.

I finished changing and rang for the chambermaid.

'What is the number of the room of Monsieur Roux and Mademoiselle Martin?'

'Nine, Monsieur.'

'Thank you; that is all.' The door closed behind her. I lit a cigarette and sat down to evolve my plan of action, to get everything quite clear before I started.

This plan, I told myself, was utterly foolproof. Here was a Gestapo agent bent on tracking down a man named Schimler. What was more, there was every likelihood that he had succeeded in doing so. That meant, then, that in all probability this agent had ferreted out information about the guests at the Réserve which would be of immense value to me. If I could get that information out of him, if I could get him to talk, perhaps I should find myself in possession of the very clue I needed. It was a real chance. But I should have to go carefully. Roux must not become suspicious. I must not appear curious. I must *draw* the information out of him, pump him very gently, make it look as though I were listening under protest. I should have to keep my wits about me. This time there must be no mistake.

I got up and walked along the corridor to room number nine. There was a murmur of voices coming from inside. I knocked. The voices ceased. There was a scuffle. A wardrobe door squeaked. Then the woman called: '*Entrez!*' I opened the door.

Mademoiselle Martin, swathed in a semi-transparent pale blue *peignoir*, was sitting on the bed manicuring her nails. The *peignoir*, I guessed, had been hurriedly snatched from the wardrobe. Roux was standing in front of the washbasin, shaving. They both stared at me incredulously.

I had opened my mouth to excuse my intrusion, but Roux got in first.

'What do you want?' he snapped.

'I must ask you to excuse my intruding on you like this. Actually I came to offer you an apology.'

His eyes flickered over me suspiciously.

'What for?'

'I was afraid that you might think that I was in some way responsible for Duclos insulting you this afternoon.'

He turned away and began to wipe the soap off his face. 'Why should you be responsible?'

'It was, after all, my mistake that led to the disagreement.'

He threw the towel on the bed and addressed the

woman. 'Have I said one word about this man since we left the beach?'

'*Non, chéri.*'

He turned to me. 'You are answered.'

I stood my ground.

'Nevertheless, I feel a certain responsibility. If I had not been so foolish it would never have happened.'

'It is now finished,' he said irritably.

'Fortunately, yes.' I made a desperate effort to touch his vanity. 'If you will allow me to say so, I thought you conducted yourself with dignity and restraint.'

'If they had not held my arms I would have throttled him.'

'You were undoubtedly provoked.'

'Of course.'

This did not seem to be leading anywhere. I tried again.

'Are you staying here long?'

He shot a suspicious glance at me.

'Why do you want to know?'

'Oh, no special reason. I just thought that we might play a game of Russian billiards together—to show that there is no ill feeling.'

'Are you a good player?'

'Not very good.'

'Then I shall probably beat you. I am very good. I beat the American. He does not play well. I do not like playing with inferior players. The American I found dull.'

'A pleasant young man, however.'

'Possibly.'

I persevered. 'The girl is pretty.'

'I do not like her. She is too fat. I prefer very thin women. Don't I, *chéri*?'

194

Mademoiselle Martin emitted a tinny laugh. He sat down on the bed, leaned across and pulled her to him. They kissed passionately. Then he pushed her away. She smiled triumphantly at me, smoothed down her hair, and resumed her manicuring.

'You see,' he said, 'she is skinny. She pleases me.'

I perched myself tentatively on the arm of a chair. 'Madame is charming.'

'Not bad.' He lit a thin black cheroot with an air of a man to whom such successes were commonplace and blew a jet of smoke in my direction. Suddenly: 'Why did you come here, Monsieur?'

I jumped. 'To apologise, naturally. I have explained. . . .'

He shook his head impatiently. 'I asked you why you came here—here to this hotel.'

'For a holiday. I spent part of it in Nice, then I came here.'

'You have enjoyed your stay?'

'Of course. It is not ended yet.'

'When do you expect to leave?'

'I have not made up my mind.'

Fleshy lids dropped over his eyes.

'Tell me, what do you think of this English major?'

'Nothing in particular. A common type of Englishman.'

'Did you lend him any money?'

'Why, no. Did he ask you, too?'

He grinned sardonically. 'Yes, he asked me.'

'And did you oblige him?'

'Do I look such a fool?'

'Then what made you ask about him?'

'He will be leaving the hotel early in the morning. And

I heard him ask the manager to book a cabin on the Algiers steamer from Marseilles. He must have found a mug.'

'Who could it have been?'

'If I knew that I would not ask you. These little things interest me.' He twisted the cheroot between his lips to wet the end of it. 'Another little thing interests me. Who is this Heinberger?'

It was said without the least hint of emphasis, the question of a man idly determined to find something of interest in an uncongenial conversation.

For no reason my spine tingled as if with fear.

'Heinberger?' I repeated.

'Yes, Heinberger. Why does he sit always by himself? Why does he never bathe? I saw you talking to him the other day.'

'I know nothing about him. He is a Swiss, isn't he?'

'I don't know. I am asking you.'

'Then I'm afraid I don't know.'

'What were you talking about?'

'I can't remember. The weather, probably.'

'What a waste of time! I like to find things out about people when I talk to them. I like to know the differences between what people are saying to you and what they are thinking.'

'Indeed! Do you find that there is always a difference?'

'Invariably. All men are liars. Women sometimes speak the truth. But men, never. That is right, is it not, *ma petite?*'

'*Oui, chéri.*'

'*Oui, chéri!*' he echoed derisively. 'She knows that if she lied to me I would break her neck. I tell you this, my friend; most men are cowards. They dislike a fact except when it is so wrapped up in lies and sentiments that the sharp edge of it cannot hurt them. When a man tells the truth he is, depend upon it, a dangerous man.'

'You must find that point of view very fatiguing.'

'I find it entertaining, my dear Monsieur. People are intensely interesting. You, for instance. I find you interesting. You call yourself a language teacher. You are a Hungarian with a Yugoslav passport.'

'I'm sure you didn't find that out by talking to me,' I said playfully.

'I keep my ears open. The manager told Vogel. Vogel was curious.'

'I see. Quite simple.'

'Not at all simple. Very puzzling. I ask myself questions. Why, I ask, does a Hungarian with a Yugoslav passport live in France? What is this mysterious little trip that he makes every morning to the village?'

'You are very observant. I live in France because I work in France. I am afraid that there is nothing mysterious about my trips to the village either. I go to the post office to telephone my fiancée in Paris.'

'So? The telephone service has improved. It usually takes an hour to get through.' He shrugged. 'It is nothing. There are more difficult questions.' He blew the ash off his cheroot. 'Why, for example, were the locks of Monsieur Vadassy's suitcase broken open in the morning and *not* broken in the afternoon?'

'Very simple again. Because Monsieur Duclos has a bad memory.'

His eyes flickered from the end of his cheroot to my face. 'Exactly. A bad memory. He could not remember exactly what was said. Bad liars never can remember these things. Their minds are choked by their own lies. But I am curious. *Were* the locks of your suitcase broken open?'

'I thought we had settled that. No, they were not.'

'Of course not. Please smoke. I do not like to smoke alone. Odette will smoke. Give her a cigarette, Vadassy.'

I produced a packet from my pocket. He raised his eyebrows. 'No case? That is careless of you. I should think that you would keep it in your pocket for safety. How do we know that this Heinberger or the English major is not at this moment stealing?' He sighed. 'Well, well! Odette, *chéri*, a cigarette? You know I do not like to smoke alone. It will not hurt your teeth. Have you noticed her teeth, Vadassy? They are fine.'

He leaned suddenly across the bed, dragged the woman backwards, and thumbed her upper lip back from her teeth. She made no effort to resist.

'Good, aren't they?'

'Yes, very.'

'That's what I like. A thin blonde with fine teeth.' He released her. She sat up, kissed him on the lobe of the ear, and took one of my cigarettes. Roux struck a match for her. As he blew it out he looked at me again.

'You had a day with the police, didn't you?'

'Everybody seems to have heard about that,' I said lightly. 'They didn't seem to like my passport.'

'What's the matter with it?'

'I forgot to renew it.'

'How did you get into the country?'

I laughed. 'You remind me of the police, Monsieur.'

'I told you that I found people interesting.' He lounged back on one elbow. 'One thing I have found out. That all men, liars or not, have one thing in common. Do you know what that is?'

'No.'

He leaned forward suddenly, grasped my hand, and tapped the palm with his forefinger. 'A love of money,' he said softly. He released my hand. 'You, Vadassy, are fortunate. You are poor and money is very sweet to you. You have no political sentiments to confuse your mind. You have an opportunity of making money. Why don't you take it?'

'I don't understand you.' And I didn't understand him for the moment. 'What opportunity are you talking about?'

For a moment he was silent. I saw that the woman had stopped filing her nails and, with the file still resting on the end of her finger, was listening. Then:

'What is today, Vadassy?'

'Today? Saturday, of course.'

He shook his head slowly.

'No, it isn't, Vadassy. It's Friday.'

I emitted a bewildered laugh.

'But I assure you, Monsieur, it is Saturday.'

Again he shook his head.

'Friday, Vadassy.' His eyes narrowed. He leaned forward. 'If, Vadassy, I had a certain piece of information that I think you could give me, I would be prepared to bet five thousand francs that today was Friday.'

'But you would lose.'

'Precisely. I should lose five thousand francs to you. But, on the other hand, I should gain the little piece of information.'

And then I saw the point. I was being offered a bribe. A sentence of Schimler's flashed through my mind. 'He won't act until he's sure.' This man had seen me talking to Schimler. He might even have seen me enter his room. I remembered suddenly the sound of a door closing after I had left room number fourteen. He obviously thought that I was in Herr Heinberger's confidence; and he was prepared to buy evidence of Heinberger's real identity. I looked at him blankly.

'I can't think what information I could give you, Monsieur, that would compensate you for the loss of five thousand francs.'

'No? Are you quite sure?'

'Yes.' I stood up. 'In any case, I never bet on certainties. For a moment, Monsieur, I thought that you were serious.'

He smiled. 'You may be sure, Vadassy, I never allow a joke to go too far. Where are you going when you leave here?'

'Back to Paris.'

'Paris? Why?'

'I live there.' I stared him in the eyes. 'And you, I suppose, will be going back to Germany.'

'And why, Vadassy, should you think that I am not a Frenchman?' His voice had dropped. The smile was still on his face, a very ugly smile. I saw the muscles of his legs tighten as though he were about to spring.

'You have a slight accent. I don't know why, but I assumed that you were a German.'

He shook his head. 'I am a Frenchman, Vadassy. Please do not forget that you, a foreigner, cannot tell a true French accent when you hear it. Do not, please, insult me.' The fleshy lids had dropped over his bulbous eyes until they were almost closed.

'Forgive me. I think it is time I had an *apéritif*. Will you and Madame join me?'

'No, we shall not drink with you.'

'I hope I haven't offended you.'

'On the contrary, it has been a pleasure to talk with you—a *great* pleasure.' There was a note of exaggerated cordiality in his voice that was very disconcerting.

'It is good of you to say so.' I opened the door. '*Au 'voir*, Monsieur, *au 'voir*, Madame.'

He did not get up. '*Au 'voir*, Monsieur,' he said ironically.

I shut the door. As I walked away his loud, unpleasant laugh rang out in the room behind me.

I went downstairs feeling several kinds of fool. Instead of doing the pumping I had been pumped. Far from skilfully extracting valuable information, I had been forced into a defensive position and answered questions as meekly as if I had been in the witness-box. Finally, I had been offered a bribe. The man had obviously realised, too, that I had faked the robbery. He had assumed, as Köche had, that I was a petty crook. A charming specimen! Schimler, poor devil, had a very slim chance of bluffing a man like that. As usual, I began to think of the crushing things I ought to have said. The trouble was that my brain moved far too slowly. I was a dullard, a halfwit.

In the hall a waiter accosted me.

'Ah, Monsieur, we have been trying to find you. You are wanted on the telephone. A call from Paris.'

'For me? Are you sure?'

'Quite sure, Monsieur.'

I went to the office and shut the door behind me.

'Hello!'

'Hello, Vadassy!'

'Who is that?'

'Commissaire de Police.'

'The waiter said that it was a call from Paris.'

'I told the operator to say that. Are you alone?'

'Yes.'

'Have you heard whether anyone is leaving the Réserve today?'

'The English couple leave tomorrow morning.'

'No one else.'

'Yes. *I* leave tomorrow.'

'What do you mean? You will leave when you are told to do so. You know Monsieur Beghin's instructions.'

'I have been told to leave.'

'By whom?'

'Köche.' All the pent-up bitterness of the day's disasters welled up within me. Briefly and very acidly I described the outcome of Beghin's instructions of the morning.

He listened in silence. Then:

'You are sure no one else is leaving, besides the English?'

'It is possible, but if so I have not heard about it.'

Another silence. At last:

'Very well. That is all now.'

'But what shall I do?'

'You will receive further instructions in due course.'

He hung up.

I stared wretchedly at the telephone. I would receive further instructions in due course. Well, I could do no more. I was beaten.

16

THE clock struck nine. It was a thin, high-pitched sound, and very soft.

I can see the scene now, clearly. There are no blurred edges. Here nothing is out of focus. It is as if I were looking through a stereoscope at a perfect coloured reproduction of the room and of the people in it.

The rain has stopped, and the breeze is once more gentle and warm. It is hot and steamy in the room, and the windows are wide open. The wet leaves of the creeper just outside gleam in the light from the electric 'candles' in their rococo brackets on the walls. Beyond the stone balustrade on the terrace the moon is beginning to rise through the fir trees.

The Skeltons and I are sitting near to the window, the remains of the coffee before us on a low table. Across the room Roux and Mademoiselle Martin are playing Russian billiards. He is standing over her, guiding the cue, and as I watch I see her press her body against his, and look round quickly to see if anyone has noticed the action. In the other corner, near the door leading to the hall, there are two small groups. Monsieur Duclos is stroking his beard with his pince-nez and talking in French to an intent Frau Vogel. Herr Vogel is saying something in halting Italian to Mrs Clandon-Hartley— an unusually animated Mrs Clandon-Hartley—while the Major listens, the ghost of a smile on his lips.

Only Schimler and, of course, the Köches, are absent.

I remember that Skelton was saying something to me about Roux and Duclos pretending to ignore one another. I scarcely heard him. I was looking round the room at their faces. Nine of them. I had talked to all of them, watched them, listened to them and now—now I knew no more about them than I had known on the day—what ages ago it seemed—when I had come to the Réserve. No more? That was not quite true. I had learned something of the lives of some of them. But what did I know about their thoughts, about the minds that worked behind those masks? A man's account of his own actions was like the look he habitually wore on his face, no more than the expression, the statement of an attitude. You could never get at the whole man any more than you could see four faces of a cube. The mind was a figure with an infinite number of dimensions, a fluid in ceaseless movement, unfathomable, unaccountable.

The Major still had that faint smile on his lips. His wife, her hands fluttering slightly as she said something to Vogel, seemed, for the first time, to be alive. Of course! Someone had lent them money. Who was it? I knew so little that I could not even make an intelligent guess.

Duclos had put his pince-nez back on his nose, and was listening to Frau Vogel's guttural French, with his head cocked patronisingly. Roux, his eyes fixed glassily on the balls, was demonstrating a stroke. I watched them all fascinated. It was like seeing dancers through a window that shut out the music. There was a mad solemnity about their antics. . . .

The Skeltons burst out laughing. I turned round feeling rather foolish.

'Sorry,' said he; 'but we've been watching your face,

Mr Vadassy. It was getting longer and longer. We were afraid you were going to burst into tears.

'I was thinking how much we identify ourselves with other people and yet how separate we are. You see, I'm leaving tomorrow morning.'

Their dismay was so well done that I had a sudden feeling that they might really be sorry to see me go. A wave of emotion swept over me; self-pity, no doubt. I fought my way clear of it.

'I shall be sorry to go myself,' I said. 'Will you be staying long?'

There was an almost imperceptible pause before he replied, and I saw her glance at him quickly.

'Oh,' he said carelessly, 'for a while, I guess.'

And then she leaned forward. 'For three months, to be exact,' she said and glanced at him again. 'There's no reason why we shouldn't tell Mr Vadassy. I'm tired of this act anyway.'

'Now look, Mary . . .' he began warningly, and I suddenly felt sick.

'Oh, what's the difference?' She smiled faintly at me. 'We're not brother and sister, Mr Vadassy. We're cousins and we're living in sin.'

'Congratulations,' I said. I still felt sick, but in a different way now. I was sick with jealousy. She smiled at me.

'Well you'd better tell about the hocus-pocus, too,' said her lover gloomily. 'It's not entirely usual in France for people in our situation to go around pretending to be brother and sister.'

She shrugged. 'It's all so absurd, really. When we came here we had separate rooms, and, because of the names on our passports and the forms you fill out and everything, they took us for brother and sister. Well then, when it turned out that we could do with one room after all, it meant that we'd either have to move to another hotel or stay here as we were.'

'Or look incestuous,' he put in unhappily.

'So, as we felt a bit sentimental about this place, we stayed. You see, we can't get married for three months yet because if Warren gets married before his twenty-first birthday we lose fifty thousand dollars from Grandfather Skelton, which would be crazy, wouldn't it?'

'Yes,' I said, but they were looking at each other and I knew now what it was that made them seem so attractive. They were in love.

'Absolutely crazy,' he said, smiling.

And then, Monsieur Duclos, abandoned by or having abandoned Frau Vogel, loomed over me.

'They are a very charming couple, these Americans,' he said.

'Yes, very charming.'

'I was saying as much to Madame Vogel. She is a most intelligent woman. Monsieur Vogel, you know, is director of the Swiss State Power Company. He is a very important man. I have, of course, heard of him before. His offices at Berne are one of the sights of the city.

'I thought he came from Constance.'

He adjusted his pince-nez warily. 'He has also a large villa at Constance. It is very fine. He has invited me to stay with him there.'

'How pleasant for you.'

'Yes. Naturally, I expect we shall discuss a good deal of business.'

'Naturally.'

'When businessmen meet for pleasure, my friend, the talk is always of business.

'Quite so.'

'Again, it is possible that we may be able to be of service to one another. Co-operation, you understand? It is most important in business. That is what I tell the work-people in my factories. If they will co-operate with me, I will co-operate with them. But they must co-operate with me first. Co-operation cannot be one-sided.'

'Of course not.'

'What's he saying?' inquired Skelton. 'I've heard the word co-operation ten times.'

'He says that co-operation is important.'

'That's fine.'

'Did you know,' pursued Monsieur Duclos, 'that Major and Madame Clandon-Hartley are leaving tomorrow?'

'Yes.'

'Someone, clearly, has lent them money. Curious, is it not? Personally, I would not lend the Major money. He asked me for ten thousand francs. A trifling sum. I should not miss it. But it is a question of principle. I am a businessman.'

'I thought it was *two* thousand francs he wanted. That was what you told me before.'

'He has increased his demands,' he said blandly. 'A type of criminal, without a doubt.'

'Personally, I should not have thought so.'

'A businessman must have an eye for a criminal. Fortunately, English criminals are always very simple.'

'Oh?'

'It is well known. The French criminal is a snake, the American criminal a wolf, and the English criminal a rat. Snakes, wolves, and rats. The rat is a very simple animal.

He fights only when he is in a corner. At other times he merely nibbles.'

'And you really think that Major Clandon-Hartley is an English criminal?'

Slowly, deliberately, Monsieur Duclos removed the pince-nez from his nose and tapped me on the arm with them.

'Look carefully at his face,' he said, 'and you will see the rat in it. What is more,' he added triumphantly, 'he told me so himself.'

This was fantastic.

The Skeltons, tired of trying to follow Monsieur Duclos's rapid French, had found a copy of *L'Illustration,* and, were pencilling in moustaches on the faces reproduced in it. I was left to deal with Monsieur Duclos alone. He edged a chair close to mine.

'Of course,' he said impressively, 'I speak in confidence. The English major would not like to know that his identity was discovered.'

'What identity?'

'You do not know?'

'No.'

'Ah!' He stroked his beard. 'Then I had better say no more. He is relying upon my discretion.' He rose, gave me a meaning look, and moved away. I saw that Köche had come into the room with Schimler. Monsieur Duclos hurried across to intercept them. I heard him announce that the rain had ceased. Köche stopped politely, but Schimler walked round them and came towards me. He was looking terribly ill.

'I hear that you are leaving tomorrow, Vadassy.'

'Yes, was that all you heard?'

He shook his head. 'No. I think that a few explanations

would be helpful. Köche is afraid that there is something going on in his hotel that he does not know about. He is worried. You, it seems, might be able to clear the matter up.'

'I am afraid not. If Köche cares to apply at the police station . . .'

'So that's it! You are from the police.'

'From them, but not of them. Another thing, Herr Heinberger: I should advise you not to talk to me for very long. I was seen leaving your room this afternoon. I have been questioned on the subject by a certain gentleman.'

His smile was ghastly. His eyes met mine. 'And did you answer the question?'

'I hope I lied convincingly.'

'That was good of you,' he said softly. He nodded to me and to the Skeltons, and walked away to join Köche.

'He looks as though he's going to fall to pieces,' said Skelton.

For some reason the comment irritated me. 'Some day,' I said rashly, 'I hope to be able to tell you something about that man.'

'Won't you tell us now, Mr Vadassy?'

'I'm afraid I can't.'

'You've cooked your goose,' he said; 'you'll get no peace now. Look, honey, Roux has finished with the table. What about a game? Do you mind, Mr Vadassy?'

'Of course not. Go ahead!'

They got up and went over to the billiard table. I was left alone to think.

This, I told myself, was in all probability my last night of freedom. These were the people I would remember. This was the scene that I would picture: the Vogels and the Clandon-Hartleys talking together, with Duclos listening, stroking his beard, waiting for a chance to break into their conversation; Köche talking to Roux and Odette Martin; Schimler sitting by himself, idly turning the pages of a newspaper; the Skeltons bending together over the billiard table. And with them all there was the warm, scented night, the drip-drip of water on the terrace, the faint hiss of the sea against the rocks at the point, the stars and the light of the moon striking through the trees. It all seemed so very peaceful. And yet there was no peace. Outside in the garden the monstrosities of the insect kingdom were creeping along the wet branches and stems in search of food; watchful, intent, preying and preyed upon. In the darkness, dramas were being enacted. Nothing was at rest, nothing was still. The night was moving, alive with tragedy. While inside . . .

There was a movement from the opposite corner of the room. Frau Vogel had risen to her feet, and was standing smiling diffidently at the others. Her husband seemed to be trying to persuade her to do something. I saw Köche break off his conversation with Roux and cross to her.

'We should all be most grateful,' I heard him say.

She nodded doubtfully. Then, to my astonishment, I saw Köche lead her over to the upright piano against the wall and open it for her. She sat down stiffly and ran her short, thick fingers over the keys. The Skeltons turned round in surprise. Schimler looked up from his paper. Roux sank rather impatiently into a chair and drew Mademoiselle Martin on his knee. Vogel glanced round the room in triumph. Duclos removed his pince-nez expectantly.

I saw Schimler lean forward, a strange look on his face

as he watched the stiff, dumpy figure, her ridiculous wisps of chiffon agitated by the quick movements of her hands and arms.

Frau Vogel, it was clear, had once had a talent. There was about her playing a curious, faded brilliance, like that of a paste buckle in a hamper of old ball-dresses. And then I forgot Frau Vogel and listened to the music.

When she had finished there was a moment of dead silence in the room, and then a burst of clapping. She half turned on her chair, flushed, and blinked nervously at Köche. She went to get up, but her husband called over to her to play again, and she sank back on the chair. For a moment she appeared to be thinking; then she raised her hands to the keyboard and Bach's 'Jesu, joy of man's desiring' stole out softly into the room.

Sometimes, after a day's work, I have gone back to my room and, without troubling to turn on the light, sunk into my easy chair and remained there motionless, relaxed, savouring the slow, pleasant ache that creeps through the limbs when they are very weary. That was what happened to me that evening as I listened to Frau Vogel playing. Only, now, it was not my body that yielded so thankfully, but my mind. Instead of the slow, pleasant ache creeping through my limbs there was the melody of a choral prelude entwining itself in my consciousness. My eyes closed. If only this would go on. If only this would go on. If only . . .

When the interruption came I did not at first notice it. There was a murmur of voices from the hall, someone hissed a request for silence, a chair grated on the floor. I opened my eyes in time to see Köche disappearing hurriedly through the door, which he closed softly behind him. A few moments later I heard it open again noisily.

It all seemed to happen in the fraction of a second; but the first intimation I had that anything was wrong was that Frau Vogel stopped suddenly in the middle of a bar. Instinctively I looked across at her first. She was sitting, her hands poised over the keys, staring fixedly over the top of the piano, as though she were looking at a ghost. Then her hands dropped slowly on to the keyboard, sounding a soft discord. My gaze travelled to the door. There, standing on the threshold, were two uniformed *agents de police*.

They looked round the room menacingly. One of them took a step forward.

'Which of you is Josef Vadassy?'

I stood up slowly, too dazed to speak.

They clumped across the room towards me.

'You are under arrest. You will accompany us to the Commissariat.'

Frau Vogel let out a little cry.

'But . . .'

'There are no "buts". Come on.'

They gripped my arms.

Monsieur Duclos darted forward.

'What is the charge?'

'That does not concern you,' retorted the leading *agent* curtly. He jerked me towards the door.

Monsieur Duclos's pince-nez quivered. 'I am a citizen of the Republic,' he declared fiercely. 'I have a right to know.'

The *agent* glanced round. 'Curious, eh?' He grinned. 'Very well, the charge is one of espionage. You've had a dangerous man among you. Come on, Vadassy. March!'

The Skeltons, the Vogels, Roux, Mademoiselle Martin, the Clandon-Hartleys, Schimler, Duclos, Köche—for an instant I saw their faces, white and motionless, turned towards me. Then I was through the door. Behind me a woman, Frau Vogel I think, screamed hysterically.

I had received my instructions.

17

I WAS taken to the Commissariat in a closed car driven by a third *agent*.

I suppose that this fact should have surprised me. Arrested men are not usually afforded the luxury of a car to convey them to a police *poste* no more than half a kilometre away. But it did not surprise me. Nothing short of a civic reception by the mayor and corporation of St Gatien would have surprised me. It had come. That which I had known all along in my heart *would* happen, *had* happened. I was under arrest again. My parole had been withdrawn. This, then, was the end. True, I had not expected quite so dramatic an exit from the Réserve; but, all things considered, it was probably better this way—I had at least been spared another night of suspense. It was almost a relief to feel that I had to think for myself no longer, that Monsieur Mathis's sarcasms could no longer touch me, that I could do nothing but acquiesce.

I wondered what the Skeltons were thinking about it all. It must have been a shock to them. Duclos, of course, would be beside himself with excitement. He would probably be telling the others that he'd known about me all along. Schimler? That *did* worry me a little. I would have liked him to have known the truth. As for the rest . . . Köche would not be surprised. The Major, however, would be horrified. He would probably advocate a firing squad. Roux, no doubt, would laugh unpleasantly. The Vogels would click their tongues and look solemn. And yet one of them would be thinking hard, one of them would know that I was neither a spy nor dangerous. That man, the man who had slammed the writing-room door, who had searched my room and taken two spools of film, who had knocked me down, whose fingers had fumbled in my pockets; he would go scot free, while I rotted in prison. What would his thoughts be like? Triumphant? What did it matter? What did it matter what any of them thought? Nothing. All the same, it would be interesting to know which of them really was the spy—very interesting. Well, I would have plenty of time in which to make my guesses.

The tyres grated on the shingle square in front of the Commissariat. I was taken into the waiting-room with the wooden forms. As before, an *agent* waited with me. This time, however, I did not attempt to talk. I just waited.

The hands of the clock in the room had crept round to half past ten before the door opened and Beghin came in.

So far as I could see he still had on the same tussore suit that he had been wearing three days previously. In his hand was the same limp handkerchief. He was still sweating profusely. One thing only surprised me. He seemed to be smaller than I had imagined. For the first time I realised what a monster my thoughts had made of him. In my imagination he had grown into an ogre, a foul, corrupt colossus of evil preying upon the innocent who crossed his path—a devil. Now I saw before me a man, fat and gross and sweating, but a man.

For a moment the small, heavy-lidded eyes stared down at me as though he were unable to remember who I was.

Then he nodded to the *agent*. The man saluted, went out of the room and shut the door behind him.

'Well, Vadassy, have you enjoyed your little holiday?' Once again the high-pitched voice took me unawares. I stared back at him coldly.

'I am to be the scapegoat after all, eh?'

He bent down, pulled one of the forms away from the wall and sat down on it, facing me. The wood creaked under his weight. He wiped his hands on the handkerchief.

'It's been very warm,' he said, and then glanced up at me. 'What did they do when you were arrested?'

'Who, the *agents*?'

'No, your fellow guests.'

'They did nothing.' I heard my own voice develop an edge to it. I knew, somehow, with half my brain, that I was losing my temper and that I could not help doing so. 'They did nothing,' I repeated. 'What would you expect them to do? Duclos wanted to know what the charge was. Frau Vogel screamed. Otherwise they just looked. I don't suppose they're used to seeing people arrested.' My temper rose suddenly to boiling point. 'Though I expect that if they stayed long enough in St Gatien they would get used to it. Next time one of the fishermen gets drunk and beats his wife you might try arresting Vogel. Or would that be too dangerous? Would the Swiss consul have something to say? Perhaps he would. Or wouldn't the Department of Naval Intelligence have enough intelligence to see that? Do you know, Beghin, that when you talked to me in that cell three days ago I actually thought that, although you might be a bullying blackguard of a policeman, it was possible that you had some sense. I thought that even if you did threaten and ask inane questions, you at least knew what you were doing. I have found since that I was wrong. You haven't any sense and you don't know what you're doing. You're a fool. You've blundered so many times that I've lost count of them. If I hadn't had a little sense and interpreted your instructions in my own way, your . . .'

He had been listening calmly; now he got to his feet, his fist drawn back as though he were about to strike me. 'If you hadn't *what?*' he shouted savagely.

I did not flinch. I felt reckless and vindictive.

'I see you don't like the truth. I said that if I hadn't interpreted your instructions in my own way your precious spy would have taken fright and bolted. You told me to question the guests about their cameras. A lunatic would have seen that that was a fatal mistake.'

He sat down again. 'Well, what *did* you do?' he said grimly: 'Fake the information for me?'

'No, I used some sense. You see'—this bitterly—'in my simple innocence I thought that if I could get the information you required without jeopardising the chances of catching the spy when he had been identified, I should receive some consideration at the hands of the police. If I had known just how badly you were going to bungle your end of the business, I doubt if I would have bothered. However, I obtained the information about the cameras by the simple process of using my eyes. When, as was inevitable, the fake robbery was discovered to be a fake, I managed to retrieve the situation by confusing the others' minds sufficiently to make them—or at any rate most of them—accept the story that the whole thing was a mistake. Now, of course, the fat is in the fire. This time I can't retrieve your mistake. You've given the alarm. The Clandon-Hartleys are leaving tomorrow in any case.

I don't suppose any of them will care to stay after this. You've lost your suspects. Still,' I shrugged, 'I don't suppose you care. The Commissaire will be satisfied. You've got someone to convict. That's all you policemen want, isn't it?' I stood up. 'Well, now that's over. I've been wanting to get that off my chest. If you don't mind, and have quite finished gloating, I'd like to be locked in my cell now. For one thing, this room is stuffy; for another, I didn't get much sleep last night. I've got a headache and I'm tired.'

He took out a packet of cigarettes.

'Cigarette, Vadassy?'

I sneered. 'The last time you said that, you had something dirty up your sleeve. What do you want now, a signed confession? Because if you do you're not going to get it. I absolutely refuse. Understand that, I absolutely refuse.'

'Take a cigarette, Vadassy. You're not going to sleep yet.'

'Oh, I see! Third degree, eh?'

'*Sacré chien!*' he squeaked. 'Take a cigarette.'

I took one. He lit his and tossed me the matches.

'Now!' He blew a cloud of smoke in the air. 'I have an apology to make to you.'

'Oh?' I put all I could into the word.

'Yes, an apology. I made a mistake. I overrated your intelligence. And I underrated it. Both.'

'Splendid! And what am I supposed to do, Monsieur Beghin? Burst into tears and sign the confession now?'

He frowned. 'You listen to me.'

'I am listening—fascinated.'

He ran his handkerchief round the inside of his collar. 'That tongue of yours, Vadassy, will get you into trouble one of these days. Has it not occurred to you that it is a little unusual for a prisoner to be sitting where you are now instead of in a cell?'

'It has. I'm wondering where the trick is.'

'There is no trick, you fool,' he squeaked angrily. 'Listen. The first thing you ought to know is that every one of the instructions you have been given has had one object—that of making the spy leave the Réserve. You were told to make those inquiries about the cameras with just that object in view. We wanted to alarm him. When that failed—and I can see now why it did fail—we told you to report the faked robbery. The man had searched your room; he had searched your pockets. I say we wanted to alarm him, not enough to put him to flight— that is why we ourselves kept away from the Réserve— but just enough to make him think that he was running a risk by staying. Again we failed. The first time I had failed to reckon on your reasoning the way you did from the facts in your possession. That was my fault. I had forgotten how little you knew. The second time I failed to reckon with your inexperience. Köche saw through you too quickly.'

'But,' I protested, 'how on earth did you expect to catch the spy like that? What was your idea? Arrest the first man to pack up and leave the Réserve? If so, you'd better arrest Major Clandon-Hartley. He's leaving first thing in the morning. If that's your idea of catching a spy, then heaven help France.'

To my surprise, I saw the beginnings of a grin at the corner of his mouth. He drew at his cigarette, inhaled deeply and let the smoke trickle out through his nose.

'But then, my dear Vadassy,' he said sweetly, 'you do not know all the facts. In particular, you are ignorant of one very important one—the fact that we had discovered the identity of the spy before you left here three days ago, that we could have arrested him at any time we wanted to do so.'

It took me a moment or two to take this in. Then hope and despair began to chase themselves through my brain. I looked at him.

'Who *is* the spy, then?'

He was leaning back, watching me with obvious interest. He flapped his hand airily. 'Oh, we'll come to that later.'

I swallowed hard. 'Is this another trick?'

'No, Vadassy, it isn't.'

'Then,' my temper rose again, 'will you explain what the devil you mean by—by torturing me like this? If you knew what I've been through these last three days you wouldn't be sitting there like a fat, complacent slug, grinning as though it were a good joke. Do you know what you've done to me? Do you realise, damn you? You —you . . .'

He tapped me on the knee. 'Now, now, Vadassy! This is a waste of time. I know that I am fat, but I am certainly not complacent. Nor am I a slug. What I have done I have had to do, as you will see if you will give me time to explain instead of losing your temper.'

'Why have you arrested me? Why are you keeping me here?'

He shook his head protestingly. 'Just be quiet, my good Vadassy, and listen. You've broken your cigarette in your emotion. Have another.'

'I don't want a cigarette.'

I watched him, cold hatred in my heart, while he lit his second cigarette. When he had done so he sat for a moment staring at the match-stalk.

'I was quite sincere,' he said at last, 'when I apologised to you. I had a job to do. You will see.'

I was about to speak, but he waved me into silence.

'About nine months ago,' he went on, 'one of our agents in Italy included in his report news of a rumour that the Italian Intelligence Department had established a new base in Toulon. In my business, of course, we hear many such rumours, and I paid little attention to this one at the time. Subsequently, however, I was compelled to take it seriously. Information about our defences along this coast was finding its way into Italy with disconcerting regularity. Our agent in Spezia, for instance, reported that particulars of a secret change in the fortifications of an island near Marseilles were being freely discussed by Italian naval officers three days after it was made. Worse, we had absolutely no clue to the source of this information. We were very worried. When that chemist walked in here with those negatives we seized the opportunity with both hands.' Dramatically his fat, baby-like hands tightened on an imaginary object.

'Naturally, you came under suspicion. When, however, we found out what had happened, how the cameras had been changed, we discarded you as unimportant. To be truthful, we nearly released you then and there. Fortunately,' he added blandly, 'we decided to wait for a few hours until the report on the camera came in.'

'Report on the camera?'

'Oh, yes. You see, that is something else you do not know about. As soon as we knew of the change we telephoned to the makers of the camera and asked who had bought the particular camera with that serial number. The reply was that it had been supplied to a dealer in Aix. The dealer in Aix remembered it quite well. As luck would have it, he was a small man and it was the only camera of that value he had sold for two years. He had had to get it specially, and was able to supply us with the name of the man who had bought it. The name corresponded with that of one of the guests at the Réserve. Meanwhile we had had the photographs examined by an expert. He was able to tell us by the position of the shadows that the photographs had been taken at about half past six in the morning, and that they had been taken with a telephoto lens attachment from a certain angle. Reference to the map, plus the fact that in some of the photographs portions of foliage were visible, showed that the photographer could have been in only one place. That place was a small, high headland, almost unapproachable except by sea.

'We consulted the fishermen in the harbour. Yes, the man in question had taken Köche's boat out at five o'clock on the previous morning. He had said that he was going fishing. One fisherman remembered it because, usually, when Köche or his guests went fishing, this fisherman would go with them to bait the hooks and look after the engine. This particular guest had preferred to go alone.

'So, we had our man. We could arrest him. The Commissaire was impatient to do so. But we did not arrest him. Why? You will remember, no doubt, that when I was talking to you in that cell I said that I was not interested in spies, but in who employed them. That was so. I was not interested in this one man. We had heard of him before, and his dossier showed that he had always been an employee. I was interested in his headquarters at Toulon. Him I could arrest at any time I chose; but first I wanted him to lead me to his superiors. To bring that about I must in some way force him to leave the

Réserve, yet at the same time let him think that he himself was completely unsuspected.'

'And then, I suppose, you thought of me?'

'Exactly. If you started making inquiries about cameras he would know what had happened to his photographs, realise that your suspicions were aroused, and go before you decided to approach the police. Then we should follow him. The only difficulty was persuading you to do this without giving anything away. Again fortune favoured us. Your passport was not in order. You had no national status. The rest was easy.'

'Yes,' I said bitterly, 'it was easy. But you could at least have told me that you knew who the spy was.'

'Impossible. For one thing, it would have appeared to have weakened our case against you, and you would have been more difficult to handle. Secondly, we could not afford to rely on your discretion. You might have confided in someone else. Your behaviour towards the man might have been unnatural. It was a pity, because, acting in what you conceived to be your own interests, you disobeyed instructions. What has worried us more than the failure of those instructions was, first, the fact that your room had been searched and, second, the attack on you last night. It meant, so we thought, that the man was proving difficult to scare. He must have found out that the cameras had been changed, of course. And he would know it was you who had his camera. He would have seen you with an identical type. The trouble was, I see now, that he thought you didn't know about the photographs. Or,' he glanced at me shrewdly, 'did you do something that I don't know about?'

I hesitated. In my mind's eyes I saw myself sitting in the writing-room, listening to the clock ticking, and staring into a mirror until suddenly the door slammed and a key turned in the lock. I met Beghin's eyes.

'There's nothing important that you don't know about.'

He sighed. 'Well, perhaps it does not matter. That is past. We come to the report of the robbery. Frankly, my dear Vadassy, I was a little sorry for you. It was an unpleasant thing for you to have to do. But it was necessary. The man who searched your room and took the two spools of film would know that he had taken nothing else. Your report of valuables stolen would puzzle him. He would be suspicious. But the situation deteriorated too quickly. We had to take more drastic measures. Hence your arrest this evening.'

'You mean that I am not really under arrest.'

'If you were under arrest, Vadassy, you would not, as I have already pointed out to you, be sitting here talking to me. You see, my good friend, we had to force his hand. But we had to do it carefully. The *agent* who arrested you was told to make it clear why you were being arrested. If Duclos had not asked, the *agent* would have announced that the charge was espionage. Now put yourself in this man's place. You know that the photographs you have taken have fallen by chance into another person's hands. What do you do? You try to get them back. Having failed, and suspecting that this person is playing some sort of game, you decide to wait. Then this person is arrested by the police on a charge of espionage. What do you think? What runs through your mind? Firstly, that the police have discovered that the photographs have been taken, secondly, that this person may, in defending himself, lead the police to you. It is time, therefore, for you to go. What is more, you have no time to lose. You understand?'

'Yes, I understand. But supposing he does not leave? What then?'

'The question does not arise. He *has* left.'

'What?'

He glanced at the clock on the wall. 'Twenty-five past ten. He left the Réserve ten minutes ago in a car he hired from the garage in the village. He was heading for Toulon. We will give him a few more minutes. We have a car following. A report should reach us soon now.' He lit his third cigarette and flicked the match across the room. 'Meanwhile I have some instructions for you.'

'Indeed!'

'Yes. For obvious reasons it is not desirable that any charge of espionage should be made just yet. The newspapers must not get too inquisitive. I propose to make the arrests on a charge of theft—the theft of a Zeiss Contax camera, value four thousand five hundred francs. Do you see?'

'You mean that you want me to identify the camera?'

'Exactly.' He stared hard at me. 'You can do that, can't you?'

I hesitated. There was nothing else for it. He would have to know the truth.

'Well?' he said impatiently.

'I could have identified it.' I felt myself getting red. 'There is only one difficulty. The camera now in my room at the Réserve is my own camera. The cameras were re-exchanged.'

To my astonishment, he nodded calmly. 'When did it happen?'

I told him. Again that faint smile puckered the corners of his mouth.

'I thought as much.'

'You what?'

'My dear Monsieur Vadassy, I am not a fool and you are painfully transparent. Your careful avoidance of the subject of the cameras on the telephone this morning was very obvious.'

'I didn't think—'

'Of course you didn't. However, as you have already found, the two cameras are very much alike. It would be an understandable mistake on your part to identify the camera we hope to find at Toulon as your own property, wouldn't it?'

I agreed hastily.

'And, of course, if the mistake is discovered later, you will be suitably apologetic?'

'Of course.'

'Very well, that is settled. He got to his feet. 'And,' he added genially, 'I see no reason why, if all goes well, you should not be able to leave for Paris tomorrow in time for your exigent Monsieur Mathis on Monday.'

For a moment I did not realise what he was saying; then, as the meaning began to filter into my brain, I heard myself babbling incoherent thanks. It was as if I were waking from a nightmare. There was that same almost overpowering sensation of mingled relief and fear: relief that it was, after all, only a nightmare, fear that it might, after all, be real and that the awakening was the dream. Fragments of the nightmare still lingered. I was afraid, afraid to trust myself to think. This was merely another trick of Beghin's, a trap, a means of gaining my confidence. My thanks died on my lips. He was watching me curiously.

'If you are telling me the truth,' I said sharply, 'if you do mean what you say, why don't you let me go now?

226

Why can't I go until tomorrow? If you have no charge against me, you cannot keep me here. You have no right to do so.'

He sighed wearily. 'None at all. But I have already told you that your assistance is required for identification purposes.'

'But supposing I refuse?'

He shrugged. 'I cannot compel you. We should have to manage without you. There are, of course,' he added thoughtfully, 'other considerations.' You mentioned, I believe, that you had applied for French citizenship. Your attitude in this matter might make all the difference between the success or failure of your application. The French citizen is required to aid the police if requested to do so. A man with so little appreciation of the responsibilities of citizenship as to refuse that aid . . .'

'I see. More blackmail!'

One of his chubby hands rested on my shoulder. 'My dear good Vadassy, I have never come across anyone so given to quibbling over words.' The hand left my shoulder, went to his inside pocket and came out with an envelope in it. 'Look! You have spent three days at the Réserve at our request and upon our business. We wish to be fair. Here is five hundred francs.' He thrust the envelope into my hand. 'That will more than cover the extra expense. Now then, we ask you to spend an hour of your remaining time here in helping us to arrest the men responsible for all your troubles. Is that unreasonable?'

I looked him in the eyes.

'You avoided the question just now. I ask it again. Who is the spy?'

He caressed his loose jowl thoughtfully and glanced at me out of the corner of his eye. 'I am afraid,' he said slowly, 'that I have purposely refrained from telling you. I am afraid, too, that I have no intention of telling you now.'

'I see. Very clever. I shall have to come with you and see for myself. And then I suppose I shall be expected to make this false identification of the camera. Is that it?'

But before he could reply there was a sharp knock at the door and an *agent* came in, nodded meaningly at Beghin, and went out again.

'That,' said Beghin, 'means that our man has passed through Sanary. It's time we went.' He walked to the door and looked back. 'Are you coming, Vadassy?'

I slipped the envelope into my pocket and stood up.

'Of course,' I said, and followed him out of the room.

18

AT ten forty-five that night a big Renault saloon swung out of the short side road leading from the Commissariat and sped east along the main coast road.

In the car besides Beghin and myself were two plain-clothes men. One was driving. The other I had recognised as he had sat down beside me in the back. It was my friend of the *limonade gazeuse*. He refused steadfastly to remember me.

The clouds had gone. The moon, high in the sky, shed a light that made the beams of the headlamps seem pale. As we left the outskirts of St Gatien, the hum of the engine rose in pitch and the tyres slithered on the wet road as we rounded the 'S' bends beyond the Réserve headland. I leaned back on the cushions, trying to resolve the chaos of my thoughts.

Here was I, Josef Vadassy, a man who, not two hours before, had been resigned to the loss of his work, his liberty, and his hopes, calmly sitting in the back seat of a French police car on its way to catch a spy!

Calmly? No, that was not quite true. I was anything but calm. I wanted to sing. And yet I was not quite sure what I wanted to sing about. Was it the knowledge that tomorrow, in almost exactly twenty-four hours' time, I would be sitting in a train nearing Paris? Or was it that soon, tonight, I was to learn the answer to a question, that my problem was to be solved for me, without a pencil and paper? I worried over these alternatives.

I think that all this was part of my body's reaction to the tension of the last three days. All the evidence points to that conclusion. My stomach rumbled incessantly. I was very thirsty. I kept lighting cigarettes and then pitching them out of the window before I had smoked them. Also, and this was most significant, I had that curious feeling of having forgotten something, of having left something behind in St Gatien, something that I should need. All nonsense, of course. I had left nothing in St Gatien that could have been the slightest use to me that night in Toulon.

The car hummed on through moonlit avenues of trees. Then we left the trees behind and the country became more open. There were plantations of olives, their leaves a silvery grey in the light of the headlamps. We flashed through villages. Then we came into a small town. A man in the square shouted angrily at us as we shot past him. 'Soon,' I thought, 'we shall be at Toulon.' I had a sudden desire to talk to someone. I turned to the man beside me.

'What was that place?'

He removed his pipe from his mouth. 'La Cadière.'

'Do you know who it is that we are going to arrest?'

'No.' He put his pipe back in his mouth and stared straight ahead.

'I'm sorry,' I said, 'about the lemonade.'

'I don't know what you're talking about.'

I gave it up. The Renault swung to the right and accelerated along a straight road. I stared at Beghin's head and shoulders outlined against the glare of the headlights. I saw him light a cigarette. Then he half turned his head.

'It's no use trying to pump Henri,' he said. 'He is discretion itself.'

'Yes, I see that.'

He threw the match out of the window. 'You spent four days at the Réserve, Vadassy. Haven't you any idea of the man we're going to arrest?'

'None.'

He chuckled wheezily. 'Not even a guess?'

'Not even a guess.'

Henri stirred. 'You'd make a bad detective.'

'I sincerely hope so,' I retorted coldly.

He grunted. Beghin chuckled again. 'Be careful, Henri. Monsieur has a forked tongue in his head and he is still angry with the police.' He turned to the driver. 'Stop at the *poste* at Ollioules.'

A few minutes later we entered the town in question and pulled up outside a small building in the square. A uniformed *agent* was waiting at the door. He walked over, saluted, and leaned through the window of the car.

'Monsieur Beghin?'

'Yes.'

'They are waiting for you at the junction of the main road and the road from Sablettes, Monsieur. The car from the garage at St Gatien returned five minutes ago.'

'Good!'

We drove on again. Five minutes later I saw the rear light of a stationary car on the road in front of us. The Renault slowed and came to a standstill behind it. Beghin got out.

A tall thin man was standing by the side of the car in front. He walked towards Beghin and they shook hands. For a moment or two they stood talking, then the tall man walked back to his car and Beghin returned to the Renault.

'That is Inspector Fournier of the dock police,' said Beghin to me as he climbed in. 'We are going to his territory.' He slammed the door and turned to the driver. 'Follow the Inspector's car.'

We moved off again. Soon now the lines of trees through which we had been driving since Ollioules thinned and we passed a factory or two. Finally we swung on to a brightly lighted road with tram tracks down the centre and cafés on the pavements. Then we turned to the right and I saw the name 'Boulevard de Strasbourg' on the corner building. We were in Toulon.

The cafés were full. Groups of French sailors strolled along the pavements. There were many girls. A handsome young coloured woman with a picture hat and a tight black dress walked serenely across the road in front of us, causing our driver to brake hard and swear. An old man was wandering along in the gutter playing a mandolin. I saw a dark, fat man stop a sailor, say something to him, and receive a shove that sent him cannoning into a woman with a tray of sweets. Farther down we passed a naval patrol going in and out of the cafés warning the sailors that it was time to get down to the tenders waiting to return to the warships. Then we came to a less frequented part of the Boulevard and the car in front slowed down and turned to the right. A moment or two later we were threading our way cautiously through a network of dark, narrow streets of houses and steel-shuttered shops. Then the houses became less frequent and there were whole streets lined only with the high blank walls of warehouses. It was in such a street that we eventually stopped.

'We get out here,' said Beghin.

It was a warm night, but as I stood on the damp cobbles I shivered. It may have been excitement, but I think that it was fear. There was something eerie about those blank walls.

Beghin touched me on the arm.

'Come on, Vadassy, a little walk now.'

Ahead of us the Inspector and three other men were standing waiting.

'It's very quiet,' I said.

He grunted. 'What do you expect at this time of the night among a lot of warehouses? Stay in the rear with Henri and don't make a noise.'

He joined the Inspector and the three men fell in behind him. Henri and I brought up the rear. The drivers remained at their posts.

At the end of the walls we turned into a street that twisted out of sight a few metres farther down. On the right-hand side was the end wall of the warehouse alongside which the cars were drawn up. On the left was a row of old houses. They were three storeys high and mostly in darkness. Here and there, however, slits of light gleamed through closed shutters. The moon cast indeterminate pools of shadow along the cracked stucco walls. Somewhere, in one of the upper rooms, a radio was croaking out a tango.

'What happens now?' I asked.

'We just pay a call,' whispered Henri. 'It'll be quite polite. Keep your mouth shut now or I'll get into trouble. We're getting close.'

The street had narrowed still more. As we rounded the bend I felt the cobbles begin to slope downwards. Dimly, I could see that there were once more high blank walls on both sides of us, walls reinforced with tall concrete buttresses. Suddenly, in the shadow of one of the buttresses, I saw something move.

My heart leaped. I gripped Henri's arm.

'There's somebody there!'

'Keep quiet,' he muttered. 'It's one of our men. We've got the place surrounded.'

We walked on a few metres. The ground became level again. Then I saw a gap in the wall on the right. It looked like the entrance to one of the warehouses, a way for trucks. The men ahead melted into the shadows. As I followed, I felt the cobbles give way to cinders. I paused uncertainly.

'Get into the side,' hissed Henri, 'to your left.'

I obeyed cautiously and my outstretched hand encountered a wall. There were no longer any movements in front. I looked up. The walls rose like the sides of a deep canyon to a wedge of starry sky. Suddenly the beam of a torch cut through the darkness ahead and I saw that the others were standing before a wooden door in the side of the left-hand wall. I moved forward. The torch lit up the surface of the door. On it were painted the words:

AGENCE MARITIME, F. P. METRAUX.

Beghin grasped the handle of the door and turned gently. The door swung inwards. Henri prodded me in the back and I moved forward after the others.

Inside the door was a short passage terminating in a steep flight of bare wooden stairs. A naked electric light on the landing above cast a cold glare on the flaking plaster wall. The Agence Metraux did not appear to be very prosperous.

The stairs creaked as Beghin began slowly to walk up

them. As I followed, I noticed that Henri, just behind me, had taken a large revolver from his pocket. The call was evidently not going to be quite as 'polite' as Henri had prophesied. My heart thumped in my chest. Somewhere in this drab, smelly, sinister building there was a man I knew. Not half an hour ago he had walked up these stairs, the stairs beneath my feet now. Soon, in a moment or two perhaps, I should meet him again. That was the part that was so frightening. He could do no harm to me and yet I was frightened. I wished suddenly that I had a mask to conceal my face. Stupid, yes. And then I began to wonder which it would be. I saw their faces as they had stood watching me when I had been 'arrested'—scared, shocked. Yet one of them, one of them . . .

Henri prodded me in the back and motioned to me to keep up with the man in front of me.

On the first landing Beghin stopped in front of a heavy wooden door and tried the handle. It opened easily and the light revealed an empty room, the floor of which was strewn with slabs of plaster fallen from the ceiling. He paused to wipe off the sweat glistening on his forehead and neck, and led the way on up the stairs.

He had nearly reached the top of the second flight when he stopped again, and motioned us to wait. Then he and the Inspector stepped on to the landing out of sight.

In the silence I could hear the watch ticking on the wrist of the man in front of me. Then, as the silence intensified, my ears caught a faint murmur of voices. I held my breath. A moment later the Inspector's head and shoulders appeared over the banister rail above, and he signalled us on.

The landing was a duplicate of the one below. There

was, however, no light. Very quietly the men ranged themselves in front of the door. I found myself pressed against the wall beside it. The voices were louder now and, although the actual words were too indistinct to identify, I could hear that the owner of one of the voices—a man—was speaking Italian.

I saw Beghin's hand go towards the handle, hesitate, then grasp it firmly and turn.

The door was locked; but the slight rattle of the handle had been heard inside. The voices stopped suddenly. Beghin swore under his breath, and rapped loudly on the door panels. There was dead silence from the room. Beghin waited a moment, then turned round quickly to Henri. Henri held out his revolver butt foremost. Beghin nodded and took it. Turning to the door again, he thumbed back the hammer of the gun, and put the muzzle diagonally against the keyhole. Then he squeezed the trigger.

The noise of the explosion was deafening. For a moment the door held. Then two of the detectives flung their bodies against it, and it flew open with a crash. My ears singing, I stumbled in after them.

It was a small room furnished as an office, but with an iron bedstead in one corner. There was nobody in it. One the far side, however, there was another door. With a shout the Inspector dashed across to it and flung it open.

The far room was in darkness; but as the door flew inwards the light from the pendant in the office flooded across to a window in the end wall. From the darkness a woman screamed. The next instant a man dashed to the window, threw it open, and flung his leg over the sill.

It all happened in the fraction of a second. The man was at the window almost before the Inspector had recovered his balance. Out of the corner of my eye I saw Beghin raise the revolver quickly. Simultaneously the man at the window turned, and his arm shot out. There was a flash and a roar. I heard the bullet thud into the Inspector's shoulder a split second before Beghin fired. There was a tinkle of glass, and the woman inside the room screamed again. Then the window slammed. The man had gone. But in the instant that he had turned to fire, I had seen his face and had recognised him.

It was Roux.

I saw the Inspector lean against the doorpost, his face contorted with pain. Then I dashed after the others into the further room.

Cowering white-faced and whimpering in the corner was Mademoiselle Martin. Beside her, his hands raised above his head, stood a thickset bald-headed man protesting angrily in rapid Italian that he was an honest businessman, a friend of France and that, as he had done nothing criminal, the police were not entitled to interfere with him.

Beghin had gone straight to the window. His bullet had smashed one of the panes of glass, but of Roux there was no sign. Over Henri's shoulder I caught a glimpse of the roof of an adjoining building about two metres below.

Beghin turned quickly.

'He's got clear over the roofs. Duprat, Maréchal, look after these two here. Mortier, you get down to the street, and warn the men there to keep watch on the roofs and shoot on sight. Then come back and see what you can do for Inspector Fournier; he's wounded. Henri, come with me! You, too, Vadassy, you may be useful.'

Sweating and cursing, he heaved himself over the sill and dropped to the roof below. As Henri and I followed,

I heard the Inspector weakly exhorting the detective, Mortier, not to stand there gaping like a fool, but get down to the street as he had been told.

I found myself standing on a low parapet running round the four sides of a flat roof with a skylight like a cucumber frame in the centre. Around it rose the blank walls of the adjoining warehouses. In the shadows cast by the moon it looked as though there was no exit from the roof. But Roux had completely disappeared.

'Have you a torch?' snapped Beghin to Henri.

'Yes, Monsieur.'

'Then don't stand about. Get over to the skylight and see if it can be opened from this side. And for God's sake hurry.'

As Henri jumped down on to the leads to obey, Beghin started walking round the parapet. I could hear him muttering curious oaths as he went. Then I saw what he was making for. In the shadow at the far corner of the roof there was a narrow gap between the converging walls. As he turned his torch on it, Henri called over that it was impossible for a man to escape through the skylight. A second after he spoke there was a stab of flame and a report from the darkness ahead, and a bullet smacked viciously into the brickwork behind me.

Beghin knelt down and lowered himself on to the leads. I followed suit. Bent double, Henri scuttled across to us out of the shadows.

'He is beyond the corner, between the two walls, Monsieur.'

'I know that, imbecile. Keep down, Vadassy, and stay where you are. Henri, get across to the wall, and work your way towards the gap, under cover. If you see him shine your torch on him. We've got him cornered.'

Henri hurried away and Beghin, revolver raised, started to walk slowly along the leads towards the gap. A small cloud obscured the moon for a second or two, and I lost sight of him. A second later there was the flash of a torch, and a moment after two shots crashed out in quick succession. The flashes came from the corner by the gap. As the echo of the shots died away, I heard Beghin calling to Henri not to go any farther.

Unable to resist the temptation any longer, I followed. As I reached the corner I nearly bumped into Beghin, who was peering cautiously into the pitch-black shaft between the walls.

'Did you see him?' I whispered.

'No. He saw us. You'd better get back, Vadassy.'

'I'd rather stay here, if you don't mind.'

'Then don't grumble if you get shot. He's on a fire-escape about twenty metres along the wall round this corner. It's the back wall of a warehouse in the street running parallel to the one we came along. Henri, you get back, and tell them in the street to get some men on to that warehouse. If the watchman is still asleep, tell them to break in. I want them to take him from the rear. And tell them to be quick about it.'

Henri crept away. We waited in silence. In the distance there were the sounds of a train shunting and of cars on the boulevard. Near at hand it was deadly quiet.

'Supposing he slips away before . . .' I began at last.

He gripped my arm. 'Shut up and listen!'

I listened. At first I could hear nothing, then, a very faint grating noise came to my ears. It was an old sound, hollow and metallic. Beghin drew in his breath sharply. I saw him edge forward to the corner of the brickwork. I bent down and moved forward until I could just see

239

over the parapet. Suddenly the beam of his torch shot out into the darkness. The beam swept over the concrete on the opposite side of the shaft. Then it stopped and I saw the fire-escape.

Roux was nearing the top of it. As the torch caught him he looked round quickly, and half-raised the revolver in his hand. His face was white, and he blinked in the light. Then Beghin's gun crashed out. The bullet hit the escape with a clang, and whined off into space. Roux lowered his gun and raced for the top. Beghin fired again, and ran forward along the guttering between the walls to the foot of the escape. I hesitated for a second before following him. By the time I reached the fire-escape he was halfway up. I could see his bulk against the sky, a shadow moving slowly across the wall. I went up after him.

A moment later I was sorry that I had done so, for I saw a movement against the skyline.

Beghin stopped and called down to me to go back. At the same moment Roux's bullet hit the rail near my feet. Beghin fired back, but Roux was no longer visible. The fat man clattered up the last few stairs. When I caught up with him he was raising his head gingerly over the top of the ledge running round the roof. He swore softly.

'Has he got away?'

Without answering me, he stepped over the ledge to the roof.

It was long, narrow, and quite flat. Near us was a large water-tank. At the far end was a triangular structure containing the door leading below. Between was a forest of square steel ventilating-shafts. Beghin drew me into the shadow of the tank.

'We shall have to wait for reinforcements. We should

never find him among those ventilators, and he could snipe us if we tried it.'

'But he may get away while we're waiting.'

'No. We've got him here. There're only two ways off this roof—the fire-escape and that door over there. He'll probably try to shoot his way out. You'd better stay here when the men arrive.'

But there *was* another way off the roof, and Roux was to take it.

We did not have to wait long. Almost as soon as Beghin had finished speaking, *gardes mobiles* with rifles were pouring on the roof through the door. Beghin shouted to them to spread out, and advance towards us. They obeyed promptly. The line began to move. I waited with bated breath.

The line had almost reached the last row of ventilators, and I was beginning to think that Roux must, after all, have given us the slip, when suddenly I saw a figure dart from behind the ventilators and make for the ledge opposite us. A *garde* shouted and raced in pursuit. Beghin ran forward. Roux leaped up on the ledge and steadied himself for an instant.

And then I understood. Between the roof on which we stood and that of the next warehouse was a space of about two metres. Roux was going to jump for it.

I saw him crouch for the take-off. The nearest *garde* was about twenty metres from him, working the bolt of his rifle as he ran. Beghin was still farther away. Then Beghin stopped and raised his revolver.

He fired just as Roux was straightening his body. The bullet hit him in the right arm, and he half-turned. Then he lost his balance.

It was horrible. For an instant he struggled to save

himself. Then, as he realised that he was falling, he cried out.

The cry rose to a scream as he disappeared, a scream that stopped abruptly with the sound of his body hitting the concrete below.

I watched Beghin walk over to the ledge and look down. Then, for the second time in twenty-four hours, I was violently sick.

When they reached Roux, he was dead.

'His real name,' said Beghin, 'was Verrue. Arsène Marie Verrue. We've known about him for years. He is —was—a Frenchman, but his mother was an Italian. He was born at Briançon, near the Italian frontier. In 1924 he deserted from the army. Soon after, we heard that he was working as an Italian agent in Zagreb. Then, for a time, he worked for the Rumanian army intelligence service. Afterwards he went to Germany for some other government, probably Italy again. He came here on forged papers. Anything else you want to know?'

We were back in the office of the Agence Metraux. Inspector Fournier had been taken away in an ambulance. Detectives were busy transferring all the papers, files, and books in the office to a van that had been summoned for the purpose. One man was engaged in ripping open the upholstery of the chairs. Another was prising up the floorboards.

'What about Mademoiselle Martin?'

He shrugged casually. 'Oh! She was just his woman. She knew what he was up to, of course. She's down on the *poste* now. We'll question her later. I expect we shall have to let her go. The one I *am* glad to get is Maletti, or Metraux, as he calls himself. He's the brain behind all this. Roux was never important, just an employee. We shall get the rest soon. All the information is here.'

He went over to the man at work on the floor, and began to examine a bundle of papers that had been found below the boards. I was left to myself.

So it was Roux. Now I knew why his accent had seemed so familiar. It was the same accent as that of my colleague Rossi, the Italian at the Mathis School of Languages. Now I knew what Roux had been talking about when he had offered me five thousand francs for a piece of information. It had been the hiding-place of the photographs that he had wanted. Now I knew who had hit me on the head, who had searched my room, who had slammed and locked the writing-room door. Now I knew, and it did not seem to matter that I knew. In my ears was still that last agonised shriek. In my mind's eye I saw Mademoiselle Martin and the dead spy standing in front of the Russian billiard table. I saw her pressing against him. But ... Roux was never important ... just an employee ... she was just his woman. Yes, of course. That was the way to look at it.

An *agent* came into the room with a package in his hand. Beghin left his papers and opened the package. Inside it was a Zeiss Contax camera and a large telephoto lens. Beghin beckoned to me.

'They were found in his pockets,' he said. 'Do you want to see the number?'

I looked at the camera in his hand. The lens and shutter mechanism were crushed sideways.

I shook my head. 'I'll take your word for it, Monsieur Beghin.'

He nodded. 'There's no point in your staying any longer. Henri is downstairs. He will take you back to St

Gatien in the car.' He turned once more to his papers.

I hesitated. 'There's just one more thing, Monsieur Beghin. Can you explain why he should have stayed on at the Réserve, trying to get his film back?'

He looked up a trifle irritably. He shrugged. 'I don't know. He was probably paid only for results. I expect he needed the money. Good night, Vadassy.'

I walked downstairs to the street.

'He needed the money.'

It was like an epitaph.

19

IT was nearly half past one when I arrived back at the Réserve.

As I walked down the drive, I noticed that there was a light in the office. My heart sank. According to Beghin, the St Gatien police had explained the situation to Köche, and prepared him for my return; but the prospect of discussing the affair with anyone was one I could not face. I tried to slip past the office door to the stairs, and had my hand on the banisters when there was a movement from the office. I turned. Köche was standing at the door smiling at me sleepily.

'I have been waiting for you, Monsieur. I had a visit from the Commissaire a short while ago. He told me, amongst other things, that you would be returning.'

'So I understand. I am very tired.'

'Yes, of course. Spy-hunting sounds a tiring sport.' He smiled again. 'I thought you might be glad of a sandwich and a glass of wine It is here, ready, in the office.'

I realised suddenly that a sandwich and some wine was precisely what I would like. I thanked him. We went into the office.

'The Commissaire,' he said as he opened the wine, 'was emphatic but evasive. I gathered that it is most important that no hint of Roux's real activities should get about. At the same time, of course, it is necessary to explain why Monsieur Vadassy is arrested on a charge of espionage

245

yesterday, and yet is back again today as if nothing has happened.'

I swallowed some sandwich. 'That,' I said comfortably, 'is the Commissaire's worry.'

'Of course.' He poured out some wine for me, and took some himself. 'All the same,' he added, 'you yourself will have to answer some embarrassing questions in the morning.'

But I refused to be drawn. 'No doubt. But that will be in the morning. All I can think of now is sleep.'

'Naturally. You must be very tired.' He grinned at me suddenly. 'I hope you have decided to forget our interview of this afternoon.'

'I have already forgotten it. It was hardly your fault. The police gave me orders. I had to obey them. I didn't like doing it, as you may imagine, but I had no alternative. They threatened to deport me.'

'Ah, so that's what it was! The Commissaire didn't explain that.'

'He wouldn't.'

He took one of my sandwiches and chewed for a minute or so in silence. Then:

'You know,' he said thoughtfully, 'these last few days have worried me.'

'Oh?'

'I once worked in a big Paris hotel as assistant manager. The manager was a man named Pilevski, a Russian. You may have heard of him. He is, in his way, a genius. It was a pleasure to work with him, and he taught me a lot. The successful restaurateur, he used to say, must know his guests. He must know what they are doing, what they are thinking, and what they are earning. And yet he must never appear inquisitive. I took that to heart.

246

It has become instinctive to me to know these things. But during the past few days I realised that there was something going on here that I did not know about, and the fact worried me. It offended my professional sensibilities. Some one person, I felt, was at the bottom of it. At first I thought that it might be the Englishman. There was that trouble on the beach, to begin with, and then I found out this morning that he was trying to borrow money from the rest of you.'

'And he succeeded, I believe.'

'Oh, yes. That young American lent him two thousand francs.'

'Skelton?'

'Yes, Skelton. I hope he can afford it. I don't think he will see it again.' He paused, then added: 'Then there was Monsieur Duclos.'

I laughed. 'I actually suspected Monsieur Duclos of being a spy, at one stage. You know, he's a dangerous old man. He's the most appalling liar, and an inveterate gossip. I suppose that's why he's such a successful businessman.'

He raised his eyebrows. 'Businessman? Is that what he's been telling you?'

'Yes. He seems to have a number of factories.'

'Monsieur Duclos,' said Köche deliberately, 'is a clerk employed in the sanitary department of a small municipality near Nantes. He earns two thousand francs a month, and he comes here every year for two weeks' holiday. I heard once that a few years ago he spent six months in a mental home. I have an idea that he will soon have to return to it. He is much worse this year than he was last. He's developed a new tendency. He invents the most fantastic stories about people. He's been badgering me

247

for days trying to get me to handcuff the English major. He says he's a notorious criminal. It's very trying.'

But I was getting used to surprises. I finished the last of the sandwiches and got up. 'Well, Monsieur Köche, thank you for your sandwiches, thank you for your wine, thank you for your kindness, and—good night. If I stay here any longer I shall spend the night here.'

He grinned. 'And then, of course, you would have no chance of evading their questions.'

'*Their* questions?'

'The guests, Monsieur.' He leant forward earnestly. 'Listen, Monsieur. You are tired now. I do not want to worry you. But have you considered what you are going to say to these people in the morning?'

I shook my head wearily. 'I haven't the slightest idea Tell them the truth, I suppose.'

'The Commissaire . . .'

'To hell with the Commissaire!' I said explosively. 'The police created the situation. They must accept the consequences.'

He got up. 'One moment, Monsieur. There is something that I think you should know.'

'Not another surprise, surely?'

'Monsieur, when the Commissaire arrived tonight, the English couple, the Americans and Duclos were still in the lounge discussing your arrest. After he had gone I took the liberty of inventing an explanation of your arrest that would clear you of all suspicion of any criminal activity and at the same time satisfy their curiosity. I told them in the strictest confidence that you were really Monsieur Vadassy, of the counter-espionage department of the Second Bureau, and that the arrest was merely a ruse, part of a special plan about which not even the police knew anything definite.'

I was startled. I gaped. 'And do you expect them to swallow that nonsense?' I asked at last.

He smiled. 'Why not? They believed your story about the theft of the cigarette-case and the diamond pin.'

'That was different.'

'Agreed. Nevertheless, they believed that, and they believed this. They *wanted* to believe it, you see. The Americans liked you and didn't want to think of you as a criminal, a spy. Their immediate acceptance of the story convinced the rest.'

'What about Duclos?'

'He claimed that he had known it all along, that you had told him.'

'Yes, he *would* claim that. But'—I looked at him squarely—'what was your object in telling this story? I don't understand what you're getting at.'

'My idea,' he said blandly, 'was simply to save you trouble and embarrassment. Monsieur,' he went on persuasively, 'if you will sleep soundly tonight, if you will keep to your room in the morning, if you will leave the affair in my hands, I can promise you that you will have to answer no questions or give any explanations. You will not even have to see any of these people.'

'Now, look here—'

'I know,' he put in quickly, 'that it was most impertinent of me to tell them this without your permission, but under the circumstances—'

'Under the circumstances,' I interrupted him acidly, 'a theft, an arrest, and a violent death all in one day would have been bad for business, so you got in first with a cock-and-bull story about my being a counter-espionage agent. Roux is politely forgotten. The police are happy. *I* am caught between two fires. Either I have to go on lying like a trooper and explain what the famous counter-espionage agent is doing back at the Réserve or I have to crawl out without anyone seeing me. Nice work!'

He shrugged. 'That is one way of looking at it. But I should like to ask you just one question. Would you prefer to make up your own explanation?'

'I should prefer to tell the truth.'

'But the police—'

'Damn the police!'

'Yes, of course.' He coughed a little self-consciously. 'I shall have to tell you, I am afraid, that the Commissaire left a message for you.'

'Where is it?'

'It was verbal. He told me to remind you that a citizen of France must be ready to assist the police on all possible occasions. He added that he hoped soon to be in touch with the Bureau of Naturalisation.'

I drew a deep breath. 'I suppose,' I said slowly, 'that you didn't, by any chance, discuss your little story with the Commissaire?'

'I did, I believe, mention it in passing. But—'

'I see. You both worked it out between you. You—' I stopped. A sudden feeling of helplessness swept over me. I was tired, tired, sick to death of the whole wretched business. My limbs were aching, my head felt as if it were falling in two. 'I'm going to bed,' I said firmly.

'And what shall I tell the servants, Monsieur?'

'The servants?'

'About calling you, Monsieur. Their present instructions are that you are officially no longer here, that your breakfast will be served discreetly in your room, that when the car arrives to take you to Toulon in time to catch the Paris train, none of the other guests is to see you leave. Am I to change those instructions?'

I stood there in silence for a moment. So it was all arranged. Officially, I was no longer at the Réserve. Well —what did it matter? In my mind's eye I saw myself walking on the terrace the next morning, I heard the exclamations of surprise, the questions, the cries of astonishment, my explanations, more questions, more explanations, lies and more lies. This way was the easier. Köche knew that, of course. He was right and I was wrong. Heavens, how tired I was!

He was watching my face. 'Well, Monsieur? he said at last.

'All right. Only don't let them bring the breakfast too soon.'

He smiled. 'You may be sure of that. Good night, Monsieur.'

'Good night. Oh, by the way!' I turned at the door and drew Beghin's envelope from my pocket. 'The police gave me this. It contains five hundred francs for my expenses during the last few days. I haven't spent anything like that amount. I should like you to give the envelope to Herr Heinberger. He might be able to make use of it, don't you think?'

He stared at me. For a moment I had the curious impression that I was looking at an actor who with one movement had wiped the make-up off his face—an actor who had been playing the part of a hotel manager. Slowly he shook his head.

'That is very generous of you, Vadassy.' He no longer addressed me as 'Monsieur.' 'Emil told me that you and he had talked together. I am afraid I was annoyed. I see now that I was wrong. However, he no longer needs the money.'

'But—'

'A few hours ago, perhaps, he would have been glad of it. As it is, he is returning to Germany in the morning. It was arranged early this evening that they should leave by the nine o'clock train from Toulon.'

'*They?*'

'Vogel and his wife will be going with him.'

I was silent. I could think of nothing to say. I picked up the envelope from the table and put it back in my pocket. Absently, Köche splashed some more wine into his glass, held it up to the light, then glanced at me.

'Emil always said that those two laughed too much,' he said. 'I found them out yesterday. A letter arrived. They said it was from Switzerland, but it had a German stamp. While they were out of their room I had a look at it. It was quite short. It said that if they wanted more money they must offer immediate proof that they needed it. They did so. Emil is right. They laugh, they are grotesque. No one suspects that they are also obscene. That is her secret.' He drank the wine and put the glass down with a bang. 'In Berlin, years ago,' he said, 'I heard Frau Vogel give a recital. Her name then was Hulde Kremer; I didn't remember her until she played tonight. I had often wondered what happened to her. Now I know. She married Vogel. It's very odd, isn't it?' He held out his hand. 'Good night, Vadassy.'

We shook hands. 'And,' I added, 'I shall hope to see the Réserve again.'

He inclined his head. 'The Réserve is always here.'

'You mean that you won't be here with it?'

'In confidence, I leave for Prague next month.'

252

'Did you decide that this evening?'

He nodded. 'Just so.'

As I climbed slowly to my room I heard the clock in the writing-room strike two. A quarter of an hour later I was asleep.

At noon that day I drank the remains of my breakfast coffee, strapped my suitcase together, and sat down by the window to wait.

It was a glorious day. The sun was pouring down and the air over the stone windowsill was quivering, but the sea was slightly ruffled by a breeze. The red rocks glowed. In the garden, the cicadas were droning. Down on the beach I could see two pairs of brown legs beyond the shadow of a big striped sunshade. On the lower terrace, Monsieur Duclos was addressing some new arrivals, a middle-aged couple still in their travelling clothes. As he talked he stroked his beard and adjusted his pince-nez. The couple listened intently.

There was a knock at the door. Outside was a waiter. 'The car is here, Monsieur. It is time for you to go.'

I went. Later, from the train, I caught a glimpse of the roof of the Réserve. I was surprised to see how small it looked among the trees.

FINE MYSTERY AND SUSPENSE
TITLES FROM CARROLL & GRAF

- [ ] Allingham, Margery/MR. CAMPION'S FARTHING $3.95
- [ ] Allingham, Margery/THE WHITE COTTAGE
  MYSTERY $3.50
- [ ] Ambler, Eric/BACKGROUND TO DANGER $3.95
- [ ] Ambler, Eric/CAUSE FOR ALARM $3.95
- [ ] Ambler, Eric/A COFFIN FOR DIMITRIOS $3.95
- [ ] Ambler, Eric/JOURNEY INTO FEAR $3.95
- [ ] Ball, John/THE KIWI TARGET $3.95
- [ ] Bentley, E.C./TRENT'S OWN CASE $3.95
- [ ] Blake, Nicholas/A TANGLED WEB $3.50
- [ ] Boucher, Anthony (ed.)/FOUR AND TWENTY
  BLOODHOUNDS $3.95
- [ ] Brand, Christianna/DEATH IN HIGH HEELS $3.95
- [ ] Brand, Christianna/FOG OF DOUBT $3.50
- [ ] Brand, Christianna/GREEN FOR DANGER $3.95
- [ ] Brand, Christianna/TOUR DE FORCE $3.95
- [ ] Brown, Fredric/THE LENIENT BEAST $3.50
- [ ] Brown, Fredric/MURDER CAN BE FUN $3.95
- [ ] Brown, Fredric/THE SCREAMING MIMI $3.50
- [ ] Buchan, John/JOHN MACNAB $3.95
- [ ] Buchan, John/WITCH WOOD $3.95
- [ ] Burnett, W.R./LITTLE CAESAR $3.50
- [ ] Butler, Gerald/KISS THE BLOOD OFF MY HANDS $3.95
- [ ] Carr, John Dickson/CAPTAIN CUT-THROAT $3.95
- [ ] Carr, John Dickson/DARK OF THE MOON $3.50
- [ ] Carr, John Dickson/THE DEMONIACS $3.95
- [ ] Carr, John Dickson/DEMONIACS $3.95
- [ ] Carr, John Dickson/THE GHOSTS' HIGH NOON $3.95
- [ ] Carr, John Dickson/MOST SECRET $3.95
- [ ] Carr, John Dickson/NINE WRONG ANSWERS $3.50
- [ ] Carr, John Dickson/PAPA LA-BAS $3.95
- [ ] Carr, John Dickson/THE WITCH OF THE
  LOW TIDE $3.95
- [ ] Chesterton, G. K./THE MAN WHO KNEW
  TOO MUCH $3.95
- [ ] Chesteron, G. K./THE MAN WHO WAS THURSDAY $3.50
- [ ] Crofts, Freeman Wills/THE CASK $3.95
- [ ] Coles, Manning/NO ENTRY $3.50
- [ ] Collins, Michael/WALK A BLACK WIND $3.9
- [ ] Dickson, Carter/THE CURSE OF THE BRONZE LAMP $3.
- [ ] Disch, Thomas M & Sladek, John/BLACK ALICE $3
- [ ] Eberhart, Mignon/MESSAGE FROM HONG KONG $

☐ Eastlake, William/CASTLE KEEP	$3.50	
☐ Fennelly, Tony/THE CLOSET HANGING	$3.50	
☐ Freeling, Nicolas/LOVE IN AMSTERDAM	$3.95	
☐ Gilbert, Michael/THE DOORS OPEN	$3.95	
☐ Gilbert, Michael/THE 92nd TIGER	$3.95	
☐ Gilbert, Michael/OVERDRIVE	$3.95	
☐ Graham, Winston/MARNIE	$3.95	
☐ Greeley, Andrew/DEATH IN APRIL	$3.95	
☐ Hughes, Dorothy B./THE FALLEN SPARROW	$3.50	
☐ Hughes, Dorothy B./IN A LONELY PLACE	$3.50	
☐ Hughes, Dorothy B./RIDE THE PINK HORSE	$3.95	
☐ Hornung, E. W./THE AMATEUR CRACKSMAN	$3.95	
☐ Kitchin, C. H. B./DEATH OF HIS UNCLE	$3.95	
☐ Kitchin, C. H. B./DEATH OF MY AUNT	$3.50	
☐ MacDonald, John D./TWO	$2.50	
☐ Mason, A.E.W./AT THE VILLA ROSE	$3.50	
☐ Mason, A.E.W./THE HOUSE OF THE ARROW	$3.50	
☐ McShane, Mark/SEANCE ON A WET AFTERNOON	$3.95	
☐ Pentecost, Hugh/THE CANNIBAL WHO OVERATE	$3.95	
☐ Priestley, J.B./SALT IS LEAVING	$3.95	
☐ Queen, Ellery/THE FINISHING STROKE	$3.95	
☐ Rogers, Joel T./THE RED RIGHT HAND	$3.50	
☐ 'Sapper'/BULLDOG DRUMMOND	$3.50	
☐ Stevens, Shane/BY REASON OF INSANITY	$5.95	
☐ Symons, Julian/BOGUE'S FORTUNE	$3.95	
☐ Symons, Julian/THE BROKEN PENNY	$3.95	
☐ Wainwright, John/ALL ON A SUMMER'S DAY	$3.50	
☐ Wallace, Edgar/THE FOUR JUST MEN	$2.95	
☐ Waugh, Hillary/A DEATH IN A TOWN	$3.95	
☐ Waugh, Hillary/LAST SEEN WEARING	$3.95	
☐ Waugh, Hillary/SLEEP LONG, MY LOVE	$3.95	
☐ Westlake, Donald E./THE MERCENARIES	$3.95	
☐ Willeford, Charles/THE WOMAN CHASER	$3.95	

Available from fine bookstores everywhere or use this coupon for ordering.

Carroll & Graf Publishers, Inc., 260 Fifth Avenue, N.Y., N.Y. 10001

Please send me the books I have checked above. I am enclosing $_____ (please add $1.00 per title to cover postage and handling.) Send check or money order—no cash or C.O.D.'s please. N.Y. residents please add 8¼% sales tax.

Mr/Mrs/Ms _____

Address _____

City _____ State/Zip _____

Please allow four to six weeks for delivery.